"I love The Art of Murder, a compelling tale, tautly told. It is laugh-out-loud funny, yet I had tears in my eyes during the poignant last chapter."

—Lynn Cline, author, and popular Santa Fe radio host

"Peggy's witty, articulate, and sophisticated murder mystery wonderfully captures the essence of Santa Fe: its Southwestern flavor, cooking, and kooky characters. A great, fun read!"

—Robert J. Guttman, Professor, Johns Hopkins University, University of Virginia

"A humorous look at the delightfully wacky life in Santa Fe, served on a platter of mystery, murder, and green chiles."

—John Sherman, Mesa Verde Press

"Peggy van Hulsteyn's signature voice—New York hip with attitude—infuses her work in The Art of Murder, the first of what we hope will be a series of Mickey Moskowitz mysteries and adventures in a Santa Fe so well-drawn the reader can smell the piñón and taste the chili."

—Paula Paul, author of the Alexandra Gladstone mystery series and other books

"Witty and atmospheric, The Art of Murder gently satirizes the foibles of Santa Fe and Los Alamos with the insights of an intrepid, introspective heroine, Mickey Moskowitz, and a cast of artists, journalists, politicians, physicists, gallery owners, and beloved relatives. The relationship of Mickey to her adoptive sister, Lupita, is key to the plot and showcases the warmth and traditions of New Mexican families. Full of quotable insights, this novel is a valuable bedside companion for these times."

—Valerie Brooker, M.L.S.

Also by the same author

Yoga and Parkinson's Disease

The Kitten Invasion

Vanity in Washington

Diary of a Santa Fe Cat

Sleeping with Literary Lions

The Birder's Guide to Bed and Breakfasts

What Every Business Woman Needs To Know To Get Ahead

Mind Your Own Business

The Art of Murder

Peggy van Hulsteyn

Outskirts Press, Inc.
http://www.outskirtspress.com

Paperback ISBN: 978-1-9772-2625-9
Hardback ISBN: 978-1-9772-2626-6

Library of Congress Cataloging-in-Publication Data
Name: van Hulsteyn, Peggy, 1944– author.
Title: The Art of Murder / Peggy van Hulsteyn.
Subjects: 1. Fiction. 2. Mystery. 3. Crime. I. Title.

Cover design by Laurie McDonald
Map by Jacqueline Rudolph
Author photo by Jeanie Puleston Fleming

Outskirts Press and the "OP" logo are trademarks belonging to Outskirts Press, Inc.

PRINTED IN THE UNITED STATES OF AMERICA

Dedicated to the memory

of my nephew

Henry Karim Zand Guttman

who loved books

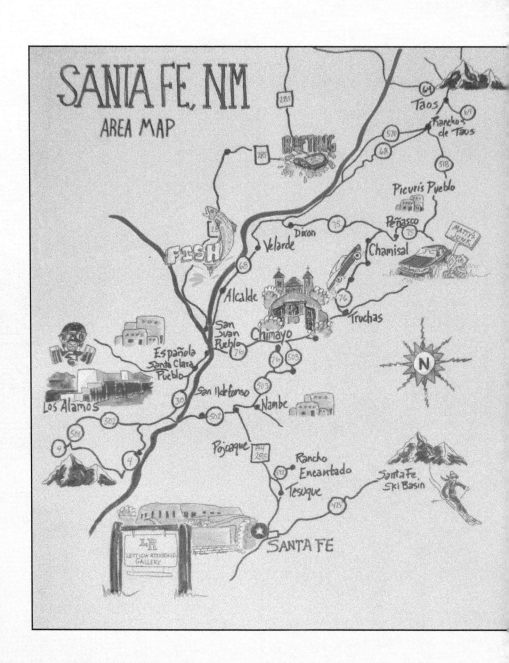

PROLOGUE

One thing most grown-ups agree upon is that life is not fair:

— Good people die young

— Children get horrible diseases

— Honorable young men get killed in wars that dishonorable old men start

— People who amass all the wealth are often not rich in spirit and generosity

— And most restaurants serve bad coffee!

Stress A+++ types like me find change overwhelming. We are not the least bit flexible about flexibility. Like cats, we love our routines, which become our shields, our protectors, our ports in the storm. Stripped of even one of our daily practices, we fear our life will unravel.

I was unraveling at the speed of light. I felt like a ball of string without beginning or end: I was my own Mobius strip. I was in a state of complete shock and denial when I found myself back in Santa Fe, New Mexico, for an occasion I had hoped never to experience.

I hate funerals.

Although the first three letters of "funeral" spell "fun," very few of them are.

Most requiems are so wretched that I'm planning to be a "no show" at my own memorial.

So what was I doing at the Berardinelli Funeral Home on Luisa Street in Santa Fe, New Mexico?

I came to bury my baby sister, Melissa, the only person I have ever loved.

I kept telling myself that any minute I would wake up and find that a brisk run down the arroyo off the Old Santa Fe Trail, followed by a couple shots of espresso, would prove that this grotesque scene was only a nightmare, some macabre figment of my subconscious.

A blur of people, some I recognized, some strangers, streamed past the simple shroud-covered pine coffin which held my sister's body.

Mel and I had shared a sardonic sense of humor, and at one point, I consoled myself, thinking this was her idea of the ultimate sick joke—that shrouded body was somebody else and Mel would pop out at any moment and yell "April Fool!" or "Got you this time!"

Get up, I silently cried out to the corpse. *We are not amused.*

As a writer, I sometimes hate myself for writing rather than living the tragic and poetic scenes in my life. I have trouble being in the moment and, to compensate, I flip into reporter mode. Even now, I was observing this whole horror show from a distance, pretending it was happening to somebody else. A stranger's sister. Not the little girl I taught how to tie her shoes and read her first book.

I was in a tailspin, having just arrived late last night on the Red Eye from New York City. Jewish Orthodox funerals are supposed to take place as quickly as possible so I rushed back to my hometown of Santa Fe as soon as I got the devastating phone call from my adopted sister and Santa Fe District Attorney, Guadalupe "Lupita" Gutiérrez.

"Mickey, *mija,* I'm so sorry. I'm calling with bad news."

"Lupita?" My mind was already shut down by the profound sorrow in her voice. "No, please no, it's not Mel—"

Hours later, still enveloped in deep shock and heavy denial, I felt as if I were starring in a surrealistic movie. *This could not really be happening, could it?*

People walking in slow motion appeared to be hugging me, uttering inane comments. *Who were they? Should I know them?* My body may have been in the room, but my mind was in a different Zip Code altogether.

I heard myself mouthing words to Mel's kindergarten teacher and her Girl Scout troop leader. But that voice wasn't mine; it had to be coming from someone else. I could barely speak. I was senseless with grief, drowning in a vat of overwhelming sorrow.

Berg, my current flame, gently held my hand while the rabbi motioned for us to be seated so he could start the service. Lupita sat on the other side of me and held my other hand. I was as comfortable as I could be in this desolate situation.

I had a quick flashback, and this time, Mel was holding my hand. We were at our parents' funeral and again were stunned that Lady Luck had bypassed our house, leaving the dirty work to her colleague, Miss Fortune, who left a woe of miseries on our doorstep.

My parents, along with Uncle Oliver, my mother's only brother, died a quick death from hypothermia when a Catamaran sailboat (guaranteed to be nontippable) spilled into the stone-cold waters of Lake Superior.

The irony of this situation was that my mother hated to travel, a so-called secret she had shared with the whole town. Her brother had been asking her to visit forever, promising her a killer trip.

It had never occurred to narcissist Muriel Moskowitz at any time in her life to suppress any thought or feeling that crossed her mind. "I hate to complain," was my mother's favorite way to begin her conversations (and the part where Mel and I rolled our eyes). "I try to keep my considerable troubles to myself," Mommy Dearest would continue with that perfectly martyred Joan of Arc look on her face. "But I just don't see why we have to fly all that way to Minnesota to see Oliver—it's either muggy and buggy or freezing cold—when my brother could just fly to us."

For once, she was exactly right; she should have stayed home.

Wherever my mother ultimately landed, I know she's still carping; that shrill voice could not be silenced, not even in death. To this day, Muriel's tape still plays over and over in my head.

Even though my parents and I had nothing in common, and I always hoped I was adopted, their death was a shock; suddenly, I was the head of the family. It was quite a transition, although I secretly loved having Mel as my only blood relative.

Keeping house and cooking were not encoded anywhere in my DNA; my specialty was reading Mel stories and sometimes making up my own yarns to keep her amused. Thankfully, there were fairy godmothers in my life and Maria Gutiérrez, Guadalupe's mother, was my own version of Cinderella's benefactress.

I think it was tasting one of the meals I fixed Mel (a peanut butter and tuna casserole, topped with orange jello, menudo, and sardines) that made Tia Maria decide there was plenty of room for two more girls in their rambling *hacienda*. When we moved to the beautiful house on Upper Canyon Road, I felt, for the first time in my life, like I was Home.

I drifted back to reality just in time for Berg and Lupita to help me into the funeral home limo (which Mel would have deemed pretentious) and we made our way to Rodeo Road and The Memorial Gardens Cemetery where Mel would be buried.

When my adoptive sister, Lupita, had called with the worst news of my life, she also offered to make all the arrangements. The Gutiérrez family has lived in Santa Fe since 1610 and knew everyone. It didn't hurt that she was the District Attorney and, though about as big as a minute, a dynamo who—in a manner uncharacteristic of Santa Fe Style—got things done immediately.

She asked if I wanted a Jewish funeral and even though I disliked both Christmas and Hanukkah, I said to bring on the rabbi.

When my flight from New York City landed, Lupita picked me up at the Albuquerque Sunport. Before heading up to Santa Fe, we detoured to our old hangout, The Frontier Restaurant, for a bag of cinnamon rolls and two cups of strong black coffee. As for the trip back, it was filled with teary talk about Mel's untimely death and the peculiar circumstances surrounding it.

"The few details the police provided are simplistic mierda," Lupita pronounced, biting hard on her third cinnamon roll. "It's your typical Santa Fe one-size-fits-all approach," she continued. "The police and propaganda experts at the Department of Tourism describe every bicycle or pedestrian accident with a banality, or worse, a cliché."

Mel's death was no exception. The preliminary report read: "Melissa Moskowitz, age thirty-one, died while cycling down Hyde Park Road after apparently losing control at high speed on the steep grade and crashing into a guardrail. The accident occurred just after 1800 hours—approximately thirty minutes before sunset." The dark side to all this is the New Mexico sky in the late afternoon; the intense sunlight is literally blinding.

The conjecture was that she was probably going fast and became distracted by the magnificent scenery. They also claimed that her helmet came off due to a broken strap.

"That might be a reasonable description for a tourist from Fort Wayne, Indiana," I blurted out, "but Mel was an experienced cyclist and never careless; she always wore a next-to-new helmet! She would never wear a helmet with a broken strap! She was uncompromising when it came to safety."

With a sweet and sorrowful recollection, I added that, "She crossed the fanatic line so many times that some of her overly lectured subjects started referring to her as the Felix Unger of the cycling world."

"Problem is that Santa Fe County deputies are spread so thin," Lupita said, shaking her head. "The Sheriff's Office needs three times the staff to cover the entire county." Lupita continued, "Many of the local police are not really local. Everyone has been driven out by the *elitista* with the opera glasses." I had to nod solemnly in agreement; it was inexcusable, but true nonetheless. "The cost of living here is so damn high that they have to commute from Española or some other low-rent district."

"That's no excuse for a shoddy report," I said. "And Mel's attention would have been heightened, not distracted, by her spectacular surroundings. She knew every coyote, every eagle, every prairie dog on her cycling routes," I said, wiping back a tear. "This city and the mountains and the basin—they were her backyard."

"You're right, mija," Lupita said, her forehead furrowing, "Mel was nothing if not vigilant."

Things got very quiet as we contemplated how our lives had been forever diminished. I felt like a time traveler, so warped with grief was my gyroscope.

Half asleep and numb with anguish, I found myself—in my mind's eye—on the ski basin road. I was driving past Black Canyon on the curvy two-lane road and remembering the ponderosas alongside creating alternating patches of shadow and light. It was late afternoon, and the sky was flooded with an intense, blinding, bright-yellow light. I could barely see the guard rail and, thinking of deer scampering across the road or an overzealous New Mexico driver charging up the hill, I pulled off to one side and waited for the sky to shift to a more gentle hue.

It would take a few more hours before my brain escaped the fog of heartache enough to allow me to begin to question why my baby sister was hurtling down Hyde Park Road on her bicycle. When it came to the tortuous route to and from the ski basin, she could tough it out with the best of them.

I awoke from this reverie to find myself at Mel's funeral with the horrible feeling that I had been totally irresponsible as her big sister. "Nancy Drew manages to keep her family and friends safe from harm," I whispered to Berg, "So, why did I screw up? No member of Nancy's cast—George, Bess, or Ned—dies. Somehow they all remain forever eighteen."

Berg looked at me, his green eyes filled with compassion.

"I should have been here to protect Mel. I was the big sister, her guardian," I cried, squeezing his hand. I blinked back an ocean of tears, consumed by my old nemesis—Jewish guilt.

I was offered a brief reprieve when Brady, my Journalism mentor and professor emeritus at the

University of Missouri School of Journalism, grabbed me from behind with one of his famous bear hugs.

"The news about Mel ripped my heart out. I can only imagine how you must be feeling." His embrace tightened, "But you have that tortured look I know so well: guilt. This wasn't your fault."

I pulled away just slightly, "Guilt? What would you know about guilt, I said with a sudden smile. You're a Unitarian."

I did what I always do when I hurt and don't want to feel; I went to work. Contemplation and introspection are not my strong suit. I wasn't planning to sit shiva. Work is my salvation, my touchstone.

I had vowed at age nineteen, when I left this New Age Disneyland (a.k.a. Santa Fe) to escape to J-school, that I would never return. (At least not for more than a weekend with the no-refund return ticket back to NYC in my virtual pocket.) But never is a long time, especially when the person whom I loved more than anyone else in the world was lying under a pile of dirt in the Memorial Gardens Cemetery.

So it was that eighteen hours after Mel's funeral, I gathered together the tools of my trade—notebook, fully charged iPhone, sunscreen, Altoids, and a discreet glow-in-the-dark can of bear mace. Hey, I'm a New Yorker!

In spite of my sorrow and lack of sleep, I had to smile when I pulled my rented beige Lincoln Town Car into the parking lot at *The Maverick,* a Santa Fe newspaper that evokes the spirit of the *Village Voice* and *The Texas Observer.* My vehicle looked like a stranger in a strange land amidst the beat-up pickup trucks. It reminded me of when I was a freshman at Santa Fe High. My clothes were straight from the pages of *Seventeen* and *Glamour*, while my classmates wore jeans and sweaters, their necks draped with heaps of Indian jewelry. I had never fit into Santa Fe, called "The City Different" by locals, and now my rental car was a misfit as well, the pariah of the parking lot, the Hester Prynne of the automotive world.

"You can't go home again," Thomas Wolfe wrote, but here I was, back in the old neighborhood.

Yesterday, at Memorial Gardens, after my sister's interment, I ran into my journalism mentor Brady. I mean, literally ran into him. I turned away from the gravesite, took a step, and came face-to-face with him. Looking utterly grief-stricken, he began expressing heartfelt condolences. He didn't get far beyond, "I'm so sorry, Mickey—" before I interrupted. Without preamble, I asked him to find me a position at his Santa Fe newspaper.

I needed a vantage point and a cover for investigating Mel's suspicious death, and once a journalist, always a journalist. How did I know I would need to play sleuth? Call it instinct, backed up by facts. My sister's last phone call was seared into my synapses—her worry palpable. I only wish I'd insisted on all the details when I could still have saved Mel.

Brady understood me better than almost anyone else, and his whispered edict came immediately. "Tomorrow, Mickey. My office."

Brady is the editor of *The Maverick*; I was his apprentice when I was in high school and known by my given name Micaela. My swinging Aunt Millie, an opera buff, named me after the character in *La Bohème* and endowed me with the nickname Mickey. Brady, the Bill Moyers of Santa Fe, is larger than life, which could account for why he goes by a single moniker. The great ones, like Voltaire, Plato, and Socrates, only need one name, as do Cher and Brady.

He changed my life in significant ways. He taught me most of what I know about reporting. Although most small weeklies eventually fold, *The Maverick* has not. It remains Santa Fe's most widely read weekly. Professor Emeritus at the University of Missouri Journalism School (my *alma mater*), the man was a complete original, and I welcomed the chance to work with him again. So, here I was at the small house converted to accommodate the offices of his weekly.

I smelled my boss's office as soon as I walked through the doorway into the reception area. Brady was an old-style journalist, and bad cigars, definitely not the chic cigar-bar variety, were his trademark. He'd gotten hooked on stogies when he was an Associated Press reporter in Cuba. Castro's best import became too expensive when Brady transferred to the Chicago Tribune but, by then, he had the cigar habit. I used to kid him that Castro must also have given him the name of his tailor since sartorial splendor was definitely not one of my editor's many virtues.

"Mickey, come in!" Brady bellowed from his back office. He has this annoying radar, always knowing something is going to happen, even before it does. It's what made him such a crackerjack reporter back in the day.

He came galumphing across the cluttered room, stepping over stacks of yellowing copies of *The Maverick, The*

New York Times, and *The Columbia Journalism Review* to greet me at the front door.

Standing amid piles of yesterday's headlines, he put a chubby arm around me and steered me toward his office. He shooed Brenda Starr, a bison-sized, tail-wagging St. Bernard, off the ancient threadbare sofa and motioned for me to sit. He removed his cigar so he could squeeze my shoulder, his version of a hug.

"I was reminded of the whisper-thin fragility of life," he continued, as he moved restlessly in the small space. "Just last Friday afternoon, at 3:32 p.m. to be precise, I had a brief chat with Mel at Harry's Roadhouse. She greeted me with 'How's my second favorite journalist? Do you have time for some lemon meringue pie?'"

Desperate for any information, any clues, I asked, "Can you remember anything else she said? How did she look? How did she seem? Maybe she told you something that could help me begin to unravel this nightmare."

"I knew you would want to know every word," said the meticulous, old-style journalist, "so I scratched out a few notes on the conversation." He handed me a pocket-sized notebook.

My brief meeting with Melissa, Friday, October seventeenth, at Harry's Roadhouse:

> Melissa Moskowitz is an eternal optimist, almost to the point of being naïve. She seems unchanged from when I first met her as a kid in junior high—a kid in love with the universe—always a isn't-the-world-the-most-wonderful-place? look on her face. How she came out of the dark, gloomy Moskowitz

household, I'll never understand. She's obviously one of the most popular regulars at the restaurant. It's like lunching with Miss Congeniality. Thirteen people stopped by for greetings and hugs.

"Bless you, Brady; you know me well," I said, holding the notebook in my lap. "Was there anything in particular that stands out in your memory of what she said?"

"She did say she'd been missing you," he added. "Said you were at a What the Hell is Fake News? conference in Mystic, Connecticut."

That "missing me" story got my old waterworks going. Brady isn't the type of man who is comfortable with a weeping woman, so I took a deep breath and tried to pull myself together.

"Mel was Harry's best customer," I said, stuffing my emotions into some stuttering chatter. "I used to kid her about owning stock in the Roadhouse, especially the pies, and she was a regular—and then some." I gulped for breath.

Brady nodded. I could tell he had to fight the impulse to squeeze my shoulder again. He cleared his throat and said, "After some chitchat about how much she enjoyed working as an aide to Senator Rendón, she said she hated to end our conversation, but she had to get ready for an informal staff meeting in a few minutes. As I was getting up to leave this lush, sun-dappled garden filled with hollyhocks, columbines, and wild yellow roses, I thought 'This place is not half bad.'"

"I could never understand how she could tolerate that guy," I said, shaking my head. "But she did feel very needed in his office. As for me, I've always thought of Arturo Rendón as a buffoon. How he ever got elected is beyond me!"

"I'm somewhere in between you and Mel on this," Brady confessed. "To be sure, Arty can be a bit of a doofus, and I personally find him self-serving. But he knows how to keep getting money for the district, and that's an art form in our poor state. The senator has a good heart and understands the people of New Mexico. He knows how to get money to keep labs going. As you know, his dad was a tech at LANL, and Arturo remains fiercely loyal." LANL is local shorthand for the Los Alamos National Laboratories. Yes, the same historic scientific laboratory that gave birth to the Atomic Age.

"Yeah, I guess," I said, shaking my head. "Did she give any indication as to what the meeting was about?"

"Not exactly. It was only days before the big fall fundraiser for Rendón—Champagne & Aspic in the Aspens—and your sister had pretty much run the show, organizing for months before. You know Mel. But there was one thing …"

Brady's expression shifted, and he looked lost for a moment, but I knew he was thinking of Mel.

"What?" I prodded. "Don't leave me in suspense."

He shook his head. "Unfortunately, Arty showed up just as Mel was about to elaborate on something she'd told me earlier regarding rancor among the ranks of the office staff—"

Practically shouting, I interrupted, "You may be onto something we can run with! During our most recent weekly phone chat, I sensed that something was not quite right at her job. She seemed uncharacteristically paranoid about having her phone conversations recorded and reverted to what reminded me of the cryptic messages we used to send each other when we were kids. All I could gather was that she needed to talk with me in person."

"Mickey." He said my name only once, but it was enough to slow me down.

He placed one hand lightly on my arm. "Mel died the day of Arty's fundraiser. She was on her way cycling back down the mountain after the event—which was a huge success for Rendón, as I hear it—and that means we have a guest list and a whole load of people who saw her just fifteen minutes or so before the crash."

I barely registered that my fingernails were digging into my palms. Brady continued. "The cops were so intent on proving it was an accident—Mel losing control of her bike and hitting the guardrail—they didn't try to find out if there were any witnesses, much less question the attendees of Rendón's fundraiser. It's shameful!"

He frowned. "We need to get hold of that list, including Rendón's supporters and staff; someone must know something."

Suddenly, in spite of the fact that I was sitting in his office, I lost it, launching into a rant. "Rendón is a political hack without a moral compass! Mel was too good for him or anybody else in his office. She excelled in physics and spent two years as an intern at The Lab developing some very sophisticated real-time cellular-biology programs. She even gave an invited talk on her work at an international symposium last spring! How the senator ever convinced her to head up his staff still baffles me!"

Mel was a PR agent's fondest dream; she was the idealism of the '60s without sex, drugs, and rock 'n' roll. She wrote an essay for her Girl Scout troop: What the USA and New Mexico Means to Me. Luckily for Rendón, much of what Mel loved about New Mexico was him. He was the loving, congratulatory dad Mel never had—Rendón was childless and had always wanted a smart, loving daughter, and Mel was right out of Central Casting.

Brady did his best to calm me down, but I realized that under all my grief was a mountain of raw fury. I was furious that the minions of the law are so understaffed that they had to rely on undertrained recruits to figure out how my sister died.

But mainly I was berating myself for not being here to save Mel—that was my job.

I looked at Brady for answers. "When she called, I should have pressed her about what was making her so guarded and cryptic. I could have jumped in to save her and I didn't. I'll have to live with that for the rest of my life."

He pinched my cheeks (which he thought people enjoyed) for a second before sighing, "You were her sister, not her keeper. You have nothing to feel guilty about."

"Kid, you need some joe," Brady said, rolling up his rumpled, once-white shirt and pouring a cup of muddy-looking coffee into a cracked blue mug. I must have been more exhausted than I realized because I actually tasted this brew before I remembered that Brady makes the worst coffee this side of the Mississippi. Before I could take another sip, a tiny fire spawned by his cigar ashes broke out in the wastebasket. Without missing one staccato beat of his sentence, my unflappable editor poured his coffee onto the flames. What could I do but follow suit? Brenda Starr put her head onto my lap and drooled all over my new Adrienne Vittadini black dress. Oh, I had missed this place!

Brady was not a touchy-feely guy. He scrunched up his face, and it took on a look of amused horror. He lit another inelegant cigar and quickly gave me an assignment.

"Mick, you need to keep busy. Take your notebook and sense of humor and head over to Leticia Rothschild's gallery on Paseo de Peralta for one of her over-the-top openings. Classy. Tasteful. Eccentric. Very *Vogue*. Our readers eat this stuff up."

I took a tiny fan out of my purse and blew his foul-smelling cigar smoke back into his face. "Brady, have you gone corporate? Or is it the lack of oxygen at this altitude? You've always hated the phony-baloney art openings."

"That's right," he said, smoothing the two or three remaining strands of hair on his otherwise bald head. "That's why I gave you the assignment. In case you forgot, living in Gotham City, we're in a town that eats, lives, and breathes art. Santa Fe is still the third largest art market in the country."

"Yeah," I said, standing up to reveal my mighty five-foot stature, "And you're an uncompromising newspaperman. I didn't leave my job in New York to cover a bunch of *chichi* art openings. I came here to find out how and why Mel died."

"I know you're an investigative reporter. Hell, I raised you from a pup. I also know that your mind works best when you're working on two things at once. You're plugging away at your first story when your subconscious is percolating along on the second article."

I looked at him incredulously and, in spite of myself, started laughing. "That's right, how could I have forgotten the second law of the Brady School of Investigative Journalism?"

"Beats me," he said, splashing club soda onto a blue bandanna and dabbing at a huge ink spot on his shirt. The spot remained unfazed. "You were my best pupil."

"Besides," he added while putting on a brown sports coat completely covered with dog hair. "There isn't a better place in town to find out what's going on than at an art opening."

"But I'm talking about Mel's death."

"So am I, and so is everybody else. It's the perfect place to start asking questions. Remember my adage, Mickey, 'In Italy, all roads lead to Rome'? In Santa Fe, 'All arroyos lead to art openings.' It's gospel in this burg. Grow up and smell the coffee, kid." With that, he poured me another cup of his foul-smelling java and ordered both me and his dog to sit. I did.

"Okay, kid, this may be my last chance to play professor to my favorite student. Here's what's going on in my world. This country has an extraordinary history of great journalists we should celebrate, starting with Samuel Clemens."

"And Nellie Bly," I chimed in.

"But my all-time hero will always be Edward R. Murrow," he continued. "Whatever happened to the credo that 'the pen is mightier than the sword'? Back in the Dark Ages, when I was in J-school, we took seriously the slogan of the *Old Gray Lady*: 'All the news that's fit to print.'"

I nodded. "When you were a guest lecturer for my honors class of the History and Principles of Journalism at Mizzou, your last lecture blew me away. You ended with, 'Most of what gets printed and broadcast nowadays isn't news, it's fear. It's a tale told by an idiot, full of sound and fury, signifying nothing.'"

On our walk to nearby Bert's Burger Bowl for lunch, Brady grabbed a copy of *The New York Times*. "Not only are we inundated with fake news and 'alternative' facts, but today's computer generation is missing the whole newspaper experience by reading stories online."

Paper in hand, he continued striding toward Guadalupe

Street. For a slightly plump man, he moved like the wind. Breathlessly, I caught up with him at the entrance of his version of Cheers.

"It's not about how fast you can read a headline on a computer," he pronounced, pulling the door open with gusto. "Reading a real newspaper is a sensual experience, one you throw your whole mind and body into."

I followed him to what was still his usual table. "Here's how it should be. You go to your preferred cafe or bar and order black coffee and doughnuts or scotch and a burger, rare. Then you spread your paper all over the table. You gaze at the paper, you feel the crispness of the newsprint, hear it crinkle, and turn the pages. Then, if you like or hate something on the editorial page, you read it to someone at the next table, get a dialogue going."

A true method actor, Brady poured a soupçon of scotch from a pocket flask into his coffee. "When I was bureau chief for *The New York Times* in Chicago, we used to run a yearly contest challenging readers of *The Times* and *The Trib* to rake us over the coals and take us to task if they didn't like our editorials. "Now what do we do?" he continued, lighting up a cigar right next to the NO SMOKING sign.

"Babble incessantly," I said, jumping in. "With the 'round-the-clock news cycle, everything is important, which means nothing is important."

"We don't need another online phony community where there is a promised intimacy among strangers. A good newspaper promotes a real feeling of community. I share the sentiments of Thomas Jefferson, who said in 1787, 'Were it left to me to decide whether we should have a government without newspapers, or newspapers without a government, I should not hesitate a moment to prefer the latter.'"

He frowned. "Let me remind you how our paper works. I am a tough newspaper man living in a computer-dominated world where most of the population can't even identify a newspaper, much less read one. I'm a pragmatist with a conscience. Hell, I know more than anyone about how our craft, if you can still call it that, has deteriorated. I'm living it. So, here's the deal I have with the folks at The Edward R. Murrow Grant Committee at Mizzou who fund the columnists who write for our paper.

"Half of the articles in the paper are about hard-hitting issues that matter to me and people who speak the truth in the West. I like to bring in guest columnists, such as my colleagues Tom Friedman, Paul Krugman, and Nicholas Kristof. Then, in the spring, Anna Quindlen and David Brooks have agreed to do a piece about something of special interest to Santa Feans. Then, I get good reporters like you to write about the local art and culture scene. We have lots of rich collectors who advertise and keep us afloat—and that's not small potatoes."

What could I say? I hugged Brady.

Which he hated. He pushed me toward the door, admonishing me: "Get to work. The clock is ticking."

I found myself wanting to call the person I turned to when I had a problem—Mel. She always knew just what to say, how to put everything into perspective.

But I would never hear her voice again. I know that in the movies people always seem to take great comfort in having soulful conversations at the gravesite. It wouldn't work for me. The memories of my sister were in my head, not on a slab of marble.

I'm an investigative reporter. I solve things. I get to the shadow side of baffling puzzles. I needed to get to work. So, I took Brady's advice and accepted his assignment to cover three art events, distasteful as that sounded.

My stalwart editor assured me he was going to nose around and try to find some leads in Mel's death, or as he put it in his own unique jargon, "Turn over some rocks." He often spoke like a character from a Mickey Spillane novel.

I walked out of Bert's primed, ready to work, and reeking of grease and cheap cigars. It took me five minutes to walk back to my rental car, and by then, I knew I needed a moment to regroup and ground myself and maybe even freshen my makeup. I hadn't bothered with mascara, liner, or blush (they don't do much for heart-break), but even my sunscreen had suffered from the stray tears I couldn't seem to fully control.

I drove from the parking lot of *The Maverick* to Berg's Canyon Road three-bedroom, two-bath Adobe Nightmare. One of the many alleged joys of living in my hometown was owning an authentic adobe. My brilliant scientist paramour fell for this ancient myth, much to the glee of roofers, stucco contractors, painters, and cleaning services. The only person, it seems, who didn't think his housing choice was positively inspired was yours truly. All during my youth, I had watched folks from back East first succumb to Turquoise Fever—wearing so much Indian jewelry they could barely waddle around the Plaza; then graduate to the Adobe Addiction—fixing up old houses that devoured all their time and most of their money. The natives and longtime residents of Santa Fe were the only ones, other than me, of course, who didn't believe this local fairy tale. They were smart enough to opt for brand-new houses with real closets in developments with sidewalks. Lupita used to laugh and tell Mel and me, "Only *gringos* want to live in a real adobe on a dirt road. We've created a cottage industry, selling them houses we've been trying to unload for centuries."

I set my bag on the catch-all table just inside the front door, slipped my feet out of my pumps, and collapsed onto the couch. I felt empty and aching and as if I were missing parts of myself, all at the same time. Oh, Mel …

I reached for the crocheted throw tucked over one arm of the couch, but my fingers closed around a soft, knitted man's sweater. I pulled its heft to my heart and buried my face in this nest of baby blue cashmere faintly scented with the aroma of freshly baked scones. I could track Berg's cooking schedule by the lovely fragrances embedded in his sweater. I sniffed again, this time, in addition to scones, inhaling the subtle fragrance of chocolate, Oaxacan to be precise, used in an award-winning mole sauce from Santa Fe's famous Chile and Wine Festival … oh, and there was the delicious savory tang of fresh-roasted green chile.

One of my lover's desirable traits: he adores going wild in the kitchen, and, unlike some of us, he can cook!

Berg (a.k.a. Lawrence Bergenceuse) was one of the few reasons I was glad to be back in the town in which I grew up. In addition to his skills as a chef, he was drop-dead gorgeous, with a razor-sharp intellect and a body equally honed.

Part of Berg's boyfriend appeal is that he is a physicist, and I have a thing for physicists; they can be exasperating but are rarely boring.

When I first moved to New Mexico at age eight, we took a school field trip to Los Alamos, the mountain-top community nicknamed The Hill. I always fantasized about what it would have been like to keep company with the ethereal and brilliant Robert Oppenheimer, who assembled at the secret city some of the greatest minds of the century and, on August 6, 1945, with the dropping of the first atom bomb, forever changed the world.

Oppenheimer was before my time, but my attraction to physicists never waned. The breed is an interesting blend of geek, genius, absentminded professor, and wonder-struck little boy. Puzzles are mother's milk to physicists, and they possess the fashion sense of a newt. One often thinks that the pairing of the striped shirt with the high-water, checked pants is their way of thumbing their nose at the shallowness of the fashion industry. Ironically, with the type of fashion savant blindness associated with this subset, they often think they look splendid. Did I mention arrogance as a predominant characteristic?

We met in Princeton when I was doing a series for *News View* on up-and-coming scientists of the new millennium. Berg impressed me with his scientific savvy, wit, and charm, but it was his beautiful body that made me break my cardinal rule of interviewing: never, ever get involved with your subjects.

Berg could have put himself through university as a male model—Michelangelo's David has nothing on my boy when it comes to a perfect physique. Berg is also blessed with a full head of curly hair—blond, in his case—but there the resemblance to the famous statue ends. Berg's face—and, yes, he is very handsome, with his patrician features, Roman nose, and sparkling green eyes—would never be described as stony. His huge smile animates his expression, and he smiles frequently, firing up that twinkle in his eyes!

We had carried on a commuting romance for the past year. Now Berg had returned from his visiting professorship at Princeton and was back "in the old neighborhood," as he put it.

So, here we were or, more accurately, at this moment, here I am, with a cat curled up on my lap. While I'd let my mind wander from my current state of misery, Magic, a lean and leggy Russian Blue, joined me to offer comfort.

Magic was named after Magic Johnson and the magical way the kitty and Berg met. Two months ago, in the middle of a monsoon downpour, Berg had driven home from work to find a cat huddled at the edge of the porch, shivering, scared, and malnourished, two glowing lights for eyes. It was the beginning of a beautiful friendship.

Now my tears came again, pouring down my cheeks and falling onto Magic's soft silver-blue fur. And then, this tiny bundle, knowing what I needed, purred his way into my heart, making the loveliest, most reassuring sounds ever. His purr was bigger than he was, and it filled the room with healing sounds.

I let myself cry until Magic stood to lick my cheek, a kind gesture I believe, but his sandpaper tongue also reminded me I was here to work.

Setting him down gently, I made my way to the bathroom, where I splashed water on my face and blotted it dry. My reflection came as a shock because all I could see in the mirror was Mel. We both had coal black hair. She wore hers loose with some natural curl; mine was straight, and I kept it in a perfect bob with every strand in place.

We both had porcelain skin, but where Mel had had a smattering of freckles on her nose, my skin was blotchy from tears. I dabbed on some light powder, noting that my worry lines were deeper than usual. Mel had almost never worried; for me, worry was my hobby.

I thought I looked a decade older than my thirty-four years with bloodshot eyes set off by dark circles.

Turning from the mirror, my gaze settled onto a bottle of a very special and expensive limited edition of Gardenia Chanel (a gift from Mel on our whirlwind trip to Paris two years ago). I took a deep breath, sprayed Gardenia into the air, and misted myself. "To you, Mel," I whispered. Then, knowing she would scold me to take care of myself in the high-desert air, I applied moisturizer, sunscreen, gloss, and drops to clear my eyes.

When finished, I thought I looked presentable, and Magic mewed his agreement.

I called my own quirky physicist, Berg, at his LANL office nearby. With feigned enthusiasm, I asked him to accompany me to tonight's art openings. Berg knew me too well to buy my act.

"Art openings? Mickey, you haven't slept in days, and your thinking is skewed. You'd rather have a root canal than go to a Santa Fe gallery."

I swallowed hard. "Brady convinced me it's a legitimate way to start asking questions about Mel's death." Magic, purring so loudly the room almost vibrated, rubbed against my ankle.

"What's that lovely sound?" Berg asked.

"That's Magic's own meditation class and his approval of my make-over. He says I'm ready for the best of Santa Fe's high society."

In the space of Berg's hesitation, I could hear him figuring out exactly what I needed.

"… then count me in."

"Thank you," I said, breathing a sigh of relief.

I have a pretty consistent history of picking the worst boyfriends on the planet. Berg, with his considerable charm and nurturing abilities, was screwing up my record. Worse yet, he was getting under my skin. In a good way.

It works better for me to keep my relationships vague and meaningless. The less I know about my beau, the better off I am. I always thought that absorbing, fulfilling careers make better lovers than men do.

In the movies, love may mean never having to say you're sorry, but in real life, it means having a hole in your heart the size of a blue whale.

Late afternoon found us rolling along in Berg's cashmere blue-and-white hard-topped convertible '56 Bel Air on Hyde Park Road, en route to the ski basin.

It was the type of crisp fall afternoon you'd like to send home to Mother. The sky was the same vibrant color as Berg's car, the golden aspen leaves were quaking in the light breeze, but I couldn't have cared less. All I could do was think about Mel.

When we drove past Nun's Curve, close to the site of Mel's death, tears burst forth unexpectedly. Within an eighth of a mile, Berg pulled his Chevy into a gravel parking lot used by hikers so he could comfort me. He shut off the engine, and we were instantly surrounded by silence, interrupted only by my weeping.

"I never cry," I sobbed softly. "The last time was when I was eleven and my collie puppy had gotten run over by a truck."

"Crying once every twenty-three years doesn't seem overly excessive," said Berg, putting his arm around me.

"Some heartless bastard ran over my sister right here, then took off. What kind of person could do that?" I let myself slide closer to Berg as tears streamed down my cheeks. I wanted him to make my pain go away, at least my vulnerable side did. My hard-boiled, practical self was sending out warning signals never to love anyone again. I told myself I needed to get out of my head before any more selves surfaced and I morphed into Sybil.

I pulled myself away from Berg's now-wet cotton jacket and wiped tears from my cheeks—at least trying to get myself back into reporter mode. "Did I tell you that Mel called me only a few nights before she died?" I asked, swallowing a hiccup.

"No! What did she say?" Berg handed me a very white hankie.

I dabbed my eyes and said, "I knew the minute she said hello that something was wrong. She seemed distracted, unfocused, very un-Mel-like." My voice was still a broken shudder. Berg patted me gently.

I tried again. "She was calling to discuss a gift for Lupita's thirty-third birthday next week—at least that's what she said, but I think it was a ruse. She went on and on about some big soirée the Governor threw for Senator Rendón and all the hotshots from around the world who showed up and showered that worm with presents. You know how devoted Mel was to Rendón, even though I tried my best to show her what a jackal he really was. But I do think she disapproved of all the expensive gifts Rendón accepted …"

Berg's nod was solemn.

I shook my head. "I thought that she sounded afraid—but I convinced myself I was imagining things— and—and—and she was very judicious in picking her words." I took a deep breath. "Something was bothering her; I know there was something vital she wanted to tell me but couldn't. Before she hung up, she said, 'I think it's time to bring in Carson Drew.'"

Now Berg tipped his head, frowning curiously. "As in Nancy ..."

"That was the code we made up as kids when we wanted to tell each other that something wasn't right."

Berg knew me well enough to know there were no words he could offer that would comfort me, so he gently kissed the still-trickling teardrops off my cheeks.

I don't remember ever in my life allowing anyone to see me cry—especially the man I was trying not to care about! I was a little embarrassed. My tears had seeped through Berg's T-shirt. My head was a silent scream telling me to pull myself together, but my heart wouldn't cooperate. I had to finish my story and own my guilt.

"I should have done something right after her phone call; it's partly my fault that she's dead. She counted on me," I said in between sobs. "We used to joke when we were kids that I was Nancy Drew and could always save the day. In Nancy's world, everything always came out right at the end. People's sisters never got killed; Nancy would not have allowed it!"

I realized, with a jolt, that I was being too vulnerable, and vulnerable people get hurt. But I was already hurt. Shattered.

My usual tried-and-true defense mechanisms were not working. It was difficult to play my usual game of turning a switch and going back to Flippant Girlfriend or Savvy and Cynical Reporter. I was not comfortable with the new soft, sloppy, and tearful Mickey—I had been trying to keep her at bay all of my life.

But it was Berg who shifted the moment. He opened his car door. "Let's go."

"What—where?"

"Let's face what we need to face and walk out to Nun's Corner. Okay? Ready?"

Was I ready? For an instant, my mind went blank.

"Mickey?" He said my name so gently.

I jerked into action, nodding my head. "Yes, ready!" Berg was right, we needed to take action, and I needed to face the place where Mel took her last breath and her last view of this world.

Five minutes later, we reached the spot where the guardrail bounded the sharpest angle of Nuns' Curve, the curve named for the nuns who died here when their car swerved off the road on an icy night decades earlier.

I'd dressed for the mountaintop party in the forest, so at least my boots were stoically prepared for this pilgrimage, even if the rest of me trembled like the aspens topping the ski valley.

No obviously recent skid marks on the asphalt— meaning no one had slowed or jammed on their brakes during the past week—and impossible to tell when or how the numerous remaining marks had been made on such a steep corner.

No tape, crime scene or otherwise. And, just beyond the battered metal roadside guard, vegetation had been trampled flat.

"So much for ensuring crime scene integrity; looks like they ran buffalo through here," I snapped, stuffing my fear and sorrow behind my trusty anger.

I remembered from the accident report that Mel's bike

had apparently hit the rail, tipping and sailing over with my sister still astride about a dozen paces from the road.

Berg helped me over the railing, and I took lead over the trampled ground. I saw some grease marks—at least I hoped they were grease. They were black. There were broken tree limbs and a torn *cholla*, a native cactus known for its ability to dismember itself and jump onto passers-by. But nothing else to see.

At least at first.

Berg carefully examined the perimeter of the scene. I did what he did, only on the other side. I spotted a rusty can of orange soda, a fast food bag, and other bits and pieces of civilization blown astray—by the same type of breeze that now rustled treetops and made me feel my sister's spirit might be paying me a flyby visit.

Santa Fe was already getting to me.

I sighed, about to turn away, when a glint of sun off metal blinded me for an instant.

"Berg!"

He was by my side in a moment. I pointed to the spot, more than fifteen feet away from where we stood and almost hidden behind a tree.

Berg used yet another hanky to retrieve the object.

He held up the rough-edged piece of plastic and metal. The metal still had very large flecks of bright red paint. Shiny red paint.

"What is it?" I asked, staring at it.

Berg stared at it too, frowning. "I'm going to take a wild guess and say it's a side marker lamp … from a very red vehicle. And it hasn't been exposed to the elements for long so …"

"How could the investigators have missed it?" My voice sounded very small.

"My guess," Berg said quietly. "It flew off and landed in a weird spot—just your amazing sixth sense spotted it."

I closed my eyes and took a deep breath. "Mel's death was hit-and-run, and her killer drove a red vehicle."

When we were back in the car, having stowed the evidence safely in the trunk, Berg took my hand. "Which way?"

"Uphill," I said.

"Uphill, it is." Berg nodded, happy to go with the flow. He turned out of the parking lot and onto the scenic road, accelerating gently.

To shift my mood from thoughts of Mel's last moments, I concentrated on the magnificent Sangre de Cristo Mountains and, I admit, my spirit lifted just a bit at the sights, sounds, and scents surrounding us. This time of year, these mountains wore spectacular fall colors, and they always reminded me of the paint-by-numbers pictures I had dabbled with as a child. There were, in my ten-year-old's memory, at least eight shades of gold to be painted onto the green.

As Berg took us higher, the evergreens looked like freshly decorated Christmas trees aglow, while falling golden and amber-hued aspen and vermillion-hued Gambel oak leaves served as ornaments. I kept these somewhat sentimental thoughts to myself; to the world at large, including Berg, I was an Oscar Wilde-type of cynic, not the sort to wax eloquent over scenery. I had already unbuttoned myself emotionally far more than was comfortable.

"Where are we going, by the way?" asked Berg, breaking my reverie.

"To Aspen Vista."

"That sounds good. One of my favorite spots to hike or ski."

"Well, prepare yourself for none of the above. I fear we're in for a New Age Easter parade."

"What?"

"Remember that article I wrote a year ago for *Vanity Fair* titled, 'In Santa Fe, Every Day is Halloween'? I'm afraid we're going to see this story come to life."

"You mean people will be in costumes? Good god, Mick, do you always have to be a method writer? Couldn't you just research your articles on the internet?"

We pulled into Aspen Vista, the crown jewel of aspen viewing. If it had been just the two of us for a romantic picnic, this would be the ultimate spot. However, Santa Fe's version of *The Canterbury Tales* would have made even Chaucer gasp at my hometown's originality, eccentricity, some would say lunacy. There were several dozen twenty-first century pilgrims milling about, everyone but The Wife of Bath, although a few of the characters looked and smelled as if they were in dire need of a shower.

The silliness of Santa Fe often makes me smile; that is, when I'm not gritting my teeth. The reason we were heading into the woods was that the Ellen Paddington Gallery was having its annual The Art of Nature Gathering, a prequel to the actual art opening later that evening at the gallery. All satirists should move to Santa Fe; you don't have to make anything up. All you have to do is look out your window.

When I was in high school, I referred to my hometown as a place so bizarre that even Jonathan Swift couldn't have invented it. Mel and I made a game of it back then, and we called it Spot the Santa Fe Originals. We used to joke that in any other town these beloved eccentrics would have been carted off to the Mansion for the Mystified. In Santa Fe, they were treated as icons, representing the tolerant spirit of the town.

Berg let me take the lead on foot as we left the parking area and followed the scenic trail that wound into the mountains. As we traversed the first half mile, it was difficult to take an accurate head count, but I guessed we'd already encountered at least fifty attendees. I recognized some of them as "eternal regulars" at all Santa Fe events.

There was the Peace Guy with his graying beard, his ponytail, his knee-length flowered house dress and sandals. A group gathered around him was performing a wedding for the Universe to evoke world peace.

As a shower of brown rice thrown by a well-wisher hit Berg on the neck, my boy whispered to me, "The peace guy looks like he's going to a unisex wedding where he plays both the bride and the groom."

"Well, if he plays both parts, at least he'll never get left standing at the altar."

"I feel like I'm in a Fellini movie," Berg said as we made our way through the last of the motley wedding crowd. "Who's that person or thing who looks like a giant radiator hose?"

The object of his inquiry slithered past us in a black full-length latex body suit.

"Oh, that's the Rubber Lady; she's been slinking through Santa Fe soirées since I was a teenager. She's the mystery woman in The City Different. Once, at some gala at the hotel La Fonda, Mel and I tried to peek under her mask. She slapped us around like a giant octopus, and we never did find out her true identity."

The thought of fun-loving Mel and how she would have adored this absurd picnic made me blink back tears. *I'll think about this later; I'm here on assignment*, I reminded myself with false bravado.

We passed a bovine woman in a Cleopatra outfit, a too-tight toga, and golden sandals, covered with golden aspen leaves. As discreetly as I could, I pointed out her special adornment: a boa draped around her neck, the live kind.

"That woman looks like an asp," said my ever-punning paronomasiac.

"A goodly portion of the residents of our fair city came here believing that they are the reincarnated Cleopatra," I explained.

Berg nodded somberly. "I'm always fascinated by how there could be hundreds, thousands, of reincarnated Cleopatras. How come no one ever comes back as one of her slaves?"

"The way my luck is going," I said, "I'll probably come back as Hamburger Helper!"

Berg, my whiz kid with the body of Adonis, started

sniffing around for food. He was like a growing teenager or a cat, always hungry. What brought out the Peck's Bad Boy in *my* boy was the sight of a Sikh, wearing a turban and full dress, heading our way with a tray of hors d'oeuvres.

"All right." Berg brightened. "At least at these shindigs, it's usually gourmet all the way. Pâté. Brie. Caviar."

Apparently, it had been some time since my lad had attended an opening, especially one of Ellen Paddington's. Brady had warned me (knowing how I like to nosh) that the bill of fare, at most openings, had slimmed considerably due to insufficient funds.

At this picnic, there appeared to be ample bounty, but it was geared, it seemed, for those who thought macrobiotic diets were a gourmet's delight.

Our solemn waiter stopped right in front of us, and with a bow, displayed his wares. My eclectic paramour, a devotee of junk food, such as green chile cheeseburgers (as well as being an aspiring, experimental chef) looked crestfallen when he saw the offerings on the tray.

"We have tofu with red chile pâté, cooked with no lard, no fats whatsoever. Or perhaps you'd like a brown rice pancake with cilantro and red chile sauce or lentil loaf with tomato topping … and autumn cabbage pie or this delicious maguro tabbouleh, which I'm sure you know is tuna. Everything is perfectly balanced to blend with the Universe and to enter your temple, the human body."

"No Frito pies hiding in there, by any chance?" Berg asked with a glint in his eye.

"Oh no, sir, Frito pies are filled with lard, meat, cheese—an affront to your holy temple. Your aura will be out of balance with the Universe. Your karma will be out of kilter."

When I was in New York City, where I would entertain my colleagues with antics about life in Santa Fe, my associates applauded me on my vivid imagination. Because I am genetically unable to speak anything but the truth, I told them that in The City Different, you don't need to evoke poetic license. It's all there in living color.

I have a lively inner life, which is why I probably turned to writing in the first place, but there is no way I could have invented the scene evolving before me. As we strolled along, our shoes crunching golden aspen leaves, my rational man of science whispered to me, "Odd's bodkins, Micaela, this place is a New Age three-ring circus."

"Why do you think I moved to the Big Apple? My hometown has way too much local color."

The rebirthing scene going on under the picnic table made Berg grimace. Someone was squirming inside a tightly wrapped Navajo rug and screaming. "Button nose, you owe me. Just for this, I'm going to force you to attend a lab party."

I made a face in mock horror and turned around to kiss Berg. At a Santa Fe art happening, it is never a good idea to take your eyes off the ball. We literally backed into a tarot card reader who had set up a booth beneath a large aspen tree. Madame sported a red turban, dimestore pearls, and a hokey-looking purple gypsy shawl. Even though she resembled a caricature, there was something sinister about her.

"Okay, missy," she said, staring straight through me, "Let's see what the cards have in store for you."

In many ways, I consider myself to be a fearless person. In my job as an investigative journalist for *News View*, I had interviewed Mafia moguls, hardened criminals in Sing Sing, and a slew of people who thought that the killing of a reporter would be justifiable homicide—but fortune-tellers always give me the creeps.

"We were just leaving,'" I said, pulling on Berg's hand and heading for our car.

"This won't take long," said Rosa, sorting her cards. She dramatically put the chosen card on top, motioned for me to come closer. "For your eyes only."

She flung the card in my hand, and I turned it over. It had but one word on it: *"MEURTRE!"*

Which, in French, is: "MURDER!"

Mercifully, we escaped from that woo-woo picnic with the real excuse that it was time to go to the actual opening at Paddington's Gallery in downtown Santa Fe.

I was uncharacteristically silent as we made our way down the mountain in the sun-drenched late afternoon. This fact did not escape Berg's detection.

"You're not going to let a character out of a ten-year-old's book get you down, are you? She seemed like a stoned 1960s actress playing a part badly."

"A part like Bette Davis played in *Dead Ringer*?" I tried for humor, but I couldn't suppress a shiver, and Berg saw that, too.

"Mickey, that woman and everyone else at that picnic would have been locked up in any place but Santa Fe. Here, they are considered folk heroes!"

"Give me the anonymity of New York City any day," I answered, trying to act more flippant than I felt, but I was still picturing Rosa the tarot reader and her MEURTRE card.

When we drove by the scene of Mel's death, an alarm went off inside of me. A cold, black anger replaced the sadness I had felt on my way up to Hyde Park. Berg glanced over my way to see if he should dry my tears.

"I've shed my last tear," I said with more conviction than I felt, as Berg, one hand on the wheel, reached out to touch me gently. "I'm tired of crying. I want justice. I want revenge. I want Mel back.

"Mel shouldn't have been killed; it isn't fair," I continued, clenching my fists. "She was a woman of integrity and a resilient fighter of causes. She was just innocently riding her bike back from Rendón's stupid fund-raising event."

"We'll find out who did this," said Berg. He gently stroked my cheek.

"I want that person executed; I want to watch them die." I was horrified to hear myself saying this. I had written several editorials rallying against the death penalty. For the first time in my life, I could understand why someone would kill another human being—an eye for an eye, a life for a life. I'd always been an advocate for gun control. I was a lifelong pacifist, but somehow, I knew that if someone handed me a gun right now and led me to Mel's killer, I could happily pull the trigger.

I was scaring myself and didn't want to frighten Berg. I flipped on the radio to the oldies station, hoping a silly song from yesteryear might soften my mood. I was also an expert at compartmentalizing, separating raw emotions from my work. I put my rage into the back pocket of my mind.

"I need to think about my two stories right now," I told Berg with more show than I felt. "Let me warn you what fun is in store for you tonight. Brady has arranged a lovely evening for us." I was trying to ease myself into a pseudosocial mood, but it was as if the furious part of me was watching and warning, "I'll be back."

"Remind me to send him a fistful of Cuban cigars as a thank you," said Berg, trying to follow my lead and cajole us into a lighter mood.

But, thirty minutes later, when we reached Santa Fe and the rambling single-story building that was Paddington Gallery on Baca Street, I sensed my rage still there, simmering and biding its time.

Fine, I told it silently. *I'm here to find out who killed Mel, and I will get to the truth even if it kills me.*

Before I was really ready, I gritted my teeth and steeled myself for this dopey assignment. Berg took my arm, and we moved toward the entrance.

The mood for the event was set when a young, spacy-looking lass with pink-and-blue hair opened the door for us. I was trying not to stare at her T-shirt that said, "Stamp out coyote art." In a rather bored voice, she greeted us with, "Welcome to Paddington Gallery." She looked like she was killing time until she got back on the bus and joined her punk rock tour.

"I'm Mickey Moskowitz, and this is Lawrence Bergenceuse. I'm from *The Maverick*, I'm here to cover the opening. Could you please let Ellen Paddington know I would like to meet her?"

One thing in Ellen Paddington's favor: She'd seen fit to stay at her gallery during the outdoor picnic for the bewildered up at Aspen Vista. I didn't even know the woman, but suddenly had a new respect for her.

"She's in the other room," the pencil-thin waif answered in a monotone voice. "Hey, Ellen!" she yelled, pointing to me with an arm tattooed with Our Lady of Guadalupe wearing a miniskirt. "This woman's a reporter."

She gestured to a white-haired woman in the crowded, adjoining room and said, "That's her."

Paddington waved and motioned for Berg and me to join her. We entered the fray, feeling for all the world like we were enmeshed in the rush hour in Grand Central Station. The narrow room where the show was hung looked like my grandmother's attic. Mediocre pictures, Santa Fe landscapes, and Western art were crammed on the wall, many hanging willy-nilly as if someone had casually tossed them up there minutes before the opening.

Every available *nicho* and shelf was stacked with paintings that looked as if they were breeding and multiplying and taking over the room. In one corner, there was a precarious stack of pots ready to be fired. The place put me in mind of a kindergarten for the arts.

Ellen Paddington looked just like her gallery. She appeared to have been designed by several of the artists-in-residence. The barrette that once held her curly white hair in place had fallen into the pocket of her rumpled blouse. The pink-and-red kimono she had draped over her orange blouse was several sizes too small so that her ample breasts seemed in danger of popping out. Her black skirt sported an abundance of moth holes and her large (I'm guessing size eleven-and-a-half) feet were bare. She looked as if Ratso Rizzo was her personal stylist.

Once I focused on her face, however, I totally forgot her shabby outfit. She possessed such serenity, such contentment, that she seemed to be an incarnation of one of the Dalai Lamas. As a Stress A+++ personality, I envied such tranquility.

Paddington shook my hand and then cupped it with both of hers. Softly, she said, "I am so sorry about Melissa. She was one of the loveliest people I've ever known. I lit a candle for her immortal soul."

Her kindness and gentleness got to me, but I swallowed the lump in my throat and willed myself not to cry.

She seemed to sense my vulnerability and focused on Berg, giving me a chance to collect myself.

"Physicist, folk dancer, chef, Telemark skier, bon vivant, a Francophile who collects esoteric French vintages, your reputation precedes you."

The woman might dress like a Salvation Army reject, but she did her homework. She put her ample arms around both of us and asked, "Have you eaten? Would you like something to drink? Do you have any questions about the show? Can I do anything for you?" She seemed so much the Jewish mother I thought she might offer us some chicken soup.

"Melissa told me that you're not much for coyote tourist art or the typical cowboy and Indians motif. Follow me. I think my back room, devoted to emerging artists, is more your style."

As we wandered through the topsy-turvy adobe gallery under her protective tutelage, her entourage of loyal artists followed us. I knew that Paddington came from an extremely wealthy Chicago family who were not pleased that she had channeled a large chunk of their fortune into the care and feeding of Santa Fe artists.

I was pleasantly surprised that the Emerging Artists Room was a horse of a different complexion, art that I responded to—metallic gouaches with Vermeer-like luminosity, pictures of amazing color and texture and use of space. There was a digital CD projected on the white, white wall that virtually compelled me to look at it—*Fantasia* meets the Zen master, O'Keeffe fuses with *2001: A Space Odyssey*.

Cynics like me hate it when they are wrong and have to undergo an attitude adjustment. Don't tell me this motley crew of artists sticking to Ellen and me like a burr to a dog created this amazing work. As if she read my mind, which is entirely possible since every other person in Santa Fe is a psychic, Ellen Paddington said, pointing to the four walls, "Look at what my kids produced; aren't they incredible?"

"I like this show very much," I said, trying to keep the amazement out of my voice. "When I interview you, I want to find out how you started this program, how you find your artists."

"The force field that brought me to this vortex of light known as Santa Fe drew me to Ellen's positive energy," interjected a tall, kooky-looking lad sporting a T-shirt that read: "Fear No Art."

Some artists, particularly the New Age ones whose mothership brought them to Santa Fe, should emulate Victorian children and be seen and not heard. Ellen smiled at the young man.

"After our opening, I hope you and Dr. Bergenceuse can join some of my artists for dessert and a Japanese tea ceremony at my home," said Ellen, pulling a crumpled map from the pocket of her blouse. "Here's how you get there."

"Don't even bother inviting her," droned one of the bored-looking ensemble of artists, an anorexic-looking maiden dressed all in black. "She's got bigger fish to fry."

"Yeah," said another of the entourage. "Mickey's leaving the low-rent district and is off to interview that miserable harpy Letty Rothschild."

One thing that had always driven me crazy about Santa Fe is that everyone knew more about you than you did yourself. As far as I was aware, Berg and Brady were the only ones who knew my plans for the evening. Was my assignment schedule posted on the Plaza?

Suddenly, I was surrounded by a Greek chorus.

"Dame Rothschild is horrible to artists."

"She humiliates us and makes us beg."

"She only shows artists she is sleeping with."

"All she cares about is having her picture plastered all over *People Magazine*."

"Interview Ellen instead. She's a true de' Medici to artists."

Finally, an exit line: "Ms. Paddington, can we set up a time for an interview?"

"Oh, by all means."

"How about tomorrow morning around ten? Here?"

"Perfect. I look forward to it."

I tugged at Berg's hand, indicating that we were ready to blow this joint. Paddington gently shook my hand and said, "Have a nice time at Leticia's."

"If that's possible," said a pony-tailed, gray-haired gentleman who escorted us to the front door. "You know that Ellen introduced Rothschild to everyone in Santa Fe's art world? And you know how she repaid her? By cutting her dead socially."

"That bitch hasn't added anything positive to anyone's life!" shouted the pink-and blue-haired woman as we hurried out the front door.

The parking lot of Leticia Rothschild's glitzy gallery on Paseo de Peralta indicated that the caviar crowd had already arrived. A shiny new herd of Mercedes, Jaguars (with a classic Jaguar X-KE leading the pack), Range Rovers, Hummers, and other assorted SUVs had been corralled into one corner of the massive parking lot. They seemed to stand in anxious anticipation, waiting for their owners to ride them out onto the open range once more. Berg parked his classic, cashmere blue- and-white 1956 Chevy Bel Air right next to Rothschild's celebrated cherry-red Rolls Royce and tossed the keys to the disdainful parking valet as we disappeared into the crowd.

"Here we are at the Ritz Carlton after Motel 6," I said to Berg as we made our way into the imposing adobe building, which looked more like a museum than a gallery.

We entered the security-flanked gallery to the scent of red sweetheart roses and strains of a Brandenburg Concerto played by the Santa Fe Symphony String Quartet. The gallery was resplendent. I hadn't seen so many flowers in one place since I covered a Mafia funeral in New Jersey.

Gallery Rothschild was magnificent in every detail. Henry Moore sculptures, Alexander Calder mobiles, and James Whistler paintings greeted us just inside the entrance. The building's design, devoid of art, had enough pizzazz to recommend it. I was ready to move in.

"Look at the incredible stone work, the massive skylights, and the wonderful wood floors," I said to Berg as we left the foyer. I was hoping the beautiful appointments might inspire my man who was, in exceedingly slow motion, remodeling his beloved Canyon Road Adobe Nightmare.

Rothschild had a coast-to-coast reputation as a twenty-four-carat bitch. I already knew from the pages of *The Wall Street Journal* and *The National Enquirer* that she was a powerful player in the cultural arena, but that she was also the art maven that the world loved to hate.

"The woman may be a shrew, but she's a shrew with good taste," I whispered to Berg.

I looked around the room, trying to soak up the atmosphere and compose a lead. What I came up with sounded more like *Entertainment Tonight* than *The New York Times* or *The Maverick*. But I think I've already revealed my disdain for art openings in the town I had never planned to write about again.

Just as I was milling about and inwardly congratulating myself on feeling anonymous in a faceless crowd, my luck changed.

"Mickey, my dear," chirped a sweet-faced woman who looked vaguely familiar. "I was so sorry to hear about Mel," she said, squeezing my hand. "She was one of my favorite students." Some old piece of data in the back of my brain kicked in and reminded me that this woman was Mrs. Cheek, my high school art teacher.

Before I could respond to her, a flock of condolence callers surrounded me. Some faces I recognized, many were strangers, but they all told me, in some form or another, that they had loved my sister. I winced inwardly, and Berg put his arm around me. I knew from a lifetime of experience that I was presenting a perfectly serene, composed exterior. Raised in a family where negative emotions weren't allowed, I was schooled in the art of being an accomplished actress. But I wished I were anywhere but here.

"Mickey, let me introduce myself," said a tall blonde, beautiful enough to grace the big screen. "I'm Sally Pommery, Ms. Rothschild's assistant. Welcome to our opening." She gently but firmly extricated Berg and me from the crowd.

"It must be hard for you talking about your sister wherever you go. This town can be incredibly small at times. I came from Los Angeles, and I still can't get over encountering people I know every place I go. And everyone's related to everyone; sometimes, it feels positively incestuous."

"You should have grown up here. I couldn't dot an 'i' or cross a 't' without someone reporting it to my parents. After high school, I took the first plane out."

"Well, for the sake of professional journalism, I'm delighted that you're back."

"What about you?" I asked. "You look like you grew up in California."

She flashed her perfect smile, and it seemed genuine.

"Like so many others, I had visions of stardom." She shrugged. "But my acting talents didn't take me beyond commercials and small speaking parts." She made a face somewhere between a grimace and a pout (either way it looked good on her). "I'd say it didn't 'help' that I wasn't partial to casting couches."

As a New Yorker, I was programmed to dislike Californians. They were all too often thin, blonde, or mellow. Sally was, in fact, all three. Like so many of them who had landed here, she was, no doubt, buying Santa Fe houses as if they were pieces on a monopoly board.

In spite of my inbred prejudices, I couldn't help but like her, even though she looked like she should be on the cover of a Beach Boys CD. She exuded warmth, sunniness, and a smooth professionalism not often seen in my hang-loose hometown. On top of that, she looked like she could handle herself on said "casting couches" and pull no punches.

"Ms. Rothschild is looking forward to meeting you. She's a big fan of your work; she read many of your pieces in *News View* when she was a curator at the Whitney. She was so pleased to hear you were going to be perking up our local paper. It's not that she doesn't admire Brady, but your articles have so much style and sophistication," Sally said as she skillfully maneuvered us toward an elegant buffet table that looked as if it had been lifted from the pages of the now-defunct *Gourmet*.

I wondered to myself if the svelte Sally would eat any of the enticing-looking appetizers. In the best California fashion, she looked as if her diet consisted of nothing heavier than a celery stick and a bottle of water.

Berg, looking inspired by the table ahead, whispered into my ear, "How is it that the genuinely lovely Ms. Pommery is married to one of my least favorite narcissists, Richard Wainwright?"

I ignored his question for the moment (it was rhetorical anyway), keeping my focus on "lovely Sally."

"Let me put you in the very capable hands of Shackleton, Ms. Rothschild's very own version of Jeeves," Sally said, backstepping gracefully. "He used to be with the Royal Family 'til Leticia stole him away, and now he rules brilliantly with an iron spatula over the kitchen."

Shackleton, also apparently a one-name phenomenon like Prince or Madonna, was a silver-haired, dapper gentleman dressed to the nines in a perfectly tailored tuxedo. In a cultivated Oxford English accent, he queried, "Might I venture to inquire what would be your pleasure this evening?"

"What are you peddling, Shack, old bean, old thing?" inquired my folksy physicist.

"I daresay, Dr. Bergenceuse, it is perfectly delightful to see you. I fancy that you are faring well in the culinary arts."

Berg grinned. "Mickey Moskowitz, meet Shackleton, the most accomplished chef this side of Chez Panisse, Lutece, and The Inn at Little Washington. He also spent some time slinging hash on the QE2 during her glory days."

"Ms. Moskowitz," Shackleton said with a click of the heels and a courtly bow. "I am, indeed, enchanted to make your acquaintance. It was my excellent fortune to have the good doctor in my Aspiring Chefs Class during the recent Chile and Wine Festival. I must say he was a most creative student, and with a modicum of practice, Dr. Bergenceuse could become a superior chef."

One of the things I find both endearing and exasperating about Berg is that he is such a Renaissance man. He and Mel were so much alike, with so many interests. All I do is work, 24-7.

"Please allow me to be of service," Shackleton said quietly. "A stimulating art opening is an aperitif in itself, but I would like to offer a few hors d'oeuvres certain to amuse and entice." With a subtle nod of his head, Shackleton conjured up two tuxedoed assistants who appeared from nowhere, with Haviland Limoges china plates in hand.

"Our theme this evening, Dr. Bergenceuse and Ms. Moskowitz, is the Art of Southwest Cooking. The fresh vegetables are from Santa Fe's historic Farmer's Market. They are complemented by Galisteo guacamole, cornmeal pizza with wild indigenous mushrooms, exotic-game pâté, and oysters with cilantro pesto. In precisely forty-eight minutes, we'll be serving a dinner of sweet potato bisque with avocado, pear, and lime; Caesar salad with blue cornmeal croutons; prawns stuffed with goat cheese on tomato coulis; and enchiladas of filet mignon with chanterelles and sorrel sauce. For dessert, we will be offering white chocolate ravioli and Southwestern fruit flan with prickly pear glaze. The wine, but of course, is Chateau Rothschild, one of the great Burgundies." Shackleton poured both of us some of the vintage brew.

"I'll try one of each, old chap," said my man of the people. He chatted up Shackleton and his assistants a bit, while I happily munched on several of the appetizers and sipped the wine. Rothschild might be a harpy, but she certainly puts out a good spread. That counts for a lot in my book.

"Let's have a look at the show," I said, remembering I soon had to file a story about the art. I stopped grazing and grabbed Berg's hand.

"Okay," my boy said reluctantly. "But let's stay for dinner. Maybe I'll get some new recipes. These hors d'oeuvres are first-rate."

"Ah, the things I must endure keeping company with a budding chef."

"It was either learn to cook or starve to death. I know you'll find this hard to believe, but bagels and espresso do not make up the five basic food groups."

"Well, they should," I said, thinking how similar Berg's wry humor was to Mel's.

Sally, who had obviously taken the course on How to Feed and Squire Reporters Around Art Openings made her way back to us. With a Pepsodent smile revealing her perfect teeth, she took us under her wing, whether we wanted to be there or not. "Did you get enough appetizers to tide you over? I peeked at the dinner. It looks beautiful enough to decorate the walls."

"Mickey, I want to introduce you to Ms. Rothschild and our featured artist, Joaquin C. de Baca. Dr. Bergenceuse, I'm sure you'd rather talk shop with my husband, Richard Wainwright. Let me find him for you."

Berg squeezed my hand hard, a gesture that I recognized as an SOS signal. When Sally was out of earshot, Berg whispered to me, "Richard Wainwright! I'd rather meet a wayward army of insurance salesmen. That asshole is the most arrogant and paranoid physicist I know. And that takes some doing. He comes from a blue-blooded family who set him up in his own private lab—corporate planes, plenty of researchers, sexy secretaries who can't type. He's nothing but a bigmouth snake oil salesman who thinks he's the greatest scientist since Oppenheimer."

As Sally made her way toward us with Richard by her side, Berg whispered, "Name your price. But don't leave me alone with that jerk!"

"You know I drive a hard bargain. How 'bout if you go to New York with me next time and see if you can't learn to discover its many charms?"

Berg, a confirmed small-town animal, made a face and said, "Desperate times call for desperate measures. You're on. But right now, as one of my favorite country ballads puts it so succinctly, 'Do not forsake me oh, my darling.'"

Sally sauntered up with Richard Wainwright, and I was stunned. The man looked about as much like a Los Alamos scientist as I did a cowgirl. Besides being a hunk, he was dressed to kill. Most scientists on The Hill could double as centerfolds for *Popular Mechanics*. Wainwright appeared to be dressed for a photo shoot for the cover of *Gentleman's Quarterly*.

He kept his eyes on me, ignoring Berg, as he extended one manicured hand. "Ms. Moskowitz, it's a pleasure to meet you. I've heard nothing but accolades about you, and I'm a big fan of your work." His steady blue-gray eyes gave me that Clintonesque you-are-the-only-person-in-the-room look as he told me, "I'd like to give you an exclusive on the breakthrough experiment my scientists and I successfully completed earlier this week."

His husky voice took on an Ashley Wilkes Southern accent as he purred, "I have a press conference coming up soon, but it would be an honor if you could drop by for a preview. My press secretary will personally deliver the invitation.

My results will put New Mexico back on the map; what we have accomplished has been the goal of fusion scientists for decades. It's truly remarkable, and you will get to see firsthand how we did it," he explained, going full throttle into his Charleston drawl.

This guy is good, I thought to myself. He's Wally from *Leave it to Beaver* all grown up, capable of adding on the softest Southern touch of gentility and all dressed up in a charcoal, perfectly tailored Yves Saint Laurent suit.

Berg was being unusually well-behaved, but I knew he had heard enough when he offered to get me another glass of Rothschild's extraordinary signature wine.

Meanwhile, Wainwright took it upon himself to continue. "I started my own lab because Los Alamos works at such glacial speed. For our team, it was absurdly restrictive having to deal with DOE's bureaucratic interference: the milestones they impose, their meetings, and the relentless documentation. My team and I sidestepped all this government garbage and focused on doing the best computer modeling, designing, and fabricating miraculously reliable targets, setting up the appropriate diagnostics, and doing the experiments. You'll be one of the first to see how we accomplished all this using my private funding."

I didn't have the vaguest idea what he was talking about, but Berg, who had returned to my side, clearly was unimpressed. My boy had had it with Wainwright's self-trumpeting and patronizing remarks, and I was hoping he wouldn't pour Letty's four-star wine onto his adversary's $200 hairdo.

"We're glacial all right; we can check out s-l-o-w-l-y that irritating little thing called 'verification' and have other labs check and double check to make certain our research is repeatable. We all remember the scientific faux pas known as cold fusion? The people who thought they had nailed it ended up with egg on their faces."

"Oh, here it comes," said Wainwright contemptuously, looking like he wanted to clean Berg's clock. He restrained himself and instead spat out, "This sounds like the idealistic utterings of a graduate student working at the elite ivory tower called Los Alamos National Laboratory. It's an irrelevant facility filled with dreamy-eyed wusses who think their job is to come up with useless ideas and outsmart each other."

Berg looked like he was ready to fling the tray of farmer's market vegetables at his nemesis. Instead, he cleared his throat and grimaced. "In the grown-up, scientific world, these useless ideas are called 'basic research.'"

A coterie of people was following this rowdy scientific little-boy debate with great fervor. They gathered around my guy, while Wainwright stood looking bored but amused. In a calm voice he replied, "Dr. Bergenceuse, unfortunately, can't sell his cutting-edge results to the world because he doesn't have any. His group just keeps testing and perfecting concepts instead of turning them over to the free market."

These were fightin' words, and Berg rose to the occasion. Looking like he was a Sunday morning orator in London's Hyde Park corner, he countered, "Dr. Wainwright is a computer jockey who has to call in somebody to help him turn on the lights in his lab. He wouldn't know a neutron counter if it hit him on the head, but somehow, he's managed to convince a few folks that his experiments are world-class. When they realize how he's hoodwinked them, there'll be hell to pay."

I stepped in to separate the two little boys to avert any fisticuffs. I steered Berg toward the food section. Shackleton popped over to offer his protégé some freshly-baked hors d'oeuvres, but Berg said in a stage whisper, "I seem to have lost my appetite. Hucksters pretending to be scientists always interfere with my digestive process."

"Let's go see the show," I said, squeezing his hand. When we were out of Wainwright's earshot, I asked, "What's with the two of you? I've seen Palestinians and Israelis in a war zone get along better than you and Wainwright. Maybe I'll set up an interview with him. I can usually analyze someone and get to their core during an interview."

"Save your breath. I'll tell you about his core. He's a fraud. He steals people's work and takes credit for research he hasn't done. He's everything that's wrong with science today."

Sally spotted us and squired us over to meet Dame Rothschild and Joaquin C. de Baca. We prepared to greet the two flamboyant characters, but instead of, "Thank you for inviting us," I let out a shriek. What happened next was unbelievable, even by Santa Fe standards.

Both C. de Baca and Rothschild came lunging toward us with knives in their hands!

I heard a scream and was startled to realize that this humiliating noise had come from me.

As my racing heart slowed to a fast jog, Leticia Rothschild stepped toward me, dramatically threw down her knife, and embraced me as if we were old friends. I backed away, and she let out a shrill laugh, almost a cackle. "Darling," she said, drawing out the short "a" vowel sound like Southern taffy, "I'm afraid I got you."

She then picked up the fallen knife and ceremoniously plunged it into her heart. "Oh, my dear, you are too delicious," she said, bending the knife backwards and forwards. "It's plastic. Just a little party favor to carry out our theme: The Cutting Edge of Art. Joaquin's art all features knives; it's his signature. We're handing the plastic knives out to our guests, just for fun."

Brady had warned me about Rothschild's rather peculiar sense of humor. Next month's show no doubt would feature explicit color photographs of public executions. But, forget about humor; her sense of style was hers alone.

Wearing a form-fitting, knee-length scarlet dress while clasping a black sequined cigarette holder, she was a knockout, a dead ringer for the stunning Paloma Picasso.

The diva of the dramatic blended in beautifully with the elegant O'Keeffes, Pollocks, Whistlers, and Gaspards hanging on the walls.

"Ms. Moskowitz, I'm so enchanted to meet you," Rothschild postured, holding out a long, elegant hand. "I trust you won't write exclusively about our little party favors. I know you have a wicked sense of humor; I've read your work. I thought the knives and, of course, the food should be your sidebar. But your main article must concentrate on Joaquin's magnificent work and the party itself."

Her words were like a command given to a private from his general. I was not amused.

"We don't use sidebars at *The Maverick*. Thanks so much for your suggestions, but it's not our style."

She glared at me with her piercing violet eyes, and I thought to myself, *The queen looks like she may be getting a little cranky; it's time to pull out the flattery arsenal.* With narcissists such as Rothschild, fawning was the sincerest way to get what you wanted. Besides, the woman was an Amazon, about six feet tall. She towered over me.

"This gallery is lovely. And your food and wine are four-star."

Bingo. This stroking of mine seemed to soothe her; her perfectly made-up face broke into a decided smile.

"Darling, I'm so glad you appreciate the finer things in life; so many of the other galleries in town are in austerity mode. You're fortunate if you manage to get tap water and peanuts. But to me, an art opening is theater; you need all the right props to put on a good show. Speaking of props, Ms. Moskowitz," she said, giving me an unwanted hug. "You have a gorgeous piece of scenery on your arm." In a theatrical gesture worthy of Blanche DuBois, she slinked over to Berg, squeezed his biceps, and looked longingly into his eyes. I was embarrassed, but not as much as Berg. He blushed for the first time since I'd met him and gave me a look that said, *You owe me big time. First, Wainwright, and now this horny cougar.*

I was so fixated on Berg and how I was going to make it up to him that I barely noticed something nibbling on my shoe, surely not mice in this opulent Spanish-style mansion. I looked down to see a Vietnamese Pot-bellied pig nipping off the bows of my new black-and-red pumps.

"Cochonette likes you, or at least she fancies your shoes," gushed Rothschild, leaning down to stroke her pet. "It's funny because she normally prefers Ballys and Ferragamos." She glanced over at my pedestrian foot-wear and gave me what I'm sure was a pitying look. Cochonette oinked in agreement.

"You must meet my artist; he's simply divine," Leticia said, grabbing us each by the arm and pulling us toward a surly looking, handsome Hispanic man with angry brown eyes and expertly cut, shoulder-length, glisten-ing black hair. He looked a bit like a retread who'd been around the block a time or two. Even so, he seemed con-siderably younger than his patroness, whom I knew to be fifty-two.

Leticia abruptly brushed aside the people surround-ing her protégé and grabbed him for a long, passionate, body-length kiss. I whispered to Berg, "Guess 'no public displays of affection' was not something Letty learned at summer camp."

They came up for air. Laughing her tinsel laugh, Madame Rothschild said, "Joaquin, darling, you must meet some of my dear friends."

I despise this type of instant intimacy. But knowing how popular Rothschild was, it was conceivable that I was indeed one of her best friends.

What next? Bridesmaid at her wedding? And this from a woman whose pig just ate my starboard shoe!

"Ms. Moskowitz is a marvelous little writer fresh from a smashing career back East," the maven with moxie said, patting me on my head. "She's trying to bring a modicum of style to our 'little' local publication, aren't you, dear?"

Her patronizing "little" description of me, reducing me to an inconsequential four-year-old, made me want to take my little hand and smash it into her beautiful face. Where was all this anger coming from? What was wrong with me? I never allow raw personal emotions to spill over into my work channel. Anger is an unprofessional emotion, and I needed to deal with it later, much later, like when I was seventy-five and hopefully tranquil. But, at the moment, I had a story to write, and the sooner I talked to Rothschild and her so-called artist, the sooner I could go home.

I squeezed Berg's hand and smiled demurely. Rothschild continued to gush. "Her friend, Dr. Bergenceuse, should be a male model."

Berg squirmed a little while Joaquin looked edgy, like his cocaine buzz was wearing off.

"And let me present Joaquin C. de Baca, the most talented, and gorgeous," she added, pinching his derrière, "artist working in the Southwest today."

She let forth one of her cackles. "He has so many talents."

"How fortunate that there's one you can hang on your walls," I said flashing my pearly whites.

Berg, who seemed to know everyone in my hometown even though he was a relative newcomer, said to C. de Baca, "I think we met on the slopes."

Suddenly the artist came to life, as if someone had pressed an "on" button on his back. Apparently, skiing was one of his "many talents."

"Right," he said, shaking Berg's hand. "I remember you took first place in the telly slalom race at the Ski Fest in February. I play around a little with the skinny skis myself."

They schmoozed about the slopes, which I affectionately called "Santa Fe's Great White Way," while I checked out Joaquin's paintings. Technically, they were excellent, and the man knew his cacti. He had the ribbed and spiny-barrel cactus, a variety of columnar organ-pipe cactus, a large display of the enormous humanlike saguaros, flat-jointed prickly pears, and a veritable garden of cholla, many sporting colorful blooms. I am somewhat of a cacti aficionado, and C. de Baca had done his homework. But huge pictures of cacti with purple knives stuck through them, in various poses, were not something I was excited about hanging in my living room. Obviously, my tastes were not shared by the general populace because there were red dots, indicating sales, on a third of the paintings.

Wincing, I went back to talk to Rothschild and C. de Baca. So far, Brady had been uncharacteristically wrong; I hadn't learned anything about Mel's murder and Santa Fe art openings were as vacuous as they were when I was in high school.

"Señor de Baca, your work is very interesting. I see we share a love of cacti."

"It sells well; people from Texas and back East seem to think cacti say Santa Fe, even though lots of what I paint, like the saguaro, are from Arizona. But they don't know the difference. So I paint them. And they buy them."

What a sense of integrity, I thought to myself. "What about the knives?"

"Let's just say I played around with knives as a boy, so I added them to my work. Adds a touch of excitement."

"Where did you grow up?"

"In New Mexico," he said, looking uncomfortable as he grabbed a glass of local Gruet champagne being passed by a server. "I'm not much of a talker; Rothschild can tell you all about me. She knows me inside and out," he said with a smirk.

"Indeed, I do," said Madame Rothschild, swooping into view. "He was a raw piece of clay," she said, blowing cigarette smoke into my face. "And I molded the clay into a piece of fine sculpture."

I was getting a little nauseated, and I could tell they were about to go at it again. "When can I interview you, Ms. Rothschild? How about tomorrow?"

"Perfect! Be a dear and make an appointment with Sally." Mercifully, our horny hostess spotted someone more important than us and led her protégé away.

"Thank God that's over," I said to Berg. *"Lifestyles of the Santa Fe Rich, Famous, and Narcissistic* has never been my favorite show."

When we were safely out of earshot and the symphony ensemble had started playing Vivaldi's *Four Seasons*, I thought it was safe to have a conversation about C. de Baca without being overheard.

"A source at *The Albuquerque Journal* told me she thought C. de Baca learned to love knives in prison."

"On the slopes, it was rumored that he did some time at the Springer Boys Reform Ranch," Berg answered as we took another glass of Chateau Rothschild.

"Dame Rothschild, no doubt, has a fascination for ex-prisoners, a la Norman Mailer. Thinks she can reform them."

"Or, more likely," said my boy, grabbing an oyster with chile-ginger salsa as we strolled by the appetizer table, "she's attracted to the danger."

"Speaking of danger, I guess you feel it's safe to indulge in more hors d'oeuvres with no fear of Wainwright's toxins infecting you?"

"He seems lost in conversation with the well-dressed Chinese contingent over in the corner. No doubt he's getting the name of their tailor."

"Obviously, you wouldn't be welcome in that discussion," I said kissing Berg on the cheek while gazing at his best formal T-shirt which he was wearing for this august occasion.

About this time, I saw a sight that made me want to duck under the tablecloth or disguise myself as one of the boys in the band. I had, after all, played a pretty mean clarinet in high school.

But it was too late. Before I could escape, the despicable person was right by my side, clutching for my hand and almost bellowing, "*La dama mas bella*, Señorita Moskowitz."

I stood speechless, and it was Berg who stepped in to rescue me, thundering, "If it isn't the king of financial appropriation, Senator Rendón!" while slapping him on the back.

If there was one person I did not want to see, it was Senator Rendón. The man was a worm.

The only reason he was here was to play politician and make nice with his constituents. I was decidedly not in his voting booth. You might have thought I was his biggest fundraiser, the way he greeted me, but I knew his effusive greetings were really about Mel.

"Mickey, *mi amiga*, I was at mass this morning at St. Francis praying for Mel. My wife and I were never blessed with children; she was like my own daughter. At least, we can be comforted knowing she is standing on the right-hand side of God, as one of his chosen ones."

I was practically an atheist (in spite of some basic training in Judaism), and Rendón's simplistic religious claptrap disgusted me. "Forgive me if I can't share your spiritual gobbledygook; all I know is that my sister is dead and buried under the dirt at Memorial Gardens Cemetery. She was far too young to be keeping any celestial beings company."

Rendón took off his tortoise shell glasses, squinted his hazel eyes, and ran a hand through his thick, silver hair, streaked with black that emerged from both temples like

vestigial horns. I wondered if he and Lucifer were bes-
ties. But for a moment, he actually looked as if he might
be tearing up. I began to shift away, but he put his arm
around me and said in a tone worthy of a politician, "My
office is pulling out all the stops looking into Mel's death.
It was probably an accident; it's easy to lose control of
a bike on that road." He frowned deeply. "But it's also
very possible a passing vehicle accidentally swerved—you
know people texting and talking on their phones—and
forced her off the road. If that's what happened, it was a
hit-and-run. We'll find whoever is responsible and pros-
ecute to the fullest extent possible. I would wring his
neck myself!"

I knew how swift and fair justice was in New Mexico!
On the Albuquerque TV stations, the prime directive
was: "If it bleeds, it leads." Drunk driving was a weekly
favorite on all three major TV networks; recently, there
had been a story reported that our very own state held
the dubious honor of being number one in pedestrian
and cyclist deaths.

In New York, I worked with Eileen Pink from
Greenwood, Mississippi. She and I had sort of a sick game
we played, vying for whose state was the bigger loser. It
turns out that New Mexico and Mississippi always ran
neck-in-neck for being the worst in the nation for practically everything. So we would take turns slipping in the
name of our respective state for the dubious honor of
most drunk drivers, most unwed mothers, worst education system, most doctors fleeing the state ...

Eileen, a crackerjack photojournalist, and I bonded
over these pathetic statistics, and about once a month,

we would have a drink at the Waldorf Astoria's Bull and Bear Bar on 49th and Lex to toast one of our state's dismal records.

The black humor appealed to my cynical nature, but now that this statistic from my impoverished state had come back to bite me, it seemed downright dismal. New Mexico was controlled by the good old boys' network. Mel and I were neither good, old, nor boys. Mel was just dead, and I had to make it right.

Someone squeezed my fingers lightly—Berg. I guess I looked like I was about to knock Rendón's block off. My lad took my hand and whispered, "I know you can't stand Rendón, but remember he was good to Mel and she was happy running his Santa Fe office."

Relieved when Rendón wandered over to a couple wearing matching (and very expensive-looking) cowboy boots and beaded leather jackets, I uncharacteristically nabbed another glass of Chateau Rothschild; I don't usually drink when I work, but this assignment warranted some serious alcohol.

Mel and I used to joke that bedfellows make strange politicians. Even when we were kids having our own private slumber parties, she and I agreed on nothing political. I've always been a leftwing liberal, and (I stopped and took a deep breath) she was a right-wing conservative.

"We tried to laugh about it. Except for a few occasions, we always tried to see the humor, even in politics. Lord knows, there is enough in this state."

"Did Mel support Rendón when he was in the state legislature?" asked Berg, taking some chile-citrus scallop ceviche when one of the servers passed it our way.

"Yes, I'm afraid so. While I was earning Girl Scout badges, she spent her after-school hours passing out pamphlets trying to get Arturo elected. Mel was a science nerd, a techie—she was always winning awards at Los Alamos. She thought her man Rendón was good for The Lab."

"She was right; he brings in tons of money for research," Berg said.

"The only time Mel and I ever had a serious squabble was when Rendón voted to cut funding for art in the New Mexico public schools." I set my unfinished wine on a passing server's tray and picked up a glass of Santa Fe Springs mineral water. I needed to clear my head. "Let's go look at some of the art work he failed to censor."

We strolled into a large, well-appointed room and admired the paintings of Leon Gaspard, Nicolai Fechin, and Ernest and Mary Blumenschein, members of the early Taos School. There was even a hibiscus by Georgia O'Keeffe.

"The really hypocritical thing is that Mel told me that Rendón fancies himself an artist, sort of a Sunday painter. Used to hang his art work all over his Santa Fe office and expected everyone to gush all over it."

Berg paused to look at the hefty price tags on the old Taos masters. "Someone must have encouraged Arturo to try art when he was a lad."

"Yeah, that's the irony. He grew up in Truchas, but his dad drove him to an art enrichment program every Saturday in Santa Fe; it was sponsored by the Santa Fe public schools."

Rendón, in that slimy way politicians have, seemed to sense that we were talking about him, and suddenly, he was by my side again. "Mickey, my dear, I know you are grief-stricken, but I'm glad to see you're back at work already."

He put his arm around me and continued his drivel. "Letty just told me the wonderful news—that you'll be covering the arts for *The Maverick*. Mazel tov."

Rendón always had the ridiculous notion that everyone in our family spoke Yiddish. Mel's religion had been worshipping nature and saving defenseless animals. Mine had been work. Neither required Hebrew or Yiddish.

"I know you'll be a mensch in honor of Mel's blessed memory and write about my art opening, the day after Thanksgiving. Letty is giving me my first New Mexico show."

Oh, be still my heart, I thought to myself. Aloud I said, "I assume you'll be donating all the proceeds to art enrichment programs in the Santa Fe school system?"

"What a good idea! I'll have to get Mel—I mean, I'll get someone right on it." He shook his head, and the expression of angst on his face actually seemed genuine. "I'm sorry; I can't get used to the fact she's gone."

I winced, desperately needing to steer him away from his current topic. "You do primitive paintings, don't you?"

Rendón blinked, then nodded. Coming up to speed, he smiled and tried his best to blush. "Just a God-given talent. I've had no training."

"Just like politics, I guess," I shot back.

Berg, brushing up on his diplomacy skills, stepped in to try to save the day. The good and bad news about politicians like Rendón is that they never knew (or cared) when they were being insulted.

"What's Rothschild getting out of it?" quipped Berg. "An appointment at the Smithsonian or an ambassadorship?"

"How did you know?" answered my least-favorite politician.

I never thought Rendón had an ounce of humor, so I guess Berg had absorbed some psychic skills at Paddington's picnic.

"November isn't such a long way off," I said. And now I felt the need to shift the subject back to my sister. "What about Mel's death? You say you're sparing no resources, but what is your office actually doing? We both know that in the last hours before her death, she was working herself to exhaustion to make sure your annual fundraiser was a great success!"

Just as he was trying to come up with a plausible answer, he was saved by the dramatic entrance of Henry Don't-Call-Me-Hank Squank, Santa Fe's king of kitsch. Even though I had never met him, I recognized Santa Fe's most notable character. Even people who didn't live in Santa Fe knew what Squank looked like. He had been in *People Magazine* more often than Julia Roberts, who lived in neighboring Taos.

We saw, heard, and smelled Squank make his way into the room. He was dressed in his signature colorful fashion, with a bright blue pair of pants artistically streaked with oils from his latest painting. A paintbrush was tucked between his broken glasses and his left ear. His once-white shirt was dirty yellow and had prominent holes on both sleeves. He was ripe. Like his art, he assailed all the senses.

A happy, smiling crowd gathered around him. The sudden appearance of the town mascot was a sign that the party was a genuine Santa Fe event. Squank, who according to his media coverage usually adored all this attention, seemed not the least bit interested in it this evening.

"Ah, sure is good to see you folks, but I've got me some pressing business with Miz Rothschild. Got to see her right away, don't you know."

His eyes were glazed, and he seemed extremely agitated. He was hopping from foot to foot, pulling on his left ear, and resembled a demented elf who had just been kicked out of a homeless shelter.

He pranced over to Leticia and said, "Miz Rothschild, I've got to talk to you right away."

She was not amused. She looked about as happy to see Squank as she would a centipede squirming in her bottle of namesake wine. Her eyes shot laser beams, and her red mouth pursed tightly. She put me in mind of an anorexic Queen Victoria. But Rothschild was astute enough to hide her murderous impulses and let her sense of public relations dictate. After all, the press, not to mention Santa Fe's crème de la crème, was watching, and Squank was their favorite puppy.

"Henry, dahling, how delightful to see you. It wouldn't be a party without my favorite artist."

Squank looked confused, as if he were dealing with at least two faces of this Eve. "I've got to see you now, don't you know."

I surreptitiously followed them, on the pretext of finding the ladies room. Good reporters are like spies in that they can make themselves invisible at a moment's notice. Rothschild was too busy doing her Cruella de Vil imitation to pay attention to me.

"You nincompoop. What do you mean by coming here now? Have you lost your mind? Get out!"

"But-but-I-I—" Squank's stutter convinced me that his supposed benefactress terrified him.

Just as things were heating up, Shackleton announced in his most formal, Jeeves-like tone, "Dinner is served."

Berg, who had followed me and was ready to add some new recipes to his repertoire, grabbed my hand and pulled me toward the library where supper was to be served. As we were looking for our place cards on the elegantly set dinner table, we were stopped by the sounds of a terrible ruckus.

I looked around to see a cherubic man with the face of a Botticelli angel sobbing like a two-year-old whose favorite toy has just been smashed.

"It's not fair," he blubbered. "She promised me a one-man show, and then this opportunistic asshole came along, and she dumped me like a box of used kitty litter." His manic voice kept getting louder and louder.

An attractive redhead sitting on the other side of Berg said, "Oh my god, who let in Jamie Inman, Santa Fe's infamous whiny wino? I thought he was blacklisted from all art openings."

"Letty better lock up her remaining bottles; Inman can drink anyone under the table, especially at openings where he's not the star," added another dinner guest.

Shackleton signaled to his waiters to start serving dinner, hoping to reframe the situation.

It was too late: Inman sobbed steadily while pouring his wine onto the tablecloth and threatening to fling whole bottles at the startled waiters.

"She's a bitch," Inman ranted. Most diners turned to watch his performance. A few ignored this apparently all-too-familiar scene and concentrated on the delicious vittles. "She's ruined my career!" Inman shrieked in a shrill and piercing voice.

"This was supposed to be my show, not that no-talent gigolo!" While everyone now watched this bizarre performance in stunned silence, Inman suddenly looked like the lead in *Friday the 13th, Part 12*. His face contorted, he ignored the onlookers and instead gazed intently at a huge C. de Baca painting, an enormous cactus with purple dots all over it. He suddenly pulled a wooden-handled kitchen knife out of his pocket (no plastic toy!), and before anyone could stop him, he ran to the painting and slashed it into shreds.

Rothschild stood up from the head of the table. I expected her to scream an outrageous stream of expletives at Inman or call her security guards. Instead, she looked like she was in a trance. She stared blankly into space, and the left side of her body was shaking.

"What's with Rothschild?" I whispered to Berg. "Is she drunk or in shock?"

Before Berg could answer, C. de Baca rushed up to Inman and twisted his arm behind his back, causing the knife to come crashing to the floor.

"I'll get you for this!" shouted Inman. The security guards, about three minutes late—in the best Santa Fe fashion—grabbed Inman and hustled him away.

Everyone was stunned. I felt sick, as if someone had punched me in the stomach. I had read about paintings being slashed, but I'd never been there when it happened. Even though I hadn't liked the painting, I felt as if I had been a witness to a brutal death.

A pall fell over the entire crowd. No one moved. Like characters in a silent movie, we drifted over in unspoken solitude to look at the mutilated painting.

We could still hear Inman screaming in the parking lot. I was mentally rewriting the lead for my story: "Rothschild's Latest Gallery Opening a Slashing Success!" (Okay, some situations warrant bad humor.) Damn! Brady was right, after all. The local art scene was anything but boring.

I tried to break the tension by whispering to Berg, "A little guerrilla theatre to liven up an average Santa Fe opening."

"Yeah," he replied, taking my hand and leading me out to the car park. "That's why I like to limit my outings to the ski slopes or hiking trails—sans woo-woo picnics! The wildlife in Santa Fe can be a little too threatening."

The words were flip. The tone was sober.

There is something good about being bad. When you declare yourself bad at something, there are no expectations. It's liberating!

Anyone who has known me for more than two minutes knows that I cannot cook. As Berg can confirm, I can and do buy the world's best coffee and bagels, but that is the beginning and the end of my repertoire.

For years, Lupita had offered me cooking lessons. But cooking is not the pastime for me. I am far too impatient to pore through cookbooks, stand in endless lines in fancy grocery stores, and keep up with the revolutionary new ovens, cookware, and assortment of spices.

Fortunately, some of my best friends are wonderful cooks.

They're also wonderfully competitive, each with a signature show-off dish that is their pride and joy. So, hosting an intimate brunch with my three best *compadres* was the perfect excuse to make Berg get cracking—eggs, that is.

It also provided the opportunity to show Santa Fe's current District Attorney and the Chief Medical Investigator the piece of red headlamp that Berg and I had discovered and retrieved yesterday—was it only yesterday!—the lonely and only piece of evidence.

What I excel in is subterfuge, making a planned, carefully crafted event seem spontaneous. So, it was that, late last night, after the excitement-verging-on-trauma of the art opening, I pressed auto-dial on my cell.

"Hey, Lupita, wasn't one of your Girl Scout honor pledges a vow that you wouldn't let your adopted sister starve to death?"

I heard a hiss and quickly adjusted my phone away from my ear, but all I could hear was annoying static.

I tried again, this time guilt-mongering via text: "Lupita, I need the curative power of green chile. Please bring a platter of your prize-winning enchiladas to a surprise brunch! When: Tomorrow. Where: The Adobe Nightmare."

What I lacked in culinary skills, I made up for in matchmaking schemes. It was so out of character for me, but I loved playing *yenta*.

Lupita and I always teased each other that we were hopeless old maids (blame local culture). I felt it my sisterly duty to find a suitable gentleman caller for *mi hermana* and beautiful best friend.

And Pygmy Koloznov—Chief Medical Investigator and Berg's close pal—was my pick.

Lupita fooled attorneys new to Santa Fe courtrooms with her God-given assets: that irresistible twinkle in her chocolate-brown eyes and her smooth as silk café au lait skin. Barely taller than my five feet, even in her customary three-inch heels, they thought she looked like a tiny and exquisite butterfly in need of their protection. They soon discovered what the court already knew—confident, feisty, and a full-on extrovert, she was a winning prosecutor. In short (pun intended), she was one tough cookie.

And then consider Pygmy K., who at first glance might be mistaken for the tall, darkly handsome, brooding Eugene Onegin. Ironically, Pygmy was the mirror opposite of Onegin when it comes to temperament. Think Ferdinand the Bull—lumbering and playful and shy and funny.

It's the perfect match, I told Berg after I'd texted Pygmy his last-minute invite—they have nothing in common!

Saturday dawned clear and crisp and kept its promise of a perfect fall morning—by ten o'clock, sunlight sparkled through the branches of piñons and aspens and ash trees outside The Adobe Nightmare.

Inside, I sipped coffee between bites of my Zabar's bagel slathered with cream cheese and jam while I put finishing touches on my pieces about last night's two art openings.

Magic, perched on the desk inches from my laptop keyboard, provided inspiration. His ears flicked from time to time when my boy shouted some pronouncement from his kitchen.

"Holy mole!" bellowed my enthusiastic chef, making both the cat and me jump.

"Hey!" I protested while Magic swatted my pencil—in a world of laptops and tablets, I still like to keep written notes.

Berg poked his head into my office, followed by one hand covered with a hot mitt that glowed with neon red and green chiles. "Wow, this is as good, or better than, Oaxacan mole. You have to taste this."

I wasn't certain if he was talking to Magic or me, but there was beautiful Berg carrying a huge spoon giving off wisps of steam, and that spoon was headed straight for my mouth.

"That smells heavenly," I said, my sniffer working overtime. "I'm picking up the scents of several kinds of divine chile, enhanced with cinnamon, cumin, black pepper, and chocolate."

"For someone who doesn't cook, you have quite the trained schnoz—cute too."

"It's a natural gift," I said, shrugging my shoulders.

"One of so many," Berg said, planting a quick kiss on my nose.

"Hmmm, nice, but I still need to finish 400 words," I said, smiling up at him. He was standing at my shoulder, scanning the screen and my story.

He acknowledged my deadline with another quick kiss, lingering even after Magic shifted his focus, leaping gracefully to the floor and stalking in the direction of the living room.

I tickled Berg's chin. "You hear something?"

Berg took a moment to consider my question. "If you mean Lupita trespassing into our living room, then yes."

Lupita called out cheerfully. "Mickey, mija? Berg? I know you guys are here because I smell those spices and chocolate. Heavenly. I hope you're decent because I've got my extra special enchiladas made from my top-secret recipe!"

I followed Berg into the living room where he took

Lupita's hot tray from her mitted hands, and I let myself be enveloped in her loving and sturdy hug. *What's happening to me?* I wondered fleetingly; by nature, I'm not a hugger—but apparently my nature was shifting, due to circumstances.

By the time she released me, Berg was in the kitchen doing those mysterious things that chefs do—at least, that's what I imagined. We joined him, and in record time, I supplied her with strong coffee and offered her an array of bagels.

She smiled a mysterious smile after the first sip of hair-on-your-chest DeLuca's brew. "Whew, just right." She nodded to the platter of bagels accompanied by the schmears of cream cheese, lox, mustard, sweet-and-sour pickled cucumber, and salt beef and, of course, a bowl of New Mexico green chile, diced and slightly chilled. "I'm feeling like a toasted onion."

"Funny, to my eyes, you look more like sesame wearing a mountain of sweet and sour creamy cream cheese!"

"Stop, you'll make me blush," she quipped. She'd just taken a huge first bite of onion bagel coated in her favorite schmears: cream cheese, lox, and chile when all three of us registered a jolt of surprise at a sharp rapping on the door. Magic jumped from the table to Berg's shoulder. We all clustered in the doorway between the kitchen and living room.

"When did we become Grand Central?" I wondered, but I smiled when I saw the huge person standing on our porch. His body filled the window while his neck and head, seemingly reaching to the clouds, stretched out of sight.

Berg swung the glass-paned door wide open with a mock bow. "If it isn't Pygmy Koloznov. *Kak zheeviosh, moy droog!*"

"*Khorasho, spaseebah,*" Pygmy said, grinning. "I'm feeling great!"

"Pygmy!" I gushed, genuinely happy at seeing him. "Come in!"

"I've brought my super brain food," he announced, holding up what was clearly a bottle of something alcoholic wrapped in cellophane. He paused for an instant, his gaze resting on Lupita, a deep red flush brightening his cheeks. As if he suddenly remembered the heavy dish balanced on one massive palm, he cleared his throat. "And, of course, my internationally renowned blini with caviar."

"To the kitchen, man!" Berg said, pushing us all in that direction.

Inside the now seemingly small space, Pygmy relinquished the bottle to Lupita, with his beguiling smile; at the same time, he guided the hot dish onto a trivet. He seemed delighted by the moustache of cream cheese with flecks of chile adorning Lupita's upper lip.

With great fanfare, Pygmy presented his offering—rows of perfectly formed blini with rich, dark caviar dabbled artistically on top. "And not to be forgotten ..." Out of a small waist pouch, he produced a container of sour cream and a small bottle of caviar, as yet unsealed and unopened.

"Second only to Iranian Almas," Pygmy announced in his deep baritone. "Bemka's Crown Russian Ossetra—to be shared with dear friends as blini represents new beginnings ..." Our Russian ambassador caught my gaze with his deep dark eyes, now glistening. "And, for dear Mel on her journey, a rebirth."

Magic, still riding Berg's shoulder, meowed what was clearly his approval.

Quickly, Lupita raised Pygmy's bottle of champagne into the air. "Shall we celebrate our renewal with a bit of bubbly?"

I clapped, taking a deep breath, so glad that my hermana had steered the moment away from tears. Pygmy, bless him, wore his Russian heart on his sleeve.

Hmmm. I watched Berg watch Pygmy watch Lupita—a kind of observational conga line. He only took his eyes off her when his plate needed tending. Berg caught my eye, offering his own hopeful wink. I knew he was thinking they looked nice together.

Lupita planted her coffee mug on the island, suddenly serious. "Okay, what have you got for me that's so important it's worth a tray of my world-famous enchiladas?"

"Not to leave out my world-famous blinis," Pygmy added.

"We want both of you to see this," I said.

Without a flourish, and without touching it directly, Berg presented the piece of broken red lamp cover, now resting carefully on paper.

Lupita stared at it as if it might stand up and explain itself.

Berg offered her his phone and his crime scene photographs, ready for her review.

After what must have been a minute but felt so much longer, she handed the phone and photos to Pygmy and said, "You did a good job, both of you. I can't believe the investigating officers missed this." She frowned. "The chain of custody is compromised because they'll say, and rightly so, that anyone could have dropped it there even a day after the accident." She popped a bit of everything bagel topped with cream cheese—and just a smidge of Pygmy's caviar—between her very red lips. He looked extremely serious, and Russians are serious by nature, so use your imagination.

"Lupita's right," Pygmy said, blushing again. "But even without cause-of-death, it's evidence we can use to do our own investigating. Unofficially, of course. Paint colors can be isolated sometimes. There are so many variations, and from this, we can get a make and model of a vehicle. And I can talk to my deputy at the Office of the Medical Investigator who handled a very superficial investigation." He handed Berg's phone back and addressed Lupita. "Let me look into this—you're too well-known pretty much everywhere in this state. While me, I can't get people to return my calls, so now I can learn some new techniques."

After a slight hesitation, Lupita nodded.

Before we could say any more, my boss, Brady, changed the subject for us by texting me: "Just sent you guest list email—open it now!"

Just like him to issue orders via text. And because Brady was Brady, I followed his orders.

When I opened his email, I saw the list of donors who'd attended Rendón's fundraiser.

By now, we were seated around the kitchen island, sipping mimosas and wiping our plates clean of second and third helpings of chocolatey mole, vodka spiked sour cream, salt beef, and tangy New Mexico green chile—all soaked up with hunks off a loaf of Berg's fresh sourdough, still warm from the oven.

My stomach hurt I was so full, but I couldn't seem to get enough, especially the chile and caviar—the first real meal I'd eaten since the news about Mel.

And, to punctuate the remains of the feast, Brady's list of attendees at the fundraiser rolled off Berg's printer.

"This reads like a who's who of Santa Fe's hoity-toities," Berg said, skimming over pages spread out on the smooth oak top.

I claimed a page and began to read, and after a minute, I said, "We saw a lot of these folks at last night's openings. I guess the overlap makes sense …"

"Richard Wainwright," Berg growled. "No doubt he wants Rendón to channel money his way." My lad waved a piece of mole-soaked bread over his head. "I wonder how Sally puts up with him."

Lupita twirled one dark curl away from her eyes with a gleaming, fuchsia-lacquered nail. "You never read *When Bad Men Happen to Good Women?*"

Pygmy snorted in appreciation. "That would top *The New York Times* list for months!" He patted the warm, aged wood table gently with one huge hand. "And speaking of not-so-great men, Rendón's been in power for decades. He's done favors for anyone who's someone—and they've favored him back."

I forced myself to focus on the pages in front of me—I didn't want my thoughts returning stubbornly to the question of how my sister put up with a staunch conservative like Rendón. *Enough,* I told myself—*Mel had her reasons and no lack of integrity. Let it go.*

Clearly reading my thoughts, Lupita spoke up—"On his good side, Rendón's protected many of Mel's most heartfelt environmental causes."

"Don't forget he's all for saving the prairie dog and a list of endangered species," Berg said, nodding.

Even as I heard them, my attention now centered on the list. Several names seemed to jump off the page. "Leticia Rothschild is on the confirmed list."

"Apparently, she's close friends with Rendón," Lupita said. "He lets her use the guest house at his ranch so she can put prospective art collectors up in style while they visit Santa Fe from around the world."

Berg harrumphed. "He was babbling last night that Leticia was going to give him his own one-man show."

"Right," I said. "And here is her edgy artist bad boy of the month, Joaquin, who specializes in stabbing his own paintings."

Berg and Lupita both leaned in to read over my shoulder. Berg pointed to a name, and Lupita said, "James Inman—that man would show up at a Tupperware party if there was free booze."

Pygmy, who had been savoring Lupita's enchiladas—already almost finished with his third large helping—examined the bite on the tip of his fork. "These rank with the best of the best on my enchilada life list," he said, sounding like a man who had reached enlightenment.

Lupita smiled—and if Pygmy's smile was Ferdinand the Bull's, Lupita's could only be described as the

Cheshire Cat, but she kept her attention dutifully on the guest list. "Your other gallery owner is on here, too," she said. "Leticia's competition, Ellen Paddington."

"And what do you know," Berg interjected, "my man Shackleton catered this VIP event." Berg licked the dollop of vodka and sour cream from his finger just as my phone dinged, signaling an incoming text.

Brady again—this time with photos from the event from *The Maverick's* archives.

I stared at them—catching sight of Mel at the edge of the photo's frame a few feet behind several musicians playing chamber instruments. She'd been caught speaking to someone, but only his arm was visible in his suit coat, a Rolex gleaming on his wrist.

Gazing over my shoulder, Lupita murmured, "Oh …" She pinched my ear. I stared hard at Lupita's expression. I looked back at the photo. "Mel looks upset," I said tightly.

"Sí, mija, I know that look—" Lupita said. "That's righteous Mel, who has God on her side."

I nodded slowly. I brushed away something wet from my cheek. "She's angry, and I don't think it's a stretch to say she's angry with the guy wearing the Rolex."

Berg leaned in to see. "We'll follow up with the photographer—it's his or her job to know who was cropped from a shot."

"Brady can follow that up," I said quietly.

"Oy …" Pygmy shook his head. "Look there, that person in the background, lurking behind the pine. Someone who's not on the guest list …"

Berg almost squeaked. "Henry Don't-Call-Me-Hank Squank."

"Lurking is kind of a signature for him," Lupita said.

Pygmy pointed. "What's that behind him?"

I shook my head as the image registered. "No, it can't be—"

"Oh, yes, it can," Berg said. "Leticia's pot-bellied pig! That beast owes you at least one shoe, button nose," he said.

"No such thing as one shoe, 'mano," Lupita said, patting his head. "That effing pig owes Mickey a pair!"

While the men settled into a debate on the attributes of various types of caviar, Lupita took my arm and led me out of the kitchen to a corner of the living room where Magic, resting on a pillow, stretched out one paw as if beckoning us to join him. For that moment, I wanted to; I wanted to curl up with him and go to sleep. But it wasn't going to happen—not now.

Lupita said, "Mr. Lucero called again, Mickey, and he sounds a little worried about Mel's casita staying empty. He's trying to keep an eye out but …"

A seeping cold feeling beginning at my feet rose through my body like an internal frost. "I don't think I can." I shook my head.

She frowned, worry widening her chocolate-brown eyes. "You can, Mickey, I'll be with you. Mel would want you to do it. And there might be clues to why she was so upset the last time she called you."

I tried to nod, but my neck had frozen from the cold.

Lupita tugged gently on my arm. "I'll be with you, and you only need to take what's most vital—any personal documents, banking info, safe deposit key—anything of value to thieves. And Mel used a laptop, right, to do all her work? So we need to look at that—"

"Of course." Suddenly, I could breathe again, and I felt the cold dissipating, banished by my new sense of purpose. "We need to go soon," I said, clasping her hand and squeezing it.

"That's the Mickey I know," she said, nodding intently. "I'll call Mr. Lucero and tell him; he promised to let me know where he'll leave the key."

Our conversation ended when Pygmy bellowed from the kitchen, "Calling all contestants!"

"Time to judge our cook off," Berg added, poking his head out of the kitchen door.

I counted up the votes, collected in one of Berg's nana's teacups. "First anonymous vote cast for Berg's extraordinary mole—hmmm, a little editorial license taken on this ballot." I winked at my lad.

"Second anonymous vote cast for Lupita's 'world-famous enchiladas,' and I quote." I blinked.

"Third anonymous vote cast for DeLuca's shipping policy!" I grinned at them all before continuing. "Drum roll, please …"

Both Pygmy and Berg obeyed my command, finger drumming the pans.

"The fourth anonymous vote is cast for—"

I took the moment, the pregnant pause, and I met my sister's dark, sparkling eyes.

"What?" She was shameful, the way she could bat those thick lashes.

And, finally, I turned my gaze on Pygmy. This time,

he did not blush. He simply smiled back at me, his handsome Russian face set with determination.

"Read it, please. This is torture," Berg bleated.

The fourth vote cast is for "the most beautiful green chile enchiladas in the world"—and again, I quote.

This time it was Lupita who blushed.

The part I love most about being a journalist is doing interviews. They give me a chance to ask probing, personal questions of total strangers. And the bizarre thing is, they usually answer them. My theory is that people, even shy ones, love to talk about themselves. We live in an extremely distracted society where no one listens to anyone. So, when a reporter seems to hang on every word, it appeals to the "unheard" everywhere.

But even with my penchant for one-on-one reporting, interviewing Ellen Paddington and Leticia Rothschild on the same day was enough to give me the bends. Talk about Beauty and the Beast. The way they each expressed concern about Mel was a good litmus test of their personalities: Paddington lit a candle and chanted a Buddhist prayer for her soul, while Rothschild offhandedly remarked, "Too bad about your sister."

Still, the two interviews meshed nicely; Paddington prepped me for Rothschild. In most towns, there are six degrees of separation; in Santa Fe, there are only one and a half. I always looked around at restaurants before I started talking about anyone; inevitably, the object of my discussion would be at the table next to me. Usually, this small-town trait of strangers knowing more about you than you knew about yourself drove me crazy. Today, it was convenient, as Ellen began our talk telling me how her life and Letty's had been intertwined for years.

"Our families have been friends for generations," Ellen said as we sat lotus style on the floor of her stark, white living room while she served me Japanese tea and rice crackers. "Letty and I even went to camp together in Maine—years before you were born," Ellen said, pushing her bushy white hair out of her eyes. "Even at twelve, Letty was a force to be reckoned with. Always a leader, she had her own elite band of girls—all at her beck and call."

"Were you friends then?" I asked politely munching the tasteless rice crackers. My eyes were watering from the strong incense burning in the far corner of the room, and the tranquil Japanese background music was making me sleepy. What I wouldn't give for a double mocha espresso! It was pretty obvious that there was no caffeine in this household.

"Well, I tried to be, dear, but she never seemed to like me much. She was always playing practical jokes on me. She was always pulling pranks on almost everyone—most of them not very amusing." Ellen paused, poured us some more colorless tea, and hesitated, as if she were trying to decide whether to tell me more or change the subject.

I helped her out by asking, "What sort of jokes?" She still seemed reluctant, so I talked about myself, an interview device I find loosens people up. "I remember when I was ten at Camp Nokomis; someone held my head under water during optional swim. Girls were always short-sheeting each other's beds, and one of my cabinmates found a snake in her bunk."

"Oh, Letty wasn't so bad," Ellen said, with a pained look that belied her serene face. "Maybe just a little high-spirited. She liked to pin a 'Fatso' sign on my back. Not just once, but time and time again. I suppose I was a bit pudgy then. Twelve-year-old girls can be unkind, and several of the kids teased me. But Letty was clearly the ringleader." She bit sharply into a rice cracker. "I'm sure it was typical preadolescent behavior."

"What was your reaction when you found Leticia was moving to Santa Fe?"

"Resigned acceptance mixed with a little dread." She brushed some cracker crumbs from her pink-and-red kimono and said, "My mother taught me always to be gracious and polite. What could I do but introduce Letty to my friends in the Santa Fe art world? I had a big party for her. Even had it catered by the O'Keeffe Café because I knew that Letty would hate the macrobiotic fare that I usually serve."

"How did your friends react to her?"

"Oh, Letty can charm the aphids off the rose bushes when it suits her purpose. She's a born performer." Ellen rose suddenly from full lotus to get us more rice crackers, which I declined (she was in excellent shape for anyone's age; my legs were going prickly and numb under me).

She continued bluntly: "Then, when she had met everyone who could do her any good, she dropped me like a plate of red-hot habañeros."

Seated again, Ellen took a deep breath and looked like she was inwardly chanting a calming meditation. Then slowly, she said, "But Santa Fe is big enough for both of us. She's stolen a few artists from me, but most of my kids are extremely loyal. Let's change the subject, if we may, and talk about my wonderfully talented artists."

About this time, almost on cue, a pretty young woman emerged from the back bedroom and asked, "Would you like some more tea? Can I fix you some lunch? A late breakfast?"

I declined, feeling I couldn't stomach any brown rice and twig tea—I needed coffee! "No, Kelly, dear," Ellen said. "Why don't you just straighten the house a bit, and then get on with your painting." Ellen, Santa Fe's artists' answer to Maxwell Perkins—the discoverer of writers such as Hemingway and Fitzgerald—rose effortlessly again, crossed to her artist-in residence, and gave her a hug. "We need to think about a show for you, as soon as you're ready."

When the now-smiling Kelly, the fledgling artist, left for her in-house studio, I asked Ellen how many artists she clothed, fed, and sheltered.

"About five at a time." Ellen answered, "but down through the years, I must have taken care of well over 200.

Kelly is a perfect example of a kid who just needs a break. She's enormously talented and does beautiful lithographs but comes from an abusive family who thinks being an artist is a waste of time." Then, in a low voice, barely audible, Ellen practically whispered, "Somewhat like my family."

"You seem to be a modern version of the de' Medicis," I said.

"Oh, that's a little grand. Artists like Kelly just need a little help—a place to live, some art supplies, food, and a lot of love."

Ellen was one of those rare gallery owners who didn't want to talk about themselves all the time. As a matter of fact, I had to drag her résumé from her. She went to Smith after growing up in Chicago in a family who thought financiers were decidedly more important than painters. After college, she married briefly, worked as a curator at the Art Institute of Chicago, and then managed first the Flatfile Photography Gallery, then the Rhona Hoffman Gallery.

"Why Santa Fe?" I asked, always curious why so many people gravitated toward the town I couldn't wait to leave.

"My grandfather had TB, so he came here as a child. When I first visited this magical place with my family when I was eleven, I knew that I wanted to live here someday."

Her eyes shone when she talked about her attachment to the art world. For the next hour, Ellen talked about "her artists" with such love and devotion that I wanted to take up painting full-time and have her manage me. (Did I mention that I'm a closet Sunday painter? I don't talk about it much because it's embarrassing in a town where every third person is a would-be artist to add to the ever-growing list.)

Ellen gave me a goodbye peck on the cheek at 11:38 a.m. At the door, I turned to her and touched her arm lightly. "You attended Senator Rendón's Aspic in the Aspens fundraiser … and I just wondered if you …"

Ellen clutched my hand and held it tightly. "I'm so very sorry, Mickey, that was your sister's last day, wasn't it?"

I nodded, and to my horror, I felt my eyes tearing up. I tried to hold back the wave of fresh emotion threatening to roll through me. If I couldn't even manage my feelings around someone as caring as Ellen Paddington, how would I deal with Leticia and other potential suspects as I searched for the truth about my sister's death? I squeezed my free hand until my nails stabbed the flesh of my palm. "Did you notice anything unusual about Mel's behavior that day? I know she worked the event for Rendón."

"Oh." Now Ellen looked at me with something resembling pity. "I only said hello to her when I arrived, dear." Paddington shook her head. "All I can say is that she seemed a bit tense, but that's normal when you're in charge of an event for 500 guests—and a fundraiser, to boot."

I nodded. What more could I ask without raising her suspicion?

"But Mickey, you're not thinking…," Ellen paused to rephrase her question. "It was an accident, wasn't it?"

"I don't know," I said, horrified to hear the words coming out of my mouth. "I just need closure, I guess."

"Of course you do, dear," Ellen Paddington said. As I turned to walk out the door, I saw that she looked troubled, as if she might need closure, too.

I grabbed a quick espresso and Caesar salad at Vinaigrette and went right to the paper to type up my notes and compose a lead. I liked it so much I just kept going and finished the whole article. I try to always be objective and not get involved with my interviewees, but I must say, I was fond of Ellen. She was the eccentric, kind mother I never had.

As I drove to Leticia's, I thought about the differences between Ellen and Letty. It was like interviewing the Buddha and Lucifer on the same day. Once again, I was beginning to think Brady was right on the money; I was actually learning something on this art beat—and although I'd only begun to look into Mel's death, my intuition told me the connections between art and politics would lead to answers. And while my experience had been bizarre, this assignment was anything but boring!

I pulled into Rothschild's Galleries at 4:49 p.m., only to be met by Shackleton, butler/chef extraordinaire, who answered the door in formal attire. His crisp English accent told me that I was expected. I decided to hold my questions for Shackleton until I could be more certain that we were not being observed. We walked briskly through myriad elegant rooms until we came to a stunning floor-to-ceiling book-lined library complete with mobile ladders overlooking a sculpture field reflected in a pristine lake. It was hard not to be impressed.

"Dahling, you're right on time. How sweet," Rothschild said in that dismissive manner that was supposed to make me feel like a slow-witted nursery school student. Madame turned to Shackleton and ordered, "A little *vin rouge* for our guest."

Chateau Rothschild, the usual. Interview or not, I was not going to pass that up.

Although just last night Rothschild had demonstrated her volatility and an ability to go off like a flash fuse, I harbored no doubts that I could handle her interview. She is her favorite subject, after all, and narcissists like her practically interview themselves.

If you have ever read my work, you know that I am the queen of the flawless interrogation, that I have a reputation for knowing just how to make reticent interviewees turn into veritable chatterboxes.

Who do you think got a prestigious journalism award for a piece on Brooklyn's most reserved mime troupe?

I pressed the record button on my cell. Going back to the conventional Q and A: name, rank, and serial number, I knew from my research at the paper's morgue that Madame Rothschild was fifty-two, so when she told me she was thirty-nine, I thought I might be writing fiction rather than nonfiction.

"What's it like being part of the Rothschild clan, such a famous and respected family?" I asked Santa Fe's most colorful gallery owner.

"Oh my god, it was like a storybook fairy tale, and I was the star, the toast of the town, the belle of the ball. It was a real-life version of the movie *Sabrina*. And, of course, dahling, I was Audrey Hepburn. I was the 'It girl' and, well, precious, everyone wished they could be me. Who could blame them?"

I laughed inwardly, while hopefully playing the part of

"the good interviewer." I had done an extensive internet search and found that Ms. Letty, as a Parisian ingénue, was apparently more roast than toast. I also called my chum from J-school, Margaret Crawford, who was on staff at *Paris Match*.

"Here's the scoop, Lois Lane," Crawford informed me. "Letty made a splash all right, an out-of-control teenager who got too much international press, the personification of the Ugly American. The Rothschilds were mortified. The final straw was when Letty, who refused to learn French, began talking incessantly about how English should be the universal language. She even had T-shirts made up with Professor Henry Higgins's quote from *My Fair Lady*. 'The French don't really care what they do actually, as long as they pronounce it correctly.'"

"The French have never realized their true strengths," Letty said now, puffing on a Camel in an opera-length cigarette holder. "They should be visual, not auditory. They are lunatics about their stupid language, and every time one of them opens her mouth, she antagonizes someone."

I barely needed to respond because Letty seemed to be standing on an imaginary stage, addressing an invisible audience.

"When I first met the Parisian Rothschilds, they were brutal," she drawled. "Ten times a day they would make fun of how I spoke French. Always in *Française*, they would badger: 'My dear, is that your best French? It's pathetic.'" Smoke snaked from between Letty's lips.

"And they never let up; that's all they talked about. They should make me ambassador to France," Letty continued, drinking her Chateau Rothschild as if it were water. "I have figured out a way the French could stop being so despicable."

I murmured what was meant to sound like admiration. I nodded, encouraging her, even as I wondered if Letty drove a red car.

"They should *fermez la bouche*! And emphasize how they look, not how they sound. They are the only people on the planet, my dear, who look perfect at all times. As Eliza Doolittle put it so well, "Words, words, words, there isn't one I haven't heard … show me!"

Letty was a method actress, and true to form, she practiced what she preached. Today, she wore a Chanel suit, Gardenia (the French perfume that reminded me of Mel), and Chanel makeup, perfectly applied. Her visual presentation was *magnifique*!

Just as I asked Rothschild for a quick review of her education and career, we were interrupted by the four-note opening of Beethoven's Symphony No. 5. It took me an instant to realize it was a ringtone on her retro-style house phone. Letty—instantly morphing from fashionista to gutter snipe—snatched up the handset while the fourth note still reverberated.

"Rosa, one more time, and I'm calling the police, cousin or no cousin!" she shouted, shaking with sudden rage. "Take your goddamn medication, and stop bothering me!"

And with that, Letty slammed the phone down with such force that the mouthpiece flew off, heading straight for me.

I ducked—my reflexes still sharp even while under the influence of the wine—and judging by the whizzing sound, the plastic mouthpiece missed my head by a hair.

Leticia didn't seem to notice my near miss, caught up as she was in the now-playing drama starring hers truly.

She shook her head, eyes wide in disbelief. "Sorry, dahling, that was my crazy cousin Rosa—"

I nodded numbly, but Leticia wasn't watching me, in fact, she was barely breathing as she continued her diatribe: "I've told Rosa to stop calling me; I've even considered a restraining order!" She managed to find her glass and finish the rest of her wine before continuing: "I've told her, 'Rosa, I only want to hear from you when you're in rehab at the psych unit of St. Vincent's Hospital, or better yet, if you're calling from Bellevue!"

She puffed on her cigarette holder so the tip of her Camel glowed red-hot, and then she waved her arms expansively—that red-hot tip flashing past my eyes. I downed the last of my wine, following her lead but for courage.

Leticia leaned closer to me, apparently to share a confidence. "Shhhh, dahling, Rosa's a relative on my father's side—he was not a Rothschild." Letty inhaled again, pausing a moment before exhaling smoke in my face. "Don't write a word of this, Mickey—but she's been threatening to murder me since we were kids in Brooklyn. Now she's moved to Santa Fe. And her aim is getting better."

Leticia paced back and forth, becoming increasingly agitated. "Santa Fe is almost too tolerant. It's known throughout the universe as a place where families can dump their dumbest son and most disturbed daughter and the town folk will treat them like royalty." She shook her head. "That's why Rosa fits in so perfectly. In any other town in America, my cousin would have been sent to the funny farm; here she gets invited to the most elite parties, even though Rosa's own menacing voices tell her that New Mexico is a nation, not a state."

She's in good company, I thought to myself—merely one of a collection of misinformed people who swear New Mexico is a country. *New Mexico Magazine* even has a column called "One of Our 50 States is Missing" with funny stories about this mix-up.

Still, Leticia railed on, "Crazy cousin Rosa thinks she's a fortune teller. She calls and shouts obscenities at me. In between calls, she mails me tarot cards that say 'MURDER' in six languages—she's nothing if not fluent."

I almost choked on my wine. I remembered the crazy fortune teller all too well!

"That fortune teller is your cousin!" I said too loudly. "I just met her at Ellen Paddington's Aspen Vista party yesterday, and she handed me the 'MURDER' card in French! I have to say, it was positively creepy."

"In reality, she's bipolar and refuses to take her medication. She hears voices and should be in a hospital." Leticia frowned, shaking her head. "And the unfortunate thing, her illustrations are elegant. She's a damn good artist—if she could just get her act together."

"And it can't be reassuring to find her cards in the mail," I said. "Do you worry that she might really harm you?"

"Oh, dahling ..." Leticia narrowed her eyes to look hard at me, and I swear I saw pity in them. "In my business, I make enemies. If I took death threats seriously, I'd never leave my home." She tossed back her head and laughed—or more accurately, cackled, and the sound sent chills up my spine. I vowed to ask Shackleton in private if Rosa had read fortunes at Aspic in the Aspens—and if she drove a red car.

"Right," I said a bit shakily. "Hmmm ..." I glanced at my notes. "Ages ago, I asked you about your education and career highlights—"

Before I could finish, Shackleton appeared out of nowhere with the retro-style telephone.

Without missing a beat, Leticia took it in hand and proceeded to bid on what I could only assume were works of art. Barely skipping a beat, she covered the mouthpiece and confided that she was bidding on the work of an up-and-coming Brazilian artist; and then, in the same breath, said, "Started graduate school at Yale but dropped out to work at Sotheby's in New York. Headed up several galleries in Chelsea, Soho, and Tribeca. Had a fabulous job at the Whitney; they loved me there and kept offering me more money and better positions. But then I came to Santa Fe one weekend to look at some O'Keeffes and fell in love with this delicious little town. The air is so good for the soul, if not the complexion. I couldn't bear to leave, so I started another gallery. A little more vin rouge, my dear?"

It took all my willpower to refuse more of that nectar of the gods, but I knew that I needed to keep my wits about me. As I was formulating my next question, Cochonette came oinking up to my feet for another go at my shoes.

With her one-of-a-kind piercing laugh, my brittle hostess went to Cochonette and nuzzled her chin to discourage the pig's little hobby. "It's my fault, I suppose," Leticia said as she blew yet more smoke in my face. "I've always allowed her to chew on non-designer shoes.

Come here, precious. Have a little drinkie with me." With that, Leticia poured the pig a thimbleful of the expensive wine I had just refused. The pig gleefully dived snout-first into the beaker.

"She just loves the Margaux, but she has never developed a taste for any wines from the Châteauneuf-du-Pape region. Colette, my former pot-bellied pig, would drink nothing else; it cost me a fortune, but I hated to deny her; she loved it so."

I knew that Rothschild could be a bitch, but I hadn't known that she was part of Santa Fe's ever-burgeoning lunatic fringe. Ah well, money has its advantages. If I gave a pet pig a primo vintage wine, I would be declared negligent by the Humane Society (or crazy, due to my yearly income). But for someone like Rothschild, it was considered charmingly eccentric.

I was thinking of quickly finishing the interview before my shoes and feet fell prey to the pig's jaw. But, about that time, two maids under the tutelage of Sir Shackleton brought in a sumptuous Thai feast, and my stomach outvoted my shoes ten to two. While I was sniffing the heavenly odors of satay sauce, the well-trained butler whipped a Belgium lace cloth onto the table and started uncovering the manna from the gods. I could feel myself salivating.

I had a sudden flashback to Mel, and my eyes filled with tears. Whenever she had visited me in New York, we had immediately headed for Sixth Avenue in the Fifties and ate our way through a string of fabulous Thai eateries: appetizers in one, entrees in another, and dessert in a third. I regularly FedExed those delicacies from New York City to Santa Fe to her and Lupita.

Leticia's prattling, high-pitched voice broke my reverie. "I heard you appreciate Thai food, precious. Since you can't get any decent authentic Thai out here in the wilderness, I had some flown in from Ugly Baby in New York."

This unctuous, high-powered woman thought she could win me over with food; she was right, of course. I stopped the recording and dived snout-first into the chicken satay, spicy beef with mint leaves, coconut soup, and steamed fish a la Bangkok. Cochonette watched me enviously from under the couch.

Rothschild thought she knew my type well enough to believe that I was a lost cause until I was sated. What she didn't know about me is that I can do several things at once and I am blessed with incredible hearing. An important part of my interviews is observing the subject in her home environment and then making these comments part of my story. I'd never seen one human take and make so many phone calls. She went from her office phone to her cell phone: a "knife" housed in a chic little turquoise and silver sheath (a gift from Joaquin, no doubt). It was like watching a skilled trapeze artist plying her trade.

What was really amazing was that she could talk on both phones at once and still manage to shout orders at a beleaguered secretary stashed in a nearby office. She could smoke at the same time and must have gone through a half pack of Kools by the time I'd almost finished my feast.

Chopsticks poised to retrieve the last bite of sweet fried banana and green-tea fried ice cream, I heard her greeting a caller curtly, "Oh, Jamie, I told you I'd get back to you!" After the briefest pause, no doubt allowing the caller (whom I assumed was Jamie Inman) to state his case, she shrieked, "I can't help it if they detest your work in Venezuela—they love their Squanks!—And if you bother me one more time about this, I'll drop you completely, you second-rate talent!"

My final bite of ice cream plopped sadly back into the tiny dish. I made a mental note to reach out to Jamie Inman when I had the chance; there's nothing more dangerous than a woman scorned—except perhaps a neurotic and spurned *primo uomo* whose art no long sells. Although Inman lived up to his reputation as insufferable, I had to cringe at the way Leticia treated him so openly as discarded trash.

As I raised my gaze from the melting dessert, I found myself looking straight into the diva's eyes. How long had she been staring at me? I suppressed an involuntary shudder and pushed words from my mouth. "I've never seen anyone use multiple telephones so effectively and so often," I flattered, making her aberration seem like a talent. "I'm impressed."

After an uncomfortably long moment, she smiled. "You should see me in the middle of the night. At least one of my phones is ringing constantly—art dealers from all over the world. It's when I do my best work."

"When do you sleep?" I asked, taking what I promised myself was the very last bite of the sweet, hot beef.

"Sleeping is for noncontenders; it's a waste of time.

I require only three hours a night." The artiste of the phone set placed two more calls while I was folding my napkin and gathering my reporter's notebook. Alexander Graham Bell would have been so proud!

"Since I've been here, I've heard Brazil and Venezuela and Indonesia . . ." I pretended to study my notes as I tried to make my question sound casual—"How much of your market is international?"

"Of course, we sell worldwide!" She raised her eyebrows so they arched like upside down Us. "Santa Fe's a small pond—but it's a prestigious pond—and it attracts wealthy buyers from every corner of the world. They come for the opera and stay for the art."

"I've heard that Senator Rendón lets your best clientele stay at his ranch, and—"

"Dahling, follow me! You're in for a treat!" Leticia pivoted with surprising grace, waving her cigarette holder (exchanged for one of her phones). "I've saved the best for last."

And, with that move, she definitely and deliberately cut off any further discussion that included Rendón.

I dutifully followed her down a sun-drenched hall lined with paintings of Helen Frankenthaler, Kathleen Morris, Jaune Quick-to-See Smith, and Susan Contreras, some of my favorite women artists. The vibrant colors of Contreras's playful works of art blended perfectly with the bright red door of Leticia's studio.

"Prepare to be wowed, my sweet—not to mention honored. I only bring the most discriminating people here. Good art, like good wine, is wasted on the ignorant."

She led me into the studio, which was bigger than

my New York apartment. It had two skylights, an adjoining patio with killer mountain views, hand-carved bookshelves filled with art books, a well-stocked corner filled with a year's worth of painting supplies—and some of the most atrocious paintings I'd ever seen.

"Mickey dear, feast your eyes upon my little dahlings, the most original works of art in this or any other gallery."

Sleep deprivation must have rendered her blind. Mary Cassatt or Georgia O'Keeffe, she was not! Apparently, her enormous ego overshadowed her training in art criticism and her ability to recognize what was commercially viable. She had created her own Frankenstein's monster and was clearly besotted with her offspring.

Then she asked me the dreaded question, "So, my dear, what do you think of my work?"

The truth is so often highly overrated, I told myself as I bravely answered, "It's completely original. I've never seen anything like it."

How to keep an egomaniac from realizing you're changing the subject? I mused in a quick conversation with myself. I cleverly answered silently, *Focus on another one of her interests. As long as you're talking about her favorite subject, HERSELF, you're in safe territory.*

A photograph prominently placed in one of her bookshelves was of Dame Rothschild rock climbing in full gear and full glory. Ah ha, this was my escape from Bad Art 101. In the interest of a good interview, I wasn't about to tell the empress she was scantily clad.

"Maybe you could give me some advice on rock climbing. I'm trying to overcome my fear of heights." Okay, this could be filed under "half-truth."

Rothschild scowled as if I'd yelled a four-letter word. "Frightey-face! You're just like Sally; she makes such a big deal that she's terrified of heights! I find you both pathetic because I love soaring to new heights wherever I am in life!"

I wagged my head and tried to show my best "shame face." I sighed for good measure. "I took a class at a climbing wall at our in-house gym at *News View*." I'd taken several actually. "It's one thing to climb indoors in the middle of the city, quite another to try it in the mountains." *Absolute truth.* "What's a good beginner's climb? Where should I start?"

Rothschild took the bait and proceeded to yammer on for about a half an hour. Oh my god, I had conjured up Climbingstein!

"You know, dahling, I'm a hard-core climber, which means I'm world-class," she said, eyeing me with pity, "and you're just a rank novice." She was clearly in her element as she pontificated about her expertise.

She batted around rock climbing lingo such as "working the moki," "war and peace on the mountain," and "cleaning the pitch" to show she was "speed soloing" and I "was out to lunch."

"While I'm 'growing muscles' and 'pulling the roof,' you'll still be 'breaking the code,'" she crowed.

I needed a Navajo code talker to decipher what in the world she was talking about, but I smiled knowingly and let her blather on.

I admit I knew more about rock climbing than I let on, but I usually find the less I seem to know, the more information I get from the person I'm interviewing.

The rock-climbing aspect of Rothschild's eclectic personality would add color to my article, and I actually was
learning some interesting things I could probably use,
that is, once I took out all the purple prose.

"The best climbing in this area is at Lost World Plateau
near Los Alamos," Leticia haughtily informed me, while
lighting up another smoke. "But it's only for virtuoso
climbers who can either 'on site solo' or at least 'rope up'
and 'rap off bat hooks with ATCs and figure eights,' not
for greenhorn rock climbers like you."

That was it! I'd had enough female bonding and was
ready to go home and see Berg. As much as I hated to admit it, having someone other than a dust bunny to come
home to was kind of nice.

But I also noticed that she was trembling—shaking
noticeably—in the same manner as she had last night at
her gallery opening when Inman had stabbed de Baca's
painting. A reaction to stress? Too much vino?

And then abruptly, she shrieked, "Sally! Get over here
right this instant, and turn those goddamn lights off!"

I barely had time to jump before Sally appeared with a
glass of water. Quietly, she handed Rothschild two small
white pills. I expected the dragon lady to fling them into
her PA's face, but miraculously, she swallowed them with
the water Sally provided. Maybe it was her daily Valium.

Shackleton, the resident valet-now-turned diplomat,
stepped forward, assuming command. "I wonder if I
could kindly ask you, Ms. Moskowitz, if it would it be
possible to resume your interview with Ms. Rothschild
tomorrow? I think she needs a little lie down now."

"Of course," I said, relieved. "In fact, I believe I have

enough to write a very original interview." I lowered my voice. "Does this happen often?"

"By 'this,' are you referring to migraines?"

By asking his own question, he had answered mine. Or, so I thought.

As Shackleton ushered me to the door, I noticed the staff continued as if these fire drills of Leticia's were a regular occurrence. Before he could close it behind me, I thanked him and then leaned in to whisper, "Did Leticia's cousin Rosa tell fortunes at Aspic in the Aspens?"

His eyebrows danced about his sparkling eyes, but his visage remained steady and serious. "Yes, I believe she did, although I did not take advantage of learning my future."

Staring at him, I hoped Rosa had not offered my sister the card: "MEURTRE!"

I crossed the parking lot and almost reached my rental car when a Ferrari cruised slowly past me—a red Ferrari. I pretended to be searching for my keys while I watched Richard Wainwright park, taking up two spaces, and then emerge from his car. He didn't seem to notice me (we were separated by about 200 feet), instead pulling his cell from his jeans pocket, and then leaning casually against a black Mercedes, while he talked into it.

When he glanced my way, I dropped my bag and bent to retrieve it—a stalling tactic. When I straightened to standing, Wainwright was walking toward Sally. She must have come from a side door of the gallery/home, and my distance vision is good enough so I saw she was not smiling. In fact, she looked spitting angry. I think she might have slapped her husband right then, except he said something, and they both turned to look directly at me. Time to leave. I climbed into my rental and started the engine. I didn't know if I was disappointed or not, but even without a sample, I could tell that the orangey fire-engine red hue of the Ferrari did not match the deeper purple red of the lamp fragment that Berg and I had found at the site of Mel's death.

I drove home (did I honestly just call Berg's Adobe Nightmare "home?") and listened to a voice mail from him saying that he was bringing me a surprise. Secretly, I had to admit that I liked someone caring about me. I also had to admit that it terrified me. So, I plugged into my style of denial and went back to work!

I brewed up some espresso, pulled out my laptop, and zipped out the two profiles, finishing Ellen Paddington first. Then, I spent more than twice the time on Leticia Rothschild because of—let's face it—her name, her colorful international reputation, and her collection of select quotes about the French, beginning with the one from *My Fair Lady* that had pissed off her relatives, the Rothschilds Français: "The French don't care what they do actually, as long as they pronounce it properly," straight from the mouth of Professor Henry Higgins.

I e-mailed both pieces to Brady, and I also sent an update to my boss back in New York City, proposing that I write an expanded piece on Rothschilds's international art trade.

I was getting some good articles out of this art beat, but I wasn't much closer to finding out who killed Mel—

instead of winnowing down the suspects, the list was growing! I still wondered about the call from Jamie Inman to Leticia during the interview. How did it factor into the dregs of their relationship? In Santa Fe, the six-degrees-of-separation thing narrowed down, predictably, to one and a half.

I expected Berg to walk in any minute now, and in the meantime, I didn't welcome time alone. I'd waved off Lupita's inquiry via text regarding going to Mel's casita this afternoon. I texted back: "Ooh, sorry my deadline's looming! Maybe tomorrow?"

Yes, okay, I lied, but it felt like my choice was lie or die! I was that terrified to walk into Mel's home, even with my other sister by my side. This was more evidence of my lifelong conviction: if you love someone, they will eventually break your heart, whether they intend to or not!

Okay, I definitely had to check the comfort I was feeling around my lad—and it was time to take a big step back, right?

"Meow!"

I flinched and gasped—before recognizing Magic's voice. Berg's gorgeous Russian Blue sat down only inches from my feet and blinked up at me.

I shook my head. "That's not fair, Magic," I said quietly. "I am not a coward."

"Mee—ow!"

"Oh, you're hungry," I said, nodding with understanding. "Just give me one minute more because something's nagging at me!"

I folded back pages of my pad until I arrived at a clean

sheet, and I wrote one question: "What is wrong with Leticia?" Then I began a list of symptoms: shaky, light sensitive, blank, almost vacuous, jerky movements, expression, intensified volatility (if that's possible)—and the "psychic" episode.

Before I got lost on Google, I set down a bowl of fresh kibble and a new can of tuna. Magic blinked up at me. I nodded. "You're welcome."

I was about to settle back into work when a familiar and very welcome voice announced, "Chocolate!"

I smiled and melted into Berg's hug. When he finally loosened his arms, he said, "After a day with Leticia the Loon, what you need is chocolate! I went to Señor Murphy Candy in Sena Plaza and asked for their most elegant, sinful chocolate—*et voila*: chile piñon brittle and piñon tortugas, crafted right here in the U.S. of A. in Santa Fe and made in very small batches, certain to amuse."

With that, he pulled out a bag of said chocolates and made the most incredible s'mores I'd ever devoured, including those eaten one summer at Girl Scout Camp when I was nine. After talking about our respective days, we fell into bed. I had to admit this living together definitely had some perks!

But even in the throes of passion, I reminded myself not to get too involved. I couldn't stand having my heart broken again. I had already lost Mel, the person I loved most in the world. As I studied his charming face on the pillow next to me, I silently recited my mantra: *She travels fastest who travels alone.* But why was I always in such a hurry? Where was I going?

I woke the next morning to my boy's shower serenade, an original composition. To the passionate strains of "You're On My Mind, But Out Of Yours," I moseyed over to my favorite adult toy, the espresso machine. I brewed up some of my special Dean & DeLuca Ethiopian Yirgacheffe, gave half of it to Berg for his commute up The Hill, and sent him off with a kiss. On his way to his car, he sidestepped Magic (returning from his nightly rounds out on the town), who slunk into the house and collapsed onto the couch. I got out my watercolors and started doodling.

There was something very freeing about not using words, a spaciousness that allowed me to see the universe in a very different way. I rarely admitted this publicly, but painting was fun for me. I did it mostly because it helped me move out of myself—or was it into myself? What I put on a page was mostly stream of consciousness, many lines going into nothingness.

Mel had dubbed it "modern abstract." I didn't take it that seriously. Most of my drawings reminded me of abstract spiders. She thought I should have a show of my work, an idea I deemed ridiculous. I saw my paintings as mediocre, but the process brought a type of joy unusual for me—I didn't think as much when I was painting and actually found the whole practice satisfying and soothing.

I put down my paintbrush, poured myself another cup of my high-priced joe, and stared out the window at the Sangre de Cristo Mountains in their golden magnificence. Gosh, I missed Mel. When the phone rang, I was glad for the distraction.

"Piece on Rothschild, her sour international diplomacy; i.e., French relations, not half bad," Brady barked. He often communicated in cryptic English, his way of conserving time and energy for the written word. "Told you art beat was lively," he said, speed talking. "Why aren't you cruising the galleries now?"

I started to explain that I was painting but thought the better of it and instead answered, "On my way, boss," in my best Lois Lane fashion.

"Good. After your gallery run, how 'bout a quick interview with Squank for your column, 'The Real Santa Fe'?"

"Excuse me, Brady, I think you have me mixed up with John Sherman; that's his beat."

"Past tense. Found out today he's moved to Key West. Left a coconut and a surfboard on my desk with a note attached to it."

Something very peculiar happens to people when they spend a few years in Santa Fe—they lose their inhibitions, their professionalism, and all they want to do is go out and play. It's as if there were a Peter Pan headhunter on every corner waiting to pick up the Lost Boys and send them to Pleasure Island.

Oh, to be sure, Sherman had been a bit of a bounder, but he had also been a super-achiever before he landed in The City Different. He had nine books under his belt, articles galore, a syndicated column, and a five-year-stint as a staffer for *Sports Illustrated*, PR director of the Indianapolis Pacers, and marketing consultant to the Indianapolis Speedway. He performed nationally at poetry slams and even wrote an opera about basketball.

Then, after adjusting to the mellow, laid-back atmosphere of Santa Fe, he decided to become a serf in "Margaritaville"? My hometown had the effect of the poppy fields in *The Wizard of Oz*—putting people to sleep professionally.

Brady ignored my drama and continued speed talking: "Squank lives at 505 Hickox. No phone. Expecting you at 11:32."

That gave me forty minutes to change gears and gather my wits, along with a new notepad and a sharpened No. 2.

I decided that before taking on Squank, I had better put in a call to Pygmy—yes, the same Pygmy whose blini recipe could make a grown reporter weep for joy. Not only was he an ace, but he was also quite the art collector. One of his many hobbies was keeping tabs on art happenings and artists.

Because of his vocation and avocation, I expected that he would know all about Squank's business relationship with Leticia and also the current and slightly peculiar international trend—Squank's paintings selling like hot cakes in countries like Venezuela and China.

"Hi, Mickey, I was going to call you today to thank you for your lovely brunch! But you beat me to it."

When I explained that I was looking for background to fill out my upcoming piece on Squank, Leticia, and her rather peculiar stable of artists, he said, "I'll be working in Los Alamos this afternoon."

I was heading that way after the Squank interview, so I invited him to meet Berg and me for a latte that afternoon at Central Avenue Grill at three-fifteen.

"That would be most excellent," he said. He lowered

his voice. "I also have some interesting information on that other question you asked me to research."

My eyes widened—Pygmy must have news on the painted metal part that Berg and I found. I swallowed with difficulty. "Already?"

"You ask me, I'm on it," he said with no bravado.

I could see how easy it would be to fall in love with the man ... if I weren't already head over heels for Berg.

"Oh, Mickey ..."

"Yes?" It didn't take a genius to know what was coming from the romantic Russian.

"It was especially nice to see Lupita."

"She said the same thing about you," I said before I realized I was pushing my matchmaking envelope. What she had actually admitted, a bit grudgingly: "The man needs a haircut and a shave and a new T-shirt ... but he makes a decent blini."

As I drove to my unexpected new beat and next interview, I wondered how Brady had set up this appointment since Squank had no phone. By carrier pigeon? Psychic messenger? An owl, on loan from Orlando's Harry Potter Land? In Santa Fe, anything was possible.

From what I had observed, Squank probably didn't have an appointment secretary. As I headed for his hacienda in the *barrio*, I wondered if he would even be at home. He was. Once he let me in, I wished he had stepped out.

Inside his tiny two-and-a-half-room house were foothills of malodorous, soiled clothes, sprinkled with half-eaten sandwiches, topped off with empty bottles. The odor of cheap wine flumed the stuffy air. Bare threads of electric wires were everywhere. And there were centipedes, my least favorite bug with their hundreds of legs (or so it seemed) doing a creepy ballet all over the floor. Let's face it, the place was a landfill.

One thing that didn't serve me well as a reporter was my excellent sense of smell. Rancid stenches literally make me sick. I have found that nausea is not a good introduction to an interview. I decided I would look around quickly, take some notes for local color, and reschedule our conversation for somewhere with fresher air.

Squank seemed oblivious to the foul odor and didn't seem to notice that I took the liberty of opening his kitchen window. In fact, he bounced around setting up his paintings, looking for all the world like a loony leprechaun. In spite of the putrid smell, I could feel the reporter in me taking over and formulating my profile on this peculiar, yet intriguing, man. With his baggy belly dance pants, Guatemalan shirt, and wispy brown beard, he looked like a cross between Yosemite Sam and Hanukkah Harry.

"That was quite a party at Leticia's the other night, wasn't it?" I said.

"Oh, that slasher Jamie is a naughty, naughty boy." Squank chortled as he spun around and around, looking like a whirling dervish on speed.

"Have you talked to Ms. Rothschild since the soirée?"

Squank's pupils darted side to side, as if the harpy from Hell might step casually out of one of his filthy laundry piles.

"Oh no, she told me at the party, I'm not allowed to talk to her unless she talks to me first. She yelled at me and told me never to crash one of her parties again or else."

He put his finger to his lip to shush me. "She is probably listening to us now. I can't talk about her. She'll find out. She knows everything."

My story antennae perked up. "Why do you think she's listening—"

"Shhhh!"

"Well, why doesn't she want you to talk without her permission—"

"Shhhhhhhh!"

The last thing I wanted to do was change the subject, but we weren't getting very far this way. I offered him my best conspiratorial nod and silently placed my finger onto my lips.

He exhaled with audible relief.

"Okay …" I said, cheerfully. "Remember the man I was with at Ms. Rothschild's?"

He nodded.

"Well, his birthday is coming up, and he just loves your work."

Sure, I was improvising my change of subject, but Berg's birthday was just around the corner, and I wanted to get him something whimsical to keep our relationship on a light note. A Squank painting was just the kitschy touch I was looking for.

He grinned. "Oh goodie gumdrops. I just love it when one of my babies finds a good home," he said in a squeaky, excited voice. "Do you know exactly where he'll put my little darling?" he asked, while patting a black abstract painting, titled Elvis, with flecks of yellow and red.

"Probably in his study," I answered, thinking that Squank would make a splendid character for that novel I was going to write someday. I'm a sucker for people who love their work, irrespective of what I think of it, and Squank was gaga over his.

"Tell me about him. Does he love Elvis? We saw The King on the Plaza last Thursday. I talk to him all the time, don't you know?" He pranced over to a canvas featuring a purple-and-green rectangle, which sported the unlikely title of *Jesus* and asked, "Is your fella religious? Would you like the Lord looking over him?"

Before I could answer, he hopped over to a free-form painting with the name *Four Bulldogs Playing Poker* and inquired, "An animal lover? If so, this one might be just the ticket."

He then lovingly stroked a picture that had the provocative title of *The Portrait of a Governor as a Young Bullfighter* and said, "A politico, perhaps? Here is our governor, don't you know? Do you think it captures her best side?"

I couldn't decide if he was putting me on or if he was being even more peculiar than usual. His paintings were all very abstract but labeled as if they were from the Velvet Merchandise School of Painting. They were derivative of paintings from the Op and Minimal Art era. In my salad days as a cub reporter, I had been a researcher at *Time Magazine* when a Josef Albers and an Al Held painting went missing from a prestigious Tribeca gallery. I did the fact finding on the two stolen paintings. Reporters are like elephants and are doomed to remember everything they've ever written. Squank must have read this piece or studied Op and Minimal Art because he had this style down perfectly: bright colors in circles and squares, often called geometric expressionism.

"You need to talk to my babies," he announced. "Stroke their frames. If you're real quiet and focused, the painting that you're supposed to have will call out to you."

He had clearly been in woo-woo land way too long. It's one thing to talk to your plants and another to have a meaningful dialogue with an inanimate oil painting. I usually have a good poker face, but trying to find just the right words to say to a picture must have shown on my puss.

"Ah, you need some time alone with your new friends. This is a very personal decision. I'll fix us some tea, don't you know."

I was becoming so mesmerized by this eccentric but endearing little man that I almost forgot the disgusting smell. Almost. While my host was out fixing us high tea, I cracked open another window and sprayed some of my perfume into the air.

Once alone, I examined all his beauties, chuckling at some of the titles: *Four Pouty Polar Bears Playing Poker With the Pope*, *The Coyote and the Road Runner Take Tango Lessons*, and *Four Poodles Take High Tea at the Palm Court*.

From a distance, you couldn't tell one painting from another except some were done in primary colors, many mostly black, while others were in pastels.

I was actually more intrigued by the photographs mounted on the starboard wall—Squank hobnobbing with local celebrities: posing with Gene Hackman, Marsha Mason, Ali MacGraw, Shirley MacLaine, Julia Roberts, Carol Burnett, and Jane Fonda. A few slightly yellowing pictures stuck up with safety pins showed him with the late Grace Kelly, Governor Nelson Rockefeller, and Greer Garson. The port wall displayed pictures of Robert Redford and the King and Queen of Spain. Did he sell his abstract velvet wares to the rich and famous?

All too soon, he was back carrying a teapot lodged on a food-encrusted, dingy, once-silver tray. "We need some goodies to accompany our tea." With that, he nonchalantly went over to his unmade bed, lifted the bedspread, and scooped up old cracker and roll crumbs and dumped them on the tray. He grandly presented it to me.

"Thanks so much," I said, picking up one of the vile-looking crackers. "I'll take one to eat on the road. I have another interview in Los Alamos in an hour."

"Did you talk to the paintings?"

"The *Elvis* spoke to me," I said.

"He's very chatty. Sometimes he sings."

"What are these?" I asked, pointing to two shiny baubles encased in the abstract painting. "I'll want to give Dr. Bergenceuse the entire history of the painting. He's quite the Elvis scholar."

"You can't tell?" he said, looking a little hurt. "Why, those are the sequins on Elvis's costume."

I tried my hardest to look ashamed while reaching into my briefcase for my checkbook. Squank, with a twinkle in his eyes, lifted *Elvis* off the wall and presented it to me. "It's a gift. Today, all paintings to beautiful women are free. But first, I'll put Dr. Bergenceuse's initials on the sequins. That way he can feel that *Elvis* is singing just to him." He pulled a paintbrush from behind his ear and added the initials LB to The King's sequins, humming the chorus of "Love Me Tender" all the while.

He then proceeded to swath my new treasure in pink toilet paper and gently guide me to the door. It was rather touching in a bizarre sort of way.

"We can finish the interview tomorrow," I said, smiling a genuine smile and hugging my newly acquired yellow-and-blue *Elvis*.

He did a little farewell jig that I took as a yes.

The Hill—Los Alamos—is the birthplace of the atomic bomb. It is renowned for having more PhDs per capita than anywhere else in the United States. The city's school system is legendary because some of these PhDs teach first and second graders. Los Alamos boasts a gorgeous, state-of-the-art library designed by the world-famous architect Antoine Predock and the city's flowing book fund never runs dry while other libraries in the state literally crumble.

The City on The Hill is like Oz sitting as an oasis of affluence on top of New Mexico, one of the poorest states in the nation. It is New Mexico's very own Emerald City, and everything the citizens want turns to gold. But if you believe the tabloids, it also boasts a seamy underside.

Countless magazine stories cover bomb-making priests, rumors of wife-swapping parties, and gossip about overeducated, underemployed spouses who serve copious martinis at afternoon bridge parties. But never have I seen television cooking shows or food magazines extolling the glories of dining in the Atomic City.

The most upscale city in the state does not waste its funds on a plethora of restaurants. Back in the day,

McDonald's and Daylight Doughnuts were my French bistros when I was hanging out there. And certainly today, I wasn't headed for The Hill as a restaurant reviewer; I had a lunch date with my favorite scientist.

Berg was in the middle of an important experiment that he had earlier explained to me this way: "I'm working with a team of cancer researchers using a technique known as flow cytometry to measure the chemical behavior of malignant cells and the T-cells that will be used to fight these malignant cells. I'm responsible for maintaining and aligning all of the lasers and spectrometers used in the experiments."

(Now you see why I let his own words do the explaining.)

If you think this city with more millionaires per capita than Santa Fe or anywhere else in the state for that matter would spend their money on five-star dining, think again. Wealthy folks watch their nest eggs like hawks. Hence, "frugal" was a favorite euphemism for describing scientists and their families. "Stingy" might be more accurate.

Raised in the most parsimonious of households, my motto has always been, "Living well is the best revenge." I could easily fantasize living on the top floor in *Upstairs, Downstairs* with monogrammed breakfast trays a vital part of my everyday routine.

Berg was my polar opposite. Had he been bequeathed P.G. Wodehouse's Jeeves the Butler or his chum, Shackleton, as his manservant, he would have taught him how to play basketball (one on one) and, over my protestations, he would have set him free.

My beau was a man of the people. Generous to a fault and supporting half the contractors in Santa Fe County with work on his house, Berg was a pushover for animal and environmental groups. That's what made him so adorable; his T-shirts did not have deep pockets, often no pockets at all.

I have to admit that as I drove past Camel Rock, two questions nagged at me: *Did I want to marry Berg? Did I want to marry anyone?*

As I spotted the dramatic basalt of Black Mesa in the foreground, I thought about seeing Berg at lunch; I hoped he wouldn't bring up the "m" as in "marriage" word again. After losing Mel, I wasn't sure I would ever be brave enough to get close to anyone again. Besides, I didn't want to rush things, as I usually did in relationships. Unlike my girlfriends, I had never once heard my biological clock ticking. I wasn't even sure I had one!

As I turned off US 285 to head north on NM 502, this mantra echoed: "I've never been very good at commitments; I am lousy at commitments!"

And I've gained notoriety for my string of bad boyfriends. Until Berg.

Also, until Berg, Mel had been the only person I ever loved without question. Except for my sister, I barely tolerated the rest of the Moskowitz clan; they seemed to feel the same about me. I had shared the same last name with my parents, nothing more. By some peculiar accident of birth, my parents and I had been housemates. Mel, on the other hand, had been my soul mate: the softer, gentler side of myself. Of course, my list of loved ones grew when Lupita's family took Mel and me into their fold. But, by now, I've made it clear that "love" is a sticky topic for me.

I wasn't very keen on marriages; I'd rarely seen a good one. My parents' union had been strictly a marriage of convenience. German immigrants, they were both practical to a fault and extremely hard workers. They knew that it took two of them to run the Moskowitz Dry Goods Store on the Santa Fe Plaza. Kissing and hugging was not their favorite contact sport, and the word "love" was forbidden in our house, except when discussing a tennis match.

Enough family history, I told myself. I tried to redirect and focus on the scenery and the sense of this area's history. Even as a teenager, when I was counting the days 'til I could escape from New Mexico, I always liked the drive to Los Alamos. I was once again struck by how much the landscape resembled an O'Keeffe painting. The piñon-dotted hills and salmon-colored mountains juxtaposed against the brilliant turquoise sky was such a spectacular sight that it sometimes made it hard to keep my eyes on the road.

I passed San Ildefonso Pueblo and crossed over Otowi Bridge and noted the little house where Oppenheimer, Enrico Fermi, and other luminaries of the Manhattan Project supposedly relaxed at dinner parties given by renowned hostess Edith Warner. According to local legend, the house near Otowi Bridge served as a sanctum sanctorum for the overworked scientists putting together the first atomic bomb. Mel and I laughingly called Warner's fabled house a "bomb shelter."

I hit the outskirts of Los Alamos and saw firsthand

the devastating effects of the Cerro Grande Fire of 2000, the once magnificent tree-laden hillsides contained black, charred stumps of ponderosas, which now resembled toothpicks. The inherent physical beauty was still intact but definitely marred by the blaze that nearly destroyed the isolated town.

I once dubbed Los Alamos "the place where New Mexico ends." The adobe architecture rules strictly enforced in my hometown had never found their way here. In Santa Fe, everything is adobe from the Five-and-Dime to La Fonda to the Allsup's on Guadalupe. In Los Alamos, everybody builds their favorite house in the style of their origins. There's Cape Cod, California Ranch, Colonial, A-Shape Ski Chalet, and Early Bomb Shelter. The small town of around 16,000 looked like a suburb in search of a city or a sub looking for its 'urb. A Midwestern town lifted by a crane and plunked down into the mountains. Many of the homes I passed reminded me of the house we had lived in when I was a small child in Decatur, Illinois—the only difference was that PhDs owned 3,000 of these homes on The Hill.

I found myself driving toward Los Alamos High School, where Mel had won so many of her science awards. She had a real affinity for math and science; I always thought I would one day be visiting her at her lab. She was what we called a "techie nerd." All through junior high and high school she was a visiting star at Los Alamos's science fairs. Mel's trophies filled our house. In fact, they became so plentiful that we used them for doorstops, paperweights, and as hooks handy for hanging clothes when our hampers overflowed.

On this route, my sister and I used to play one of our favorite Hill games: Count the Churches and Temples. I could almost feel Mel in the car with me as I enumerated the names of the Unitarian Church, the Los Alamos Jewish Center, the United Church of Los Alamos, and the Immaculate Heart of Mary Catholic Church, all on just one street: Canyon Road. On Santa Fe's Canyon Road, there was an art gallery every few feet, while Los Alamos's Canyon Road had a church or temple on every corner. As I wound my way to downtown Los Alamos, I thought it was the height of incongruity that a town filled with rational scientists should have a house of worship at every bend of the road. Then again, the legacy of The Bomb wasn't easy to square with anyone's god.

I arrived at the Blue Window Bistro on Central Avenue fifteen minutes early. I ordered a latte, and I took out my cell phone to check in with Lupita; I prefer to show up way ahead of time, while Berg is notoriously late. But, this day, he surprised me by walking in minutes before our appointed rendezvous time!

He took a blue and red bandana from around his neck and wiped his sweaty face. "I jogged over from my office at P Division."

Eyes wide open, I said, "You're actually right on time—let me call my source at *Ripley's Believe It or Not*."

"It's not every day I get to enjoy *dejeuner* with the beautiful and illustrious Mickey Moskowitz." He got that funny look, adding, sheepishly, "And my watch is still on Pacific standard time."

I smiled. "I invited Pygmy to join us."

Berg smiled too. "He called—he's running late."

"Did he tell you—?"

"About his new info?" Berg spoke cheerfully, but I heard how serious he was behind the cheer. "He's going to share it with us, *mi amor*."

Katie, the owner, breezed over to us, looking apologetic. "I'm so sorry; we just sold our last chocolate mousse." The Bistro is Berg's hangout, and Katie's mousse is his favorite.

Berg smiled graciously. "I will survive, barely. And next time, I'll call in advance."

We both ordered the Cobb salad and held hands like two teenagers at Pop's Soda Shoppe. Who knows what might have happened if my cell phone hadn't started ringing off of the hook?

It was Brady, talking faster than usual. "Mickey, hightail it to the Y near Tsankawi Ruins. There's been a climbing accident. Leticia Rothschild is dead."

"Mick, are you okay? You're so pale."

I heard Berg talking in a foggy voice through an inverted megaphone. He sounded concerned. "Something about Mel?"

I snapped out of my dazed and seemingly frozen state, embarrassed. I had been on the police beat in J-school, and for a while, was a crime reporter at *News View*. Covering accidents was business as usual, and I didn't even blink when photographing dead bodies, some of them quite grotesque. I could have been Hard-Hearted Hannah's twin sister—that is, until someone killed mine.

"It's Rothschild. Died in a climbing accident at the Y near Tsankawi." My voice sounded like a frightened four-year-old, a fact that didn't escape Berg.

"I'll drive you there."

"You will not," I said, trying to pull myself together. "It's my story, and you're in the middle of an experiment. You have to present your data at an APS meeting in Monterrey in two months. Don't worry about me. I'm fine."

Berg hesitated, but he's known me long enough to recognize when I'm riding my stubborn streak.

"Call me when you get there," said my mother hen of a paramour.

Why was I feeling like such a wimp? I prided myself on my independence and my ability to handle any situation.

"And they say nothing exciting ever happens on The Hill," I answered, trying to make light of the situation. Vulnerability wasn't my favorite color.

I gave Berg a breezy little kiss and made my way the three and a half miles to the split known as the Y, where two canyons diverge, near Tsankawi, an ancient Pueblo ruin built on top of a mesa. I pulled into the gravel parking area, glancing automatically at the dozen vehicles parked in the lot. But aside from the officially marked law enforcement vehicles, it was impossible to tell which belonged to hikers and which belonged to journalists and TV reporters and the gruesomely curious.

The sight of police cars and neon yellow hazard tape almost made me sick. From the top of the mesa, the mountain where Mel had died loomed in the distance. I just kept picturing her on that lonely mountain road, bleeding and then dying alone. Why hadn't I been there?

Stop it, I warned myself. *Stay focused, you're a professional! You are on assignment!*

A deep breath helped, although I was still shaky, so I looked around and took in the majesty of my surroundings.

The Y, with its magnificent adobe-colored rock formations, looked like it was lifted from a tourism ad touting the charms of New Mexico. The Anasazi, the ancient Indians who had once lived here, certainly knew the meaning of "location, location, location." When Mel and I were little, we always thought all exotic rock structures, such as these, looked like luscious wedding cakes. Chocolate. Carrot cake. In the winter, iced with frosty snowflakes.

We had joked only recently that we probably concocted this desert dessert fantasy because our sweets intake had been limited to apples and prunes by our all-too-utilitarian mother.

My cell phone rang; it was Berg, checking to make sure I got there okay. He was like the poster boy for Boyfriend of the Year, which is what worried me. With my track record, I could probably even screw up this relationship. In my book, familiarity breeds contempt, not everlasting romance.

I put on my track shoes, which I always kept in my car, even the rentals. New Mexico hiking trails were not for amateurs wearing high heels, although Mel and I used to laugh at the yokels from back East who wore short shorts and sandals even on the most treacherous of trails. These tourists often made the six o'clock news, suffering from hypothermia and lamenting, "But I thought it was hot in the desert."

I wrapped a cashmere sweater around my shoulders and climbed over a fence to cover the 300 yards to reach The Y. I dutifully signed my name at the trail register. I thought about my fear of heights and my fledgling rock-climbing career. Leticia would be offering me no more advice, except serving as an example of what not to do. My would-be mentor had the hubris of the narcissist who believes she is far too important ever to be in harm's way.

Even though my reporter's instincts always told me to be the first one on any scene, be it crime or art opening, I stopped for a second to pick up a piece of yellow glass gleaming in the brilliant New Mexico sunlight. I was a bag lady—most writers are. Maybe it had something to do with Rothschild's death. Maybe it was merely a shiny bauble, but into my fanny pack, it went.

The retrieval of her body had been completed by the EMTs. The assemblage of the thin blue line and the fourth estate gathered on the top of the cliff around a handheld gurney that would transport Rothschild's body over the rough trail to the Office of the Medical Investigator's transport vehicle. A gaggle of officers of the law interviewed the climbers who had discovered the lifeless Rothschild. I was amazed to see so many law enforcement officers from so many jurisdictions already here. It looked like a mini cop convention—officers from Los Alamos, nearby Española, the Santa Fe County sheriff, officers from San Ildefonso Pueblo, and a couple of officers from Santa Fe's police department.

I whipped out my press pass and reporter's notebook and got in on the act. A young, blonde, twenty-something woman who looked like she could pose for a Sierra Club poster was crying and visibly shaken as she answered an officer's questions. "We were about two miles in, red pointing the crux (meaning they had reached the most difficult part of the 2,000 foot climb) on Cat Burglar, when we saw this big lump at the foot of the cliff—she must've fallen from the top, and that's a forty-foot drop!"

The young climber's sobs increased in volume, and I took the opportunity to enter the law enforcement circle to hand her a tissue. Her sturdy male companion, equally shaken but trying not to show it, interjected, "At first, we thought it was just a bag of garbage." He paused to blow his nose. "People often come here to dump illegal trash."

"It was awful," said the woman, her mascara running down her face. "She was all bloody and broken-looking. Rock climbing is supposed to be fun."

I looked down at the black zip bag that held Leticia Rothschild's body, and it was all too easy to imagine her wounds, even as the vision of Mel's lifeless body kept flashing before me.

"Mickey, you look white as a Russian snowfall," boomed the baritone-voiced Pygmy. "Berg phoned me to make sure you were okay," he said. "Take some deep breaths. Like this."

A huge teddy bear of a man, he squatted down and breathed so loudly he sounded like Darth Vader on speed. I couldn't help but laugh.

"What do you think happened?" I asked him.

"Probably just a routine climbing accident—a forty-foot fall, equipment failure, operational error, distraction, miscalculation—happens all the time."

"But?"

"She was wearing a medical alert bracelet."

I felt my eyebrows rise sharply. "Hmmm, what for?"

"Seizures."

"Oh." I shook my head. "That could explain the weird symptoms …" I quickly related the list of physical symptoms that she had demonstrated during my interview with her.

He nodded. "That could explain them … those are

symptoms of epilepsy." He shrugged. "And because Rothschild is a high-profile figure, we would be doing an autopsy anyway. And now I'm very curious ..."

"Autopsy?" I said; my mouth seemed to be filled with particles of dry grit. I wondered if I should have insisted on an autopsy for Mel.

"Why would she take those risks each time she climbed?" I asked, feeling a bit faint.

"She was a driven woman, an alpha female," he said, tipping his head. "For alphas, it's all about risk."

"Oh ..." My voice was almost too faint for me to hear.

"You still don't look well, Mickey," he noted. He poured me some very black tea from a canteen he carried over his shoulder.

As I sipped, I tried to slip back into my smart-ass demeanor. "Tea always works for the characters in Agatha Christie novels. No reason it shouldn't work for me, old chap," I chirped in my best English accent. Even though I am a certified coffee addict, the tea was soothing.

Just as two very fit EMTs were about to carry out the body, who should appear looking like a character from a Disney cartoon but Squank, waving his colorful artist's palette in the air. *How had he gotten from Santa Fe to Tsankawi so quickly?* For an instant, I pictured him hitching a ride in the trunk of my rental, hugging his *Elvis* painting! Oh, I was losing it!

"Hi, Mickey. Hi, Pygmy," he said, placing his easel and paintbrushes on top of a large rock. "Are you climbing? Are you picking daisies? I came to paint the clouds and the pretty rocks. Aren't the blue skies beautiful?"

He started dancing around like a loony leprechaun.

"It was a yellow day. The blue sky turned bright yellow. It's a sign. There are evil spirits here, don't you know?" He started spinning around, looking like Rumpelstiltskin on steroids.

Suddenly noticing the body bag and gurney, he stopped his prancing and looked chagrined. "They told me ... but I still don't understand. I wonder if she was mad at me. She was really mad at me last night."

Pygmy and I glanced at each other. And the question raced through my mind: "Was Squank just being Squank, or had he pushed Leticia Rothschild off the cliff?"

And was I crazy to even wonder about that?

Pygmy started asking questions. I took out my notebook.

"What are you doing here, Squank?"

"This is my painting place, it's magic—the Lost World Plateau," he answered, prancing again. "Spirits and ghosts visit me here. They tell me what to paint, don't you know?"

"Do they ever tell you to kill someone?" Pygmy asked in a voice much less booming than usual.

"Oh no, never. They're nice ghosts."

I thought to myself, *Squank is either the best actor this side of Robert Redford or else his combination plate is two tortillas short of an enchilada.*

"What is a yellow day?" I asked. "Does it have to do with the spirits?"

"Oh no, the spirits only come out when the skies are blue. Today was the first time I've ever seen one."

"Describe it."

"It was scary—like the gods of the mountain were angry and throwing yellow thunderbolts. On and off. On and off. I hid under a tree so they couldn't see me. They sounded like mean thunder."

"Can you draw a picture to show Pygmy and me?" I asked. By this time, a group of officers and deputies had gathered for Squank's performance.

"Oh no. I only paint pictures of nice things."

A young female officer wearing a Los Alamos police uniform stepped up. "Squank, why don't you come with us and draw us pictures of the good spirits? We have police artists who want to hear your story of the yellow day. They're used to sketching portraits that are anything but nice."

Squank looked nervous and turned his anxious face toward me. "Should I go with 'em, Ms. Moskowitz?"

"I don't think you have a choice, Squank. Pygmy Kolozmov is a friend of mine, and he'll treat you fairly." Pygmy gave me a nod of appreciation. "Besides, he has delicious tea and cookies."

I thought to myself, *Even if Squank had to spend a night in the slammer, it would only improve the caliber of his life.* The air quality and the cuisine in jail had to be an order of magnitude better than at his adobe abode.

Even in sleepy New Mexico, the death of a high-profile art dealer is big news. A gaggle of reporters arrived with their photographers, and I smelled a big story. The competitive journalist in me took over.

Pygmy must have noticed the color coming back into my cheeks.

"You know, Mickey, in a few minutes we are going to politely ask all press to leave the premises."

"Even me?"

"Even you, but you know some MIs are almost human, and though I can't play favorites, I'll put you on the top of the list to call when we have made our preliminary report—in a few hours. I have your cell phone number memorized."

Ah, the advantages of having an overprotective boyfriend, I thought, smiling at Pygmy. "Sounds good."

As he nodded, he dug into the pocket of his pants and produced a folded piece of paper. "For you, for later."

I took the paper, reading his expression, which was back to dark and brooding. It had to be information he'd dug up on the car that hit Mel and her bike. "What you wanted to tell me—?"

"Yep. Sorry I couldn't make lunch he said, but at least you know why." He brightened. "With your permission, I will call Lupita to share the news in confidence."

I nodded and couldn't help but smile just a tiny bit. "Thank you. That saves me a phone call on a busy day."

He offered me a salute as I gathered my things.

I used to kid my paramour that he had been in Santa Fe, the New Age capital of the universe, long enough to qualify as a psychic. As if on cue, the first notes of Pachelbel's "Canon in D" emanated from my cell; my ringtone for Berg. We agreed to meet in Los Alamos in ten to fifteen minutes. Pygmy's folded paper was burning a hole in my pocket now, and I couldn't move fast enough.

When Berg walked into the Blue Window Bistro, Katie, smiling brightly, brought him a very large chocolate mousse, freshly confected. I ordered my heart's desire, caffeine on top of caffeine—in this case, espresso and a Mexican chocolate brownie.

Katie breezed away with her coffee pot, and I slid the

paper over to Berg. I had opened it on the way over from Tsankawi. I didn't need to look at it again; I had memorized the information: Phoenix Red—the default paint for touching up 1989 Honda Accords.

"Okay," I said to Berg. "Let's pretend we're Hercule Poirot and Inspector Japp."

"Or Peter Wimsey and Harriet Vane. Or Nick and Nora Charles?"

"Then there's always my mentor, Nancy Drew."

"Am I supposed to play Ned Nickerson or George Fayne?"

That's what I loved about Berg—like Mellie, he always knew how to make me laugh.

"Shall I round up the usual suspects and seat them around this table?' he asked.

Assuming this is foul play instead of a climbing accident brought on by health issues ... I mused. "I think in the case of Rothschild, if we wanted to round up the usual suspects who hated her and had motive, we'd need to move into Bandelier National Monument."

"How about Squank? Rothschild was brutal to him at the party, and he seemed terrified of her. Or maybe one of his ghosts told him to push her off the cliff," I said, speaking my earlier unspoken question.

"He's either an amazing actor or the most unstable fellow in Santa Fe; in any other town in America, he would be institutionalized. In our fair city, he's a folk hero," said Berg, holding up his cup to signal Katie he was ready for some more chocolate.

"So, let's just say, for the sake of argument, that it was murder," I whispered. "What was his motive?"

"Permanent insanity."

I sipped my espresso. "How about Ellen P.? I really like her, but she has to resent how horribly Rothschild treated her: how she humiliated her and how she stole her artists."

"But I thought Ellen was as pure as the driven snow," Berg said. "A devout Buddhist, a spiritual being."

"She seems that way, but I've learned in Santa Fe, it's a good idea to apply Shakespeare's theme of appearance versus reality. Some of the folks who appear most spiritual, in reality, are just mean-spirited."

Berg nodded somberly. "Which is why the only spirits to pray to are being fermented in the wine caves of the Rhone Valley."

"Who knows?" I said. "It's possible Ellen has been plotting her revenge on Rothschild since they were girls at summer camp. Letty short sheets her bed, calls her a fatso. Ellen pays her back by killing her. Seems fair to me."

Berg kept a straight face. "Let's admit it; Rothschild was the Mr. Potter of Santa Fe, the most hated person in town."

"Jamie Inman had motive to kill her. He said as much at Joaquin's opening."

"For that matter, according to the artists at Ellen Paddington's party, she wasn't exactly Gallery Owner of the Year."

"That's true," I said. "I even heard of some Los Alamos artists who hated her."

"She was an equal opportunity offender."

"How about Joaquin C. de Baca?"

"What?" Berg sipped from his cup and licked his lips in appreciation. "Kill the goose that laid his golden egg?"

"Maybe she left everything to him. Hmmm … I need to check out her will to see who her beneficiary is."

Berg studied me with raised eyebrows. "Think her only friend was her pig."

"Or how about Shackleton? He knew every skeleton in every closet."

"I've always wanted a mystery to end with, 'The butler did it.'"

I dislike parties intensely. Truth be told, I don't like people all that much. Mel thought that I was such a party pooper that, by age twelve, she had already dubbed me Mickey the Misanthrope.

As a reporter, I could pick and choose whom I conversed with; when I stopped asking questions, the interview was over. At parties, on the other hand, especially when the invitations sported your address, you were expected to chat up your guests and pretend as if you were having a good time.

My memories of my childhood parties didn't exactly conjure up a warm, fuzzy Hallmark card commercial. To say my mother was utilitarian was like saying Fidel Castro wasn't exactly a fashion plate. Every year for my natal day, without fail, I got a sensible pair of cotton underpants. If it were a particularly good year, in addition, I got what every little girl dreams of for her birthday—a matching pair of white anklets.

Food is the cornerstone of any soirée, right? It sets the mood, the tone. Here's what my mother served at my eighth birthday party: her not-very-good version of tuna noodle casserole, cottage cheese, runny applesauce, and prune juice. I was always hoping she dished up all that bland food so we would have plenty of room left for elegant ice cream and cake. Ha! Her dessert, which sent all the guests running for the front door, was rice pudding. In retrospect, I think she must have thought she was cooking for Meals on Wheels.

With these pathetic recollections of not-long-enough-ago fêtes fresh in my mind, why in the world was I throwing a party tomorrow for Berg's forty-second birthday? Had I taken leave of my senses? No, I was (dare I admit it?) a woman in love. One of the multitude of ways my man and I differed was that he was a social butterfly and loved parties. I even nicknamed him "the folksy physicist." And I think I just described how, when faced with the choice between a "do" or a root canal, I often opt for the dental chair.

The good news about cooking up birthday parties for physicists is that these shindigs are a piece of cake to pull off. While Berg was happily whipping out equations and curled up with tomes such as *Treatise on the Analytical Dynamics of Particles and Rigid Bodies*, *Theory of Atomic Spectra*, and *Principles of Plasma Physics*, I planned his party under his very nose. He never even noticed.

I had filed my basic story with Brady on Leticia Rothschild's untimely death, and being the newspaperwoman that I am, I pitched *Art News* for a piece tentatively titled, "Retrospective of an Art Collector's Life and Death." They practically screamed, "Yes!"

Pygmy, true to his word, called me with the preliminary report on her death: severe injuries consistent with a fall—fractured skull, shattered bones, broken ribs, hematoma of tissues damaged by trauma causing blood to extravasate into surrounding interstitial tissues, external lacerations, and abrasions—which basically translated to the fact that poor Leticia was all banged up the way anyone would be after falling forty feet off a rocky cliff!

I hadn't liked the woman, but I could still feel sorry for her dying that way.

"What about the seizures?" I asked Pygmy.

"No conclusive physical evidence—a small cut inside her mouth, but that could have been part of the fall, and no involuntary bowel release, but that doesn't mean she didn't have a seizure."

"Oh …" Enough of that topic for now. So, I'd changed the subject very quietly, whispering into my phone, "Are we on for cocktails, as prearranged?"

And Pygmy, who knew when to keep on the q.t. said, "*Da!*"

And so it was that Pygmy took Berg to La Posada for a birthday drink. While the boys were downing their Sazeracs or Moscow mules, I was trying desperately to get his place in good enough shape so I didn't have to administer tetanus shots to all incoming guests.

As I swept a few remaining dust bunnies back beneath the fridge, I checked my phone and found a text from Pygmy reassuring me that everything was on track.

Berg assumed that he and Pygmy were having libations to set the mood that would transform them into genuine soccer maniacs. Pygmy and I cooked up the viewing of the game of the year, the World Cup broadcast live from Chicago's Soldier Field, as a way of luring the lads back to our house for the surprise party. The physicist and the medical investigator were sport fanatics; if they could have played shortstop or third base for The Orioles, they would have given up science and medicine in a heartbeat.

The two obsessed sports fans met when they were students at Cambridge, where they got hooked on soccer. When they reconnected in Santa Fe, one of the first orders of business was to organize a local team, where the two diehards served as co-captains.

Tonight's game had special significance because the son of one of my boys' British teammates was on the English team. Nobody took the words "root, root, root for the home team" more literally than Berg and Pygmy!

Berg had already arranged his own playing field of snacks on the coffee table next to the TV. He had informed me that the wise fan has everything at the ready pregame because "soccer is a continuous game; the clock stops only at halftime."

To keep in the spirit of the game, I had arranged a poster of Brazilian legend Pele on one side of the TV and an almost life-sized picture of Pygmy and Berg, in their soccer finery, on the other side. The game was afoot!

I kept looking out the window, watching for Berg's car to pull up, and when I saw it, I gave the dozen assembled guests the high sign, and *en masse*, they turned their eyes to the TV screen.

I despise clichés, and nothing is triter than the typical surprise party. So, I nixed the traditional happy birthday cheer and instead instructed the guests to completely ignore Berg's entrance.

Berg walked in to find his amigos eating his food,

watching his TV, and paying absolutely no attention to the fact that the king had arrived at his castle. The only clue Berg had that the cake might be a post-game snack was when my birthday boy spied five-year-old Vicente Gutiérrez holding a tiny sign that read, "It's Berg's birthday. Rah!"

Berg came over and kissed me. "Does this mean I can't watch the game?" he said with a big grin. I could tell that my master of understatement approved of my efforts.

"DVR," I said.

I had instructed everyone to come dressed in swing dance garb or their version of it. People sported outfits that Jay Gatsby and Daisy Buchanan would have killed for.

I was big on party themes, but I had a well-deserved reputation as the worst cook on three continents. So, when I announced that I had "fixed dinner myself," a collective moan filled the room.

"Your culinary skills consist of making coffee and slicing bagels," said Pam, a research scientist at LANL and the first of Santa Fe's version of the Greek chorus. To set the proper tone, I had instructed Gerald Gutiérrez (Lupita's father and Mel's and my adoptive dad) to hand out Alka-Seltzer tablets as party favors.

"Mickey doesn't know the difference between a food processor and a word processor," added Gail, a reporter at *The Maverick*.

"You've cut me to the quick," I said. "And I've prepared all of my mother's favorite recipes." With that frightening pronouncement, I went into the kitchen and pulled out a groaning board of monstrosities from the fifties.

"It's a white-bread feast," I announced, pretending

to enjoy being a hostess. "The classic sour cream-onion soup dip, macaroni and cheese, lime green Jell-O mold, and the pièce de résistance, Mother's famous tuna noodle casserole."

"This takes me back to my childhood," chimed in Denise, Berg's personal assistant. "And honey, that ain't good."

Before I could delight the crowd further with the promise of Twinkies for dessert, the cavalry, Santa Fe-style, stepped in to save the day.

"Everyone knows that *gringas* can't cook," announced Lupita, making a dramatic entrance, marching into the kitchen while carrying a platter of her legendary stacked green enchiladas. "Step aside, and we'll show you how it's done."

In a festive parade, the entire Gutiérrez family ceremoniously strutted in, each carrying dishes that had delivered me from starvation in my childhood. I could smell the savory fragrance of green chile stew, carne adovada, chiles rellenos, posole, calabacitas, sopaipillas, and steaming, handmade tortillas. I knew that the birthday boy, my aspiring chef, would love all of these Gutiérrez family signature dishes. While Pygmy stood staring at Lupita, his mouth gaping open in admiration, I took Berg's hand and led him to the buffet table laden with his soon-to-be-favorite dishes. I even prepared his plate of food for him, an unusual act for someone as domestically disabled as me.

As Berg and our guests chowed down, looking very contented, and Mama Gutiérrez offered seconds and thirds, I thought back to how the Gutiérrez family had transformed my life. As a child, I was always certain that my birth certificate had been forged. I suspected I was adopted and was secretly waiting for a wizard, a la Harry Potter, to pop in to reveal the name of my real parents. I knew I couldn't really belong to Marvin and Muriel Moskowitz—we were nothing alike.

After my parents' unexpected death, Guadalupe's parents adopted Mel and me. The minute I took a bite of their incredible food, I knew that this was the family for me. The vittles were symbolic of their love and nurturing. In stark contrast, my mother handed us a box of macaroni and cheese (a generic, bad imitation of Kraft) and said, "Make it yourself. I'm too tired."

And to paraphrase Shakespeare, if food be the music of love, Maria Gutiérrez, Lupita's mother, played a gastronomic symphony every time she went into the kitchen.

On my cue, trumpeter Jan McDonald struck up his little big band in a rousing version of "Las Mañanitas." At that exact moment, Maria marched in carrying pumpkin flan, candles glowing. This seemed the perfect moment to unveil Squank's painting, Berg's big gift!

Over by the white kiva fireplace, I had perched the *Elvis* portrait on an easel and put a black velvet cloth over it. Pygmy nudged Berg over to my makeshift stage. Berg tried his best to act embarrassed, but I could tell by the sparkle in his blue eyes that he was pleased. To the world, Dr. Lawrence Bergenceuse was a distinguished scientist; to me, he was just an overgrown little boy. McDonald signaled the drummer to let forth with one of his most dramatic drum rolls while I unveiled the abstract *Elvis*.

"It's a Squank original," I proudly announced.

"Which is why we have no idea what it is," said Jacquelyn, Lupita's younger sister.

"Leave it to Squank to turn velvet into Op or Minimal Art; his work is derivative of Ellsworth Kelly or perhaps Helen Frankenthaler," said Pygmy, a passionate art collector and art historian.

"You folks have no imagination. Anyone can tell it's Elvis," I protested.

"So, that's what you look like when you've been making cameo appearances in shopping malls across America for thirty years," added another cynic.

"He looks better than Marley's Ghost."

"Which shows what you know," said Pygmy as he shuffled his ungainly gait up to examine Berg's birthday present. I noticed that Lupita had one appraising eye on Pygmy, even as she conversed quietly with her sister and her mother.

Pygmy made a guttural noise of appreciation. "A Squank has become quite the collector's item in certain circles. His abstract, kitschy velvet paintings are all the rage, especially in parts of Asia and Venezuela."

Suddenly, we were all startled by loud and fast honking outside. Like the sheep we humans easily become when we herd together, we moved as one to the front portal, where our guests politely made way for the birthday boy *et moi*, and we made our way to the front step and stared—at an undeniably strange sight: a white Cadillac convertible idling beneath a security light. Two men were seated in front, while in back, a little leprechaun stood alone, doing his characteristic jig while blowing kisses to his rapt audience.

"It's Squank," I said, somewhat stunned, as he plopped back down and the collective spell was broken. "And that's Rendón riding shotgun!"

Berg squeezed my shoulder. "And Richard Wainwright behind the wheel," he said.

"What the heckski are they doing here?" I asked, apparently channeling Squank. But before anyone could answer, Wainwright gunned the engine and drove away.

Back inside minutes later, the mysterious visitation still unexplained, Berg stepped up to the plate, so to speak, to examine his new prize.

"This isn't any old Squank painting," I said with mock pride. "It's a one-of-a-kind, custom designed for you. Feast your eyes on *Elvis's* sequins." I pointed dramatically to the initials, LB. "Personally monogrammed for Dr. Lawrence Bergenceuse, the world's cutest Elvis fan."

"This is the best birthday present I've ever gotten," Berg whispered into my ear. "It's even better than my first box seats to the Orioles-Blue Jays game."

I could feel myself blush. Egads! What was happening to my carefully built up protective armor, which had kept gentlemen callers at length for most of thirty-four years? I sounded like a lovesick teenager. This rush of intense feelings was making me uncomfortable. I was used to being a solo act with neon signs flashing: "Detached."

Berg and I moseyed out to the backyard to take advantage of our own private dance band. Berg's spacious redwood deck was actually finished, in a miraculous feat in his never-ending work in progress: evolving adobe. Tonight, the deck, surrounded by piñon trees and yellowing aspens, doubled as a dance floor. I signaled Jan to strike up his band so that Berg and I could lead our guests to jitterbug, a feisty swing number by Cab Calloway, and Morgenblätter, a lilting waltz by Strauss.

Berg was a fabulous dancer, and I was not half bad, thanks to my girlhood ballroom dance lessons paid for by my toe-tapping grandpa.

It was difficult to remember my vow of not getting too attached when we were waltzing. Even in his blue jeans and T-shirt, Berg looked like he was in Hapsburg Vienna, waltzing around the Schoenburg Castle.

"Let's go back inside," Berg whispered into my ear after the last twirling waltz step.

"What for? Are you ready for a sachertorte and café with schlagobers? Me, after all that spinning, I'll have a Dramamine on the rocks."

"I want to have another look at my birthday present."

We sashayed into the living room, and this time, the surprise was on me. At first, I thought I had consumed too much champagne. But when I blinked, I still saw … nothing.

Berg's birthday present had vanished!

The morning after Berg's birthday party—ending with a missing painting—I awoke to a dark and stormy morning, to paraphrase Snoopy. It had been a magnificent Indian summer with crisp cool days, shimmering yellow aspens, and red ristras rustling in the soft breezes. Now, in the best New Mexico fashion, right before Halloween, winter had come blasting in with a vengeance. Everything in this part of the world was so dramatic, especially the weather.

I had been up half the night listening to the howling winds knocking over summer chairs and sending torrents of arctic air through our not-so-air-tight adobe. I had on a cuddle-skin nightgown, a robe, and three blankets, one of them electric—and still I couldn't get warm. Even my usual cozy snuggle with Berg couldn't take the chill from my bones. I thought of the Day of the Dead, celebrated in the Southwest and in Mexico immediately following Halloween, and I shuddered as I pictured witches or ghosts or worse whirling around the blustery skies. With my eyes closed, I could see skeletons and skulls spinning ominously around in the tempest. The Day of the Dead was a popular holiday in

Santa Fe, and as a kid, it had always given me the creeps. It still did.

The wind was still shrieking when I crawled out of bed at 7:30 a.m. Berg, who had an early breakfast meeting in Los Alamos, had left the house an hour earlier. I'd been awake enough to hold my own in this exchange with him:

Berg: "Thank you for the party fun ..."

Me: "Mmmm ..."

Berg: "Lupita called, said everyone's offended that we frisked them at the door before leaving ..."

Me: "Very funny ... did you happen to find your *Elvis* in the refrigerator or the laundry basket?"

Berg: "Nope. And I don't think we can file an insurance claim since you've confessed that Squank refused to take your moola."

And then, Berg had kissed me on the forehead, the cheek, and the tip of my nose before he let me slip back into sleep.

Now, I punched KHFM, 95.5 FM up to almost a deafening level, hoping the sound of Vivaldi or Purcell might drown out the roar of the north wind. I fixed myself an espresso, thinking it might wake me up and convince me I was on the Left Bank instead of the Arctic Express. The creaky, clanging drafts of howling wind seemed to fill every crevice of the house. This type of weather was typical of northern New Mexico's late fall, and even as a bold ten-year-old hooked on Nancy Drew, it had frightened me. My no-nonsense mother had chastised me for being such a big baby and ordered me to stop being so sensitive and overly dramatic. "It's only wind," she scolded, "and we have a store to run."

I was actually thankful that I had an interview with Squank at 9 a.m.—I'd pushed it back a day because of Leticia's death. Being alone in this house was giving me the willies today because there was a storm brewing. The sound of the wind seemed so mournful, so foreboding, so sinister. This scaredy-cat image was not compatible with the profile of a hard-boiled New York City reporter that I had so carefully cultivated. I told myself I was being ridiculous.

I fixed myself a poppy-seed bagel from my special stash that I had FedExed in from Zabar's. I know it was self-indulgent, but Santa Fe, with all its five-star restaurants and good coffee bars, could not produce a decent bagel. There are certain necessities of life, and in mine, good bagels were right up there with good sex and good wine.

I looked over the notes I had gathered from *The Maverick's* rather limited morgue on Squank. There was such a mythology about him that it wasn't obvious what was true and what had been created by Squank himself or by Santa Feans who love their folk heroes, even if they have to invent them.

There were as many theories about his life as there were ideas about what happened to the Anasazi Indians.

I arrived at Squank's on the dot of nine. Punctuality is one of my better virtues. Unfortunately, it is not a trait highly regarded in this part of the world—obviously not by Squank, who opened the door wearing a long white nightshirt and matching nightcap. He looked like Ebenezer Scrooge right before the spirits visited.

"Oh, my stars. Is it morning already? I was up painting half the night and lost track of the time, don't you know. Oh, and I wanted to fix you one of my special breakfasts. Hecky darn."

"Oh, that's quite alright, I've already eaten. But it's nice of you to offer. I'll just bet you're quite the cook."

He beamed. "Well, I do have a reputation in that direction. You just sit yourself down, Mickey, and I'll be with you in two-thirds of a jiffy."

I walked around his domicile, which appeared unchanged from the time I had come here to buy Berg's painting; it still looked like it had just been robbed. But the horrible odor from my visit two days ago seemed to be gone. I couldn't decide if my allergies were so severe I couldn't smell anything or that the stench had been frozen because he seemed to have no working heat. I put on my winter gloves and ear muffs; glad I'd stashed them in my jacket pocket.

On the artistic side, there were a few new pictures of abstract purple coyotes adorned with green and blue kerchiefs. On his celebrity wall, there was a recent picture of Leticia hugging Squank, looking like they had just won first prize on *The Bachelor Meets The Bachelorette*. Where had this come from? Curiouser and curiouser.

He reappeared in about five minutes, dressed like a poor man's Beau Brummell. He had on red pants and boots, a flaming pink silk shirt with several holes and ink spots adorning it, and a huge purple chapeau with a large ostrich feather sticking up on the left side, hiding half of his face.

"Wanted to look kind of splashy for the photographer.

What do you think?" With that, he pirouetted around the room and took a bow or two.

It was hard not to be charmed by this peculiar little man. With some interviews, I had trouble thinking of appropriate adjectives to describe my subject; this would definitely not be a problem in his case.

"You look terrific," I said, smiling my approval. "The photographer will be here in about an hour."

He pushed an assortment of clothes, books, and paints over to one corner of the ratty couch and beckoned me to sit down with him.

"Squank," I said, in my most professional reporter's voice. "Your background appears to be a mystery. All the articles I've read about you have different facts. How do you explain that?"

His face broke out in a toothy grin. "Oh shoot, Mickey. People need to have a little intrigue in life. For some reason, I can't quite fathom folks 'round here seem to like to make up tales 'bout me. So I just let 'em think what they will. Seems to amuse 'em."

I pulled out my notes. "One article states that you have a PhD in philosophy."

"That's what some folks think."

"I also have a clip here that says you only went through the fifth grade."

"I've heard that rumor myself." He squirmed around on the couch, looking as restless as a tone-deaf, hyperactive four-year-old who had been dragged to a three-hour concert of Handel's *Messiah*.

Jeez, this was going to be one of those interviews where I get no straight facts. This guy was either really crazy or one of the slyest foxes I've ever met—and I've met my share.

"What about Harvard? Were you ever a professor there?"

"I spent some time there, don't you know. Cambridge is such a lovely spot in the spring. Walks down the Charles River. Watching the crew sculling along. Ah, takes me back, it does."

This man could be a politician, so successfully was he avoiding my questions.

"I heard you were an associate of Timothy Leary's at Harvard."

"Timmy was my friend. He taught me how to cook. I'll invite you and your fellow over sometime for Steak O'Leary."

"Were you his student? His chef?"

"I surely do miss him. He's in outer space now, don't you know."

He's not the only one, I thought to myself.

"What about your family?" I asked, hoping a change of subject might give me something to write in my notebook.

"All dead, sad to say."

"I heard that your father died in a mental institution and that several of your relatives suffered from severe depression."

"Ah, do you know a family today that doesn't suffer from depression? We live in difficult times, my dear child."

So far, this interview was going to be miniscule—about a one-by-one column inch.

"Squank, some say that you came to Santa Fe after

you lost your job at Harvard. Is it true you were dismissed during the sixties on drug charges?"

"Mickey, don't believe everything you hear."

"Well, what about drugs? You seem to associate with a lot of the known druggies in this town."

"That's not hard to do. Every third person in Santa Fe has a drug problem, don't you know."

This was turning into a big pile of nothing. "Tell me about all the celebrities you know. Your photo wall of the rich and famous is quite impressive."

Finally, his face lit up, and he was off and running. "I just love famous people. Something about them just makes my blood run like an arroyo in springtime. They excite me. Stimulate me. Keep me young." His eyes grew animated, and he started pulling on his left ear in a rhythmic way, as if he were teaching it to dance. "Whenever there is someone I particularly admire, I write to them. And gosh darn, don't you know, most of them write me back. You want to see my scrapbook?"

He leaped up and came back with this overflowing scrapbook filled with letters. "Here's my first letter from O'Keeffe. Even though she was rather full of herself, I loved to visit her at the ranch. God rest her soul, she's up in heaven, probably barking orders at St. Peter. She was one of a kind and a good friend."

He flipped the page. "Here's the lovely Miss Greer Garson. She gave me front row tickets when she appeared at the College of Santa Fe in *The Madwoman of Chaillot*. And I even got to go to the party afterwards. She was the dearest woman I've ever known. She had a complexion a thirty-year-old would kill for."

He was on a roll now, and so was my tape record-er. Finally, some conversation that could turn into copy. "Now Bobby Redford. He's got a big collection of my paintings. Has them decorating a whole room at Sundance. Flew me up there in his private jet to arrange my little babies in just the perfect spots. He's one fine man. Just as natural as the day is long."

I kept trying to figure out his accent and speech patterns. Hills of Kentucky? Southern Georgia? North Carolina Tidewater? Or, like with his mysterious past, was he reinventing himself every five minutes? Maybe as the spirit moved him, he changed his accent as quickly as he changed his facts.

He danced around the couch, looking like his lepre-chaun avatar searching for the perfect four-leaf clover. "I love showing my scrapbook. I surely do." He sat on the floor in the lotus position and leafed through the aged, yellowing pages. "Why, let's see. Here's Grace. Why, it nigh broke my heart when she died in that car accident. It was like losing one of my own, don't you know."

He leapt up to the couch and pulled out a picture of a young Grace Kelly at the Rancho Encantado resort with her regal arm around who else, but Squank. "What a beauty. And as sweet as cotton candy. I don't believe a word of those horrid things they've written about her. She was an innocent, a child, a lover of beauty."

For the life of me, I couldn't imagine Princess Grace with Squank's abstract, kitschy pictures ennobling the palace. I couldn't resist asking, "Did she buy your paintings?"

"Oh, my yes," he answered, with a why-do-you-ask? expression plastered over his elfin face. "She was going to raffle them off at one of her charity balls."

For the next half an hour, we leafed through a scrapbook that looked like a treatment from *Entertainment Tonight*.

Gene Hackman
Jessica Lange and Sam Shepard
Ted Danson
The King and Queen of Spain
Oprah
Carol Burnett
Shirley MacLaine
Ali MacGraw
Marsha Mason
Julia Roberts
Wes Studi
Calvin Trillin

I rarely saw any of these people on my outings to Kaune's grocery, and if I had, they wouldn't have looked twice. What was Squank's appeal?

"I've got some blank pages, don't you know." Like a little kid showing me his finger painting, he turned to the back of the scrapbook where there were empty pages waiting to be filled by tomorrow's celebrities.

"I'm so excited that Jane Fonda finally moved here. I sure do like that little gal."

I reminded myself that I was not here as a reporter for *People Magazine* (although I would have been paid more, if I were) but as an investigative reporter. After this puff piece was filed, I had a possible murder to write about.

"What about Leticia Rothschild? Did she make your scrapbook?"

Suddenly, his demeanor changed, and his face went white. "Oh no," he said, cowering a bit. "She wouldn't have cottoned to my scrapbook. Would have thought it was stupid. She thought everything I did was stupid."

He looked genuinely agitated, so I thought I had better change the questioning somewhat, but I still wanted to know more about her.

"What about that picture on your wall, of you and Leticia? She's hugging you."

He got a half-smile on his face and answered, "She was nice that day. But she was usually mean. She just pretended to be nice."

He twirled around, looking like Rumpelstiltskin. "Once, though, she gave me ice cream and cake and a new paint set and jelly beans, all on the same day."

I decided I had warmed him up enough; it was time for the $64,000 question. "Were you with Leticia when she fell?"

"Oh no, oh no, the yellow day killed her!" He was up and twirling now.

Speechless, I wondered if I should try to calm him or push the questions, but he filled the silence.

"I know, but I'm not allowed to tell. I'll get in trouble if I do." He walked around the room in half circles with his head hung low, like a child who had just been bawled out for not cleaning up his room.

"I don't want to talk about this stuff anymore. It's not nice to talk about the dead." He walked toward the back of the house, beckoning me to follow. "I've saved the

best for last, don't you know. You need to meet my kids."
His eyes were piercing into mine, and his mouth broke
into a huge grin, revealing several missing teeth.

I must have looked puzzled. I had no idea that he had
any living family. I thought his kitschy paintings were his
only babies.

"Don't introduce my kin to many folks. They're kind
of finicky-like." With that pronouncement, he turned on
one of his fleet of computers, which briefly emitted a
high, shrill sound.

He led me out to what passed for the backyard. Snow
was just beginning to sputter. The sky was still grey and
threatening. I took one step, and a gust of wind pinned
me against an overflowing garbage can. Who lived out
here in this squalor? The Addams family? For a moment,
I heard the shrill almost-whistle from his computers.

I wrapped my down jacket closer around me and
pulled my wool cap over my ears. I was freezing. Was
this some misguided tribute to the Day of the Dead
ceremonies? Were we going to talk to dearly departed
Squanks whom he buried in his backyard? Perhaps bring
them some of their favorite food. Help! Get me back to
New York! At least I sort of understood the street people
there.

"They like it better if I leave and let y'all get acquaint-
ed on your own. They're kind of persnickety that way."

I had no idea what he was talking about. His eccentricity seemed to be slipping into dementia.

And then, he said words that pierced my heart and
froze my blood.

He said, "Your sister was a good girl, Ms. Moskowitz;

too good, don't you know. Ms. Rothschild didn't like your sister."

Before I could really register what he said or what was happening, he slammed his door, and I was left out in the backyard alone. Or I thought I was alone. Suddenly, like some horrible circus act, out of the nowhere came what looked like a million snarling, barking dogs—big dogs! Oh, my god. This was his family!

I screamed for him to rescue me, but he was nowhere to be seen. I had covered stories about Santa Fe's vicious packs of dogs and how they had mauled and killed children. I was all too aware that when I took walks around the block or up in the mountains, dogs seemed to be everywhere except on the end of a leash.

But this was no article; this was real. I felt like I was the lead in an Alfred Hitchcock movie. I stood alone, clinging to the smelly garbage can, feeling like I was in suspended animation. Maybe this was only a dream—granted—a nightmare.

There were five of them—two Dobermans and three pit bulls, almost on cue, baring their teeth and snarling. The Dobermans rushed toward me like I was dinner.

In a split second, I was aware of my pants being ripped and a sensation of pain and numbness in my left leg. The first time I screamed, I couldn't hear the sound—it was drowned out by the deafening growling and barking.

I had taken survival 101 classes in New York, and I knew I had better pull out some of those lessons fast while I could still think, so I dug into my shoulder bag and almost cried when my fingers quickly curled around my canister of Mace!

The second time I screamed, I had the canister ready and aimed—but the instant before I pressed the trigger the shrill noise stopped! And—I shook my head and blinked—his pack of snarling dogs morphed instantly into adorable little puppies. They started licking my hand and rolling over on their backs for tummy rubs.

He came bouncing out of the back door, cackling, "How did you like my trick? A friend taught me how to do it. Wasn't it fun?"

My response? I raced toward the open door, and from the corner of my eye, saw him tossing each of the dogs a treat for performing so well.

"You can't leave," he called out plaintively on my heels. "I have another trick to show you."

But by then, I'd already dashed out the front door.

The poor, unsuspecting photographer was getting out of his car as I was rushing to mine.

"What happened to you?" he asked, wide-eyed.

I looked down and saw the gaping tear in my Adrienne Vittadini slacks. *Ouch*—my leg hurt, and so did my wallet, as they cost ninety dollars on sale! But at least I didn't see blood.

"I'd drive away as fast as you can, and I'm not joking," I called back. "Or at least take your pictures with your telephoto lens, and whatever you do: stay out of the backyard and don't go near his dogs!"

It came to me minutes later, when I'd almost reached downtown Santa Fe and my sense of humor was back—I should have told him with just the slightest touch of irony: I doubt there will be a story to run, but there will be a hefty kill fee to pay if it isn't.

The rest of the day passed in a fog. Back at The Adobe Nightmare, I touched in with Brady about my "experience" with Squank and was relieved to hear the photographer had survived and returned with some charming photographs of him and his split-personality canines. I agreed to put together Squank's profile, but I told Brady I'd like a few days to put my thoughts into any comprehensible order—the man baffled me.

By the time Berg checked in after lunch, I'd gone to bed, where Magic was keeping me company. He brought food and affection and the news that he would be working late on his project.

Just when I thought the day couldn't get worse, Lupita called with the worst news possible for me at that moment.

"I'm picking you up tomorrow morning at nine," she said.

"Okay …" My she's-up-to-something antennae were up and twitching.

"Mija, you have to face it sometimes, and Mel's landlord is worried about her casita … about no one staying there."

I groaned and Magic meowed. "I'm not ready."

"You'll never be ready, mija," Lupita said gently. "Neither will I. But we can do it together. And we need to do it for Mel."

When we finished our phone call, I turned the ringer off and pulled the blanket over my head.

Mel's casita is in Santa Fe's South Capitol neighborhood, nestled beneath a globe willow tree, and rubs shoulders with two tall ponderosa pines; cosmos lined her walkway and sunflowers of various varieties and other native flowering shrubs filled her planters. She'd painted these same brightly colored flowers on her mailbox, and birdfeeders and suet hung from the trees. Lupita and I made our way to her front door, holding hands. I was marveling at my strength until I saw the greeting on her door mat: "I Love Nancy Drew!"

Blinking back tears, I glanced toward Lupita as she squeezed my fingers hard. Without releasing me, she inserted Mel's key into the lock and turned.

We stood on the threshold for seconds that felt like minutes. "Okay," I said so softly that Lupita leaned closer to hear. Together, in sync, we crossed into her home. I half expected the air to smell stale and close but it didn't. It smelled like crushed pine and herbs. In fact, everything seemed normal—eerily so because I expected my sister to walk out of the kitchen wearing a smile on her face and an apron tied around her waist to say, "You're just in time for veggie quesadillas!"

I must have stood staring at the place I thought Mel should be because Lupita patted me lightly on the back. "What are we looking for?"

"What …" I shook off my overwhelming mix of emotions. "We're looking for is anything out of the ordinary."

"Oh, good, that clarifies things," Lupita said. "I can start in the kitchen and move to the living room." At a glance, I blanched when I saw Mel's grocery list attached to the fridge with a bright "Save the Prairie Dogs!" magnet.

"I'll take the bedroom and bathroom," I said, nodding shakily to reassure us both that I was up to the task. At least the casita was small—Mel's bedroom doubled as her office.

I did my best to keep my eyes off of reminders of Mel's life interrupted—her handwashed bike shorts hanging over her shower bar; *Sierra Club Magazine* opened to an article on the meltdown in the Arctic and the loss of polar bear habitat; her Piglet, loved since she was five years old, tucked between her pillows on the bed.

But, of course, everywhere I looked, Mel was right in front of me. I felt another wave of grief coming on—and I pinched myself so hard my eyes watered. *Get tough, Mickey, and stop stalling!*

I got to work—checking under her mattress, in cupboards, between the pages of her matched set of Nancy Drew mysteries on her bedside table, even the pockets of her jackets hanging in the closet.

Nothing.

I checked in with Lupita. *Nada* on her end, too.

"The usual stuff," she said. "A few bills, notices, a few to-do lists, but nothing about work and nothing ominous." She looked toward the phone resting in its base. "The messages record on the machine, so I checked—just a couple of political robo calls and her landlord telling her the drip irrigation guy was stopping by to check the system."

We both sighed in unison, and then Lupita shrugged. "I'm going to check a few more places, just in case."

"Me too," I said.

Four minutes later, I found it—the letter Mel had been writing to me.

She'd folded it and tucked it into the pocket of her terrycloth dressing gown hanging on the bathroom door. And she'd written it in code!

My eyes filled with tears when I saw Mel's handwriting; it was as if she were in the room with me. But I brushed the tears away a little harshly. *Stay focused,* I snapped silently.

The letter was written in our secret code, devised when she was eight and I was ten, an idea we hit upon after excessive reading about the adventures of our heroine. We devised a game called What Would Nancy Drew Do?

This game was to deal with our own form of internal security from the spy that lived among us, our mother. Mata Hari or even Snoopy Sniffer couldn't hold a candle to Muriel Moskowitz.

When we were older and dating (always someone our critical mother disapproved of), or if we wanted to go to a movie considered unsuitable, or pal around with "questionable" chums, then Mel and I resorted to our secret code:

Dear Nancy,

I need to see you right away. Something is very wrong here in River Heights; even life in the Drew household is being affected. As Hannah Gruen put it last night at one of her famous dinners, "With everything going on in town, I don't even feel secure in our once semi-tranquil homestead. I'm especially worried about your safety."

This case needs your sleuthing skills and the legal savvy of Carson Drew. I need to give you the details in person. I don't trust e-mail, faxes, phones, or even snail mail. Big Brother is watching. Come immediately. I'll call George, and we'll all hatch something out over lemonade and Hannah's cheese puffs, Twisted Candles peach cobbler, and Larkspur Lane sandwiches.

Your chum, Bess

I felt my tears falling onto Mel's letter. Thank God nobody was around to see the gritty, hard-boiled reporter acting like a sob sister. Damn, why didn't I get this when there was still time to fly out to Santa Fe and talk to my sister? Mel might still be alive, and the two of us would be somewhere sipping silver margaritas, plotting what to do. To quote Bobby Burns: "The best-laid schemes o' mice an' men/Gang aft agley."

Her letter was crystal clear if you knew our code. River Heights was Mel's job. Security could mean lots of things—security in her office, the city of Santa Fe, or because she had worked for a powerful senator, even national security. Mel had obviously been worried about her own safety. And something illegal was going on. The food was just for fun.

This letter only proved what I already knew; life is unfair. The fact that Mel, the kindest, gentlest person I had ever known, was dead while that opportunistic Rendón was planning his first art show was proof positive that justice did not reign supreme in this universe.

What was happening to the carefully controlled world that I had constructed? I liked answers, concrete results achieved with a minimal amount of feelings. My role as an investigative reporter was all about problem-solving. I did my research, knew my facts, and wrote solid stories. There was an order, a symmetry, to it. Now nothing made sense; my world was spinning out of control. My beloved baby sister was dead, and I wasn't any closer to finding out why.

My Santa Fe stories were about as absurd as Santa Fe itself. What happened to Rothschild? Was her death an accident or did someone push her off that cliff?

Who in the world would want to steal Berg's abstract *Elvis*? Was there a connection between the theft of the kitschy painting and Rothschild's death? And how could they connect to Mel's death? Did Squank purposely try to terrorize me with his stupid dog trick or was he a candidate for The Home for the Bewildered? More questions were stacking up by the hour, and I think Alice's bizarre world in Wonderland was more orderly than mine in Santa Fe!

I showed the letter to Lupita before I tucked it away into a zippered pocket of my shoulder bag. Neither of us spoke. I took one more look around Mel's home because I didn't think I'd be back for at least a little while. I gathered up Piglet, and then I stepped out and let Lupita lock up.

We drove downtown to the Plaza to Tia Sophia's, a popular hangout that served native New Mexican food, and we were seated at Lupita's regular table by 11:15 a.m. Tia's had been one of Mel's favorite spots; I winced as I thought how hard it was, in a small town, to avoid places that evoke memories of her.

My gloomy mood lifted as I glanced at the menu.

"As usual, I'm starving," I said. At that moment, a vaguely familiar face showed up and asked, "The usual, Mickey?" I recalled that the waitress Paula was a nodding acquaintance in high school who somehow remembered that on my return visits to Santa Fe I always ordered blue corn guacamole enchiladas with Christmas, light on the cheese. Christmas, as all good New Mexicans know and the novitiate tourists quickly learn, means some of each, both red and green. This question was asked so many times a day throughout the state that in last year's legislature, it was made the official state question. Without blinking an eye, I answered, "Christmas."

There's a reason my hometown is called The City Different. You never know what you're going to get in Santa Fe. People have been known to show up three months late for a business appointment, yet a waitress who only sees me every six months remembers my enchilada order! Even King Solomon would be baffled by the contradictions in this bizarre burgh.

Lupita ordered a Caesar salad with red chile croutons and an extra order of sopaipillas, a type of puffed fried bread that resembles little pillows that melt in your mouth.

She was petite with a metabolism that fat farms around America would kill for; she could eat four baskets of sopaipillas and never gain an ounce.

She stretched now and tipped her head while she considered me. "It was good you—we—faced Mel's casita together. I watered her plants while you were in the bedroom."

"Good." I nodded. She was right; I was relieved to have that first visit out of the way. And there was Mel's letter, confirmation that her life had been in danger, even if it wasn't direct evidence. For a moment, I smiled, imagining how a meeting with detectives would go if I presented Mel's letter as evidence of a threat. *Well, we had this code from Nancy Drew …*

"I forgot to ask you," Lupita said, "if anyone confessed to stealing Berg's *Elvis*?"

I shrugged. "Not yet. But I'm thinking maybe Squank regretted giving it to me, well, to Berg, and he took it back. We were all outside for a while—it's possible he snuck in and made it disappear …"

"Maybe it was the Art Police. Let's face it; Squank has abstracted, gentrified, and in the process, ruined our pure style of Mexican velvet painting, an art form in its own right. He's taken all the earthiness, the soul out of it."

Paula zoomed in to deliver my steaming enchilada plate, the salad, and the sopaipillas.

Our conversation temporarily halted as we dived snout-first into the glorious food.

"Next to your green stacked enchiladas, these are the best in the world."

"See, Ms. New York City, you haven't lost the taste for our native food."

"Any people who can concoct these types of victuals," I said as I poured some honey into a fluffy, lighter-than-air sopaipilla, "are my kind of people."

While I was stuffing a second sofa pillow into my mouth, Lupita continued her theory about Berg's missing painting.

"And did you think perhaps that relatives of Ellsworth Kelly, Josef Albers, Milton Avery, Al Held, and their band of merry men might have organized a posse to round up Squank's paintings? They probably were offended that he made Kelly's abstract concepts so concrete."

"Or as goofy and mysterious as he is, he could have been Kelly in a former life."

"Maybe he's moved into his Velvet Art Elvis Period."

"Well, he should move on to his next incarnation," she said, with her impish Cheshire Cat-like grin. "It's like trying to mix New Mexican food with Chinese; it's the worst of all possible worlds. You're hoping for the perfect carne adovada or kung pao chicken, and you end up with chop suey! Maybe someone is trying to tell Squank to find another line of work."

"But," I countered, "Pygmy says Squank's paintings are collectors' items in the Far East."

"So what?" Lupita speared a red chile crouton. "Ducks' feet are considered a delicacy in that part of the world."

I was enjoying our irreverent banter so much that I dreaded bringing up a real question.

But Lupita beat me to it. "What could be going on in Rendón's office? Lord knows the senator is somewhat of an opportunistic slimeball—always glad-handing anyone who could help him—he's always known which side his tortilla is buttered on. I've always found him an embarrassment to New Mexicans. He's a buffoon but seems like a harmless one."

"You know he was never on my A-list; he and I are on opposite sides of every issue. But Mel loved him for the generosity he showed her—the new car, the scholarship, the things a *real* father does for his daughter—and Berg swears he's keeping The Lab afloat."

Lupita slathered extra honey butter onto a sopaipilla. "He's joined at the hip to The Lab."

I shook my head. "Rendón doesn't have the imagination to do anything very clever; Machiavelli, he's not."

"But he has a shrewd staff who know how to pull his strings."

"Well, I wish someone would pull a few strings and help the Santa Fe PD with Mel's murder. Nothing seems to get solved around here. We're clearly not in River Heights, where everything is tied neatly in a bow by the end of the book."

Lupita brushed a crumb from the corner of her mouth, dabbing with her napkin. "Life isn't a Nancy Drew mystery, mija," she said softly.

I set my fork on the edge of my plate, my appetite suddenly gone. "Have you heard anything official from Pygmy or anyone at OMI?" I asked.

"Nope. And he's not one of the boys; he's an out-sider—and until he wins the trust of the compadres, he'll be out of the loop."

"How long does it take to be accepted by the locals?"

"Oh, you know the answer to that question, Mickey, about 200 years, if you're on good behavior. The sun is going to come out in its own good time; so no matter what you do you can't really hurry it along, even if you stay up all night."

"Patience was never one of my virtues."

I felt yet another tear trickle down my cheek. She came over to my side of the booth and gave me a hug, then handed me a Kleenex. I wiped my cheek, blew my nose, and sniffled, "Nancy never cried."

"She never lost her sister."

We were tussling over which of us would get the check when my phone rang.

Brady.

I felt a twinge of anxiety—what had I forgotten?

She snatched the check from my fingers just as I clicked talk. "Brady?"

I listened to his deep voice, his punctuated message, already nodding my head. "Right, Richard Wainwright's big announcement and press conference, of course, I didn't forget—I'm driving! In fact, hands-free, boss. I'll call you when I'm there."

Lupita made a face at me—already sliding out of the booth—as I shoved my phone into my briefcase/shoulder bag. "I'll get the next check—I'm supposed to be in Los Alamos five minutes ago."

"Wait! Wainwright's big announcement on fusion—"

"You got it," I said.

W as I still operating on New York time? As soon as I got in the car, my phone dinged to remind me of the event—starting in a little less than two hours. I needed to clear my head and find some peace and serenity, so I took the circuitous route to Los Alamos. I drove south on 25 to pick up 550 toward the Zia, San Ysidro, and Jemez Pueblos. I drove past beautiful Jemez Springs, with its curative hot waters, and the magnificent Valles Caldera National Preserve before reaching the turn-off to Los Alamos.

It is the height of incongruity to have, in the midst of all this splendor, the laboratory where the atomic bomb was developed. Dr. Oppenheimer, expressing regret years later for his role in unleashing nuclear terror, might have felt inclined to lament, "Welcome to Los Alamos, Destroyer of Worlds."

I turned into the parking lot at Fuller Lodge, a few minutes early for the Wainwright event. I sat on a bench in front of the historic building, to absorb my surroundings and consider why I was here. Wainwright had scheduled a press conference in this very building to announce his breakthrough research in laser fusion. It was

Chutzpah (with a capital C) for his private research team to announce a major scientific breakthrough in a competitor's backyard.

Three nights ago, when I met Richard Wainwright at Leticia's party (was it only three nights ago?), he'd struck me as a man who would think it great fun to thumb his nose at his former employer, Los Alamos National Laboratory; the man had an ego the size of Alaska and the money to back it up.

"Ms. Moskowitz?"

I looked up to see an earnest PR flack from Wainwright Laboratories Inc., who seemed to have a radar gun with my name on it. She handed me a slick brochure regarding the press conference and said, "If you'd like to follow me in …"

I shook my head and smiled. "In a minute. I'm testing my equipment. Don't want to miss a syllable."

"We'll be starting in a few minutes," she said, smiling, too. She turned back toward the lodge, leaving me with, "If there's anything I can do to help you with your story, just ask."

"Okie dokie," I said, thinking Wainwright must believe I'd be placing a piece on his earthshaking announcement with *The New York Times*.

Enjoying the Fuller Lodge setting while testing my recorder, I gazed at the houses on Bathtub Row where Manhattan Project leaders lived in the 1940s—the only residents important enough to rate a bathtub.

"If these walls could speak, button nose," said Berg, hugging me from behind, "what stories they could tell about Oppenheimer and Fermi and Bethe and Rabi and

186 – PEGGY VAN HULSTEYN

Bohr—unique and brilliant scientists, all assembled here to work on one huge project. It's ludicrous and pathetic that Dickie Wainwright can claim that he is the heir to their throne."

The earnest looking Wainwright PR flack briskly informed us that it was time to gather inside. As I entered with Berg by my side, I blinked at the memory of the exuberant girl with freckles squealing with delight as her name was called as a winner. The Lodge served for years, and still serves, as the hub of social events, and this was where Mel had accepted many of her awards.

Fuller Lodge is a magnificent log cabin filled with politically incorrect deer and elk heads mounted on the stone walls and twenty or so beautiful Navajo rugs in various shapes and hues. Stunning pieces of black pottery created by New Mexico's most famous potter, Maria Martinez, from nearby San Ildefonso Pueblo sat on prominent display on a very large fireplace built with local stone and granite.

The hall, which looked like it could accommodate an audience of a hundred or more, was rapidly filling up. Seated in the first three rows were Wainwright's loyal followers, decked out in their finery. The back ten rows were occupied by LANL scientists, reporters, and a gaggle of science wannabes anxious to claim that they were part of the action.

As we waited for the festivities to begin, I asked Berg to describe the targets used for the Inertial Confinement Fusion experiment that Wainwright is going to brag about. "Be patient with me. Pretend you're describing them to a ten-year-old."

"It's elementary, my youngish Micaela. Merriman's been working for the past few years with folks from the Los Alamos supercomputer teams to come up with new target designs for the National Ignition Facility at Livermore. His newest one looks like a tiny metal cylinder not much larger than a big grain of rice. But don't let the simple appearance fool you; it's extremely sophisticated and complex on the inside. It took two months to design and fabricate."

"This sounds like Star Trek starring Thumbelina," I replied.

Looking slightly exasperated, Berg finished his explanation. "When the target passes its final inspection, it'll be logged in and placed in a special container with a unique identification number. It will then be stored in a safe alongside two other recently fabricated targets."

I held up my palm and whispered, "Enough education for now; the press conference is about to commence." I grimaced when I read that Senator Rendón was giving the introductory remarks. A tall, thin man, apparently a member of Wainwright Laboratories Inc, stepped to the podium to introduce Mel's former boss. "Please welcome Senator Arturo Rendón, second in command on the Senate Foreign Relations Committee. Thanks largely to his continued interest in and support of our research efforts, WLI has been able to accomplish the miracle that our Director, Richard Wainwright, will be describing."

If I hadn't disliked Rendón so much, I would have described him as "dapper," even "debonair." With that enviable silver hair and those strong eyebrows. He wore an expensive-looking English tweed jacket, complete with a Dunhill pipe tucked into the top left pocket. Rendón ceremoniously strutted to the lectern and proceeded to give the same speech I'd heard him give dozens of times before, patting himself on the back for being the brains and money bags behind keeping New Mexico's national laboratories afloat in these perilous times—while also making sure that cutting-edge independent labs found backing, too.

I had a flashback to the time when Mel told me she was going to work for Rendón. It was the closest we had come to a fight. I felt myself tearing up and tried, for some comic relief, to play my favorite game, Dress the Scientist. Mel and I used to joke that most of the scientists at The Lab looked like they had been dressed by a blind drunk. I looked toward the back of the room where the scientific contingent was seated and noted the sartorial display: checks with plaids, too-short pants that the kids called "high waters," the requisite polyester on parade, and a gaggle of bad haircuts. Many of them look like they could pose for a Sears catalogue. The representatives from the media and the Wainwright entourage, seated toward the front of the room, looked downright chic with their suits and dresses. But Wainwright, standing at Rendón's shoulder at the dais, stood out from the crowd. With his impeccable Armani suit and perfectly cut hair, he looked like the centerfold for *Men's Vogue*.

Rendón finally wound down from his favorite topic, himself, to spout a brief intro for Wainwright, before returning to his seat.

Then Wainwright was off and running. "I'd like to thank the fourth estate for being here on this august occasion. I realize that this press conference was called on short notice, but I'm sure your organizations will find the information I provide well worth your while. And my special thanks to Senator Rendón for your gracious introduction.

As most of you are well aware, there has been a move afoot in the scientific community for the past sixty years or so to harness the energy released when nuclei of deuterium and tritium collide to create miniature suns in a controllable fashion so that they can be used in what I like to think of as a fusion furnace. This is no simple task because in order for these nuclei to collide, they have to be heated to temperatures of millions of degrees Fahrenheit.

So, what actually happens when, for example, a deuterium nucleus and a tritium nucleus collide? We get new particles, namely a helium nucleus and a neutron, as you can see in this picture. But we get even more because the mass of these two new particles is less than the mass of the deuterium and tritium combined. This is the key to the whole problem because, as Einstein predicted a century ago, the mass loss shows up as energy. In layman's terms we have $E = mc^2$."

"Oh god," Berg sputtered. "The instant gratification physicist is such an arrogant asshole. Just wait until you hear the rest. He'll be claiming to the world that he's succeeded when everybody else has failed; he's going to be the attorney, judge, jury."

If Wainwright heard this aside, he ignored it. Giving Berg a dismissive glance, he cleared his throat and continued. "I'll describe what my team and I have accomplished by making an analogy that all of you will appreciate. In prehistoric times, humans were aware that fire could be devastating—forest fires and volcanic eruptions come to mind. Eventually, however, human ingenuity found ways to tame this destructive force and put it to good use. Using the same approach, WLI has taken the first step toward harnessing thermonuclear energy so that it, too, can be useful rather than destructive."

This was where my mind started to drift. I was thinking of Mel and the events that led up to *her* destruction. Another one of Oppenheimer's quotes came to mind: "There are no secrets about the world of nature. There are secrets about the thoughts and intentions of men." I was angry and ravaged by my loss but determined to discover those secrets. Mel's world had been destroyed, but I was dead set on keeping mine from imploding.

When my reverie ended and my thoughts returned to Fuller Lodge, Wainwright was still droning on: "Ever since the late nineteen forties, when the first thermonuclear device was exploded, there has been great interest in producing a machine that would simulate miniature hydrogen bombs but would release their energy in a controlled manner. In case you have forgotten, deuterium and tritium, the fusile materials, are simply heavier isotopes of hydrogen."

This prompted Dr. Lee, Berg's research partner, to pipe up. "Why are you embarrassing yourself and wasting our time with this sophomoric lecture. What do you have to show us?"

This suggestion evoked a smattering of applause from the plaid shirt and checkered pants crowd as they stood to leave the hall.

The PR flack was waving her arms, trying to block the escapees, while Wainwright, clearly flummoxed, sputtered, "Dr. Lee, your insolence is unprofessional and totally unwarranted. Please show me the courtesy of allowing me to continue."

Wainwright coughed and continued, "Here's what the world demanded and what our team was able to accomplish. We have actually managed to produce a prototype for a miniature fusion furnace, or, if you prefer, a room size replica of the sun! I'll give you a few seconds to let the significance of this sink in.

We were able to produce the prestigious number of extremely hot deuterium and tritium nuclei needed to create this furnace by shining light beams from our huge laser onto a tiny target which I, personally, designed and helped produce."

At this time, the moderator very quietly held up a poster board sign toward Wainwright: "10 MINUTES!"

Wainwright nodded at this time management warning and commented, pompously, "It'll only take a few seconds to humiliate my scientific brethren by letting them know that the secret to the whole thing was right in their grasp and they never recognized it. My unique target was designed after I spent weeks analyzing the Los Alamos and Livermore targets to find out what was wrong with all of them. And sure enough, there was a flaw in the choice of materials, one that I was able to correct."

A voice from the back of the room yelled out, "Cut to the chase, Wainwright! We didn't come here for a high school physics lecture. Describe your experiment; show us your data!"

"I regret, Dr. Merriman, that I am not at liberty to discuss the details because the information is proprietary at this moment. The information you are requesting will be presented in the next issue of *Physics Today Letters.*"

"Okay," Merriman continued. "But you better have something that's really worth the time all of us have wasted in attending this adolescent performance."

"That's my boy!" Berg almost shouted, which drew an exceedingly contemptuous look from Wainwright.

I poked Berg's arm to get his attention "According to Brady, there's a rumor going around that Wainwright made Fuller Lodge an offer it couldn't refuse. He paid them double what the time slot went for, and it was hard to turn down Big-Daddy-Dollars' cash money in these hard economic times."

"Yeah," Berg muttered, "but the arrogant SOB conveniently forgot that the lodge's scheduling office just fit him in between their regularly scheduled events."

Before he could ask if there were any other questions, a cleaning team, complete with vacuum, had their own way of giving Wainwright the axe. One of the merry maids started sweeping, another turned on the vacuum cleaner, another began to dust the Maria Martinez pottery.

The moderator announced, "I'm certain that our audience enjoyed your fascinating account of how you, almost single-handedly, were able to succeed in this critical energy research project where so many of our greatest scientists have failed. Please join me in thanking Dr. Wainwright."

Unfortunately for Richard, there was no applause except from the first three rows, because everybody else had left. Berg nudged me to head out, but just as I was about to follow my boy, who should appear but Lupita, looking bright-eyed and anxious to talk.

Lupita hugged me and said, "Hey, how about sharing some of your special java with your best girlfriend? God only knows what's in that joe The Lab serves—glow-in-the-dark plutonium latte, no doubt." She spoke in her usual irreverent brassy style but lowered her voice so only I could hear her last remark.

"What are you doing here?" I asked incredulously, even as I pulled my thermos out of my oversized bag and poured her some of my special brew of café au lait.

"You know I always like to be where the beautiful people hang out. Seriously, girlfriend, I thought you and I could go on one of our incredible shopping expeditions."

She and I are so close I usually can interpret anything she says, but I was totally baffled by this conversation, thinking that I had misheard over the continuing noise of the cleaning crew.

"This is top secret," she said, motioning me away from the crowd, over to the hallway by the ladies room. "Mija, there's a chance I've found the car that hit Mel. My Tia Concha just called me from her home in beautiful downtown Chamisal. She heard a rumor at her sewing circle that the car is at Matty Martinez's auto shop."

"And how did she—how could your tia know—?"

"Ssshhh." She raised a finger sharply to her lips. "Wait until we're on the road. I'll tell you all about it."

I found Berg talking with Dr. Harry Merriman, and I managed to whisper in his ear, telling him that I was leaving with Lupita. Although he took a moment to banter a bit with the charming Ms. Gutiérrez, when he kissed me goodbye, I could tell he was totally preoccupied, discussing his latest experiment.

As we walked out of Fuller Lodge, Lupita pulled keys from her purse and said, "We'll take my car, The Red Beast. Your buggy looks too Anglo."

I loved riding in her pristine 1956 Chevy Bel Air that had been in the Gutiérrez family since it was a puppy. It had been treated as lovingly as any of the children, and it was a beauty with its immaculate paint, white tires, and glistening chrome. The classic car had been proudly passed from one family member to another.

Several other survivors of Wainwright's interminable presentation passed us by—recognizable by their truly bad outfits. I warded off my impatience to hear Lupita's explanation by concentrating on her Bel Air. "When did you get the keys to The Beast?"

She unlocked the driver's side and gracefully settled behind the wheel. Reaching across the car, she unlocked my passenger door, and I slid onto red-and-white leather. I breathed in the scent of classic Chevy while she continued: "It all started when my boss, the governor, announced on the front page of *The New Mexican* that he'd never ridden in a lowrider. I decided I had better start driving The Red Beast to work to show him some of the treasures of life in the state he claims to represent. I took him on his first lowrider excursion; we cruised the Plaza, and he loved it."

"Okay, enough about the governor. How in the world did your Tia Concha know to keep her ears to the ground about a stolen Honda Accord?"

"So," Lupita said, "after you and Berg found the broken piece from the car, and then Pygmy tracked down the most likely year, make, and model, I put the word out to my sources. Most of New Mexico's stolen cars go straight over the border to chop shops in Mexico—but sometimes somebody decides to siphon off a less-than-Mercedes-model to our local New-Mex ring. Easy extra bucks and nobody misses the beater. Matty's is a favorite destination. So, if someone local were trying to ditch a car because it's evidence, well ..."

"Makes sense," I said. "And I'm guessing Tia Concha is one of your sources?"

"Sí! Mi tia Concha called me and said she heard through the grapevine about a recent addition to the cars in Matty Martinez's auto shop, a Honda Accord. She did some surveillance and ordered me to get up here pronto because she could see through her opera glasses that Matty and his merry men had just gotten in a shipment of midnight black paint."

I chuckled, thinking of the incredibly intricate threads of northern New Mexico Hispanic families, while she continued: "So, mija, her friend Maria (with whom she plays cards on Thursdays) told Tia Concha that her nephew's son (who works with Matty on the weekends) told her he hated to paint over the awesome Phoenix Red but those were his orders."

After checking her view in the mirror, she turned the key, and the engine started with a throaty growl before settling into a purr.

We drove out of the parking lot heading toward Central Avenue, and she said, "I'm taking the route through Chimayo and Trampas, and we'll get to see a few of their spectacular wildflowers." After a few minutes, she turned onto 502, and soon we passed LAM, the very small Los Alamos Airport. As we began the descent off the mountain, I gazed out the window at the glorious New Mexico turquoise blue sky and the undeniably breathtaking horizons. I guess she heard me sigh.

"Hey, Mickey, you kind of missed our big blue sky, no? Not like that pathetic grey thing you call a sky in the Big Apple."

She could always make me laugh. "New York City has lovely skies," I said, defending my adopted hometown.

"Yeah, three days out of the year. Here we have sunshine and blue skies all year long."

"You sound like a 1940s song, 'Blue skies, nothing but blue skies.'"

"You, of course, prefer gray skies, gray buildings, gray people."

"Okay, so sometimes I do miss the mountains, the skies, and the green chiles." I tipped my head, an admission. "But," I said quickly, pouring myself more of my special imported coffee. "I didn't miss all the car graveyards and everybody's 1950s kitchens that are now glutting the arroyos."

"Oh, come on, Ms. White Bread, where is your soul and sense of humor? You never did develop an appreciation for our native, primitive, indigenous art form, Art in the Arroyos. Trashy Charm, we call it."

"How can I ever repent for being so politically incorrect?" I bantered. "How about if I write a piece for *News View* praising New Mexico's two greatest crops—green chile and dead cars?"

Butterflies rose in my stomach as I suddenly remembered we were not on a joyride, but instead were trying to find the car that ran my sister off the road to her death.

Lupita had laughed at my article idea, but now, she touched my arm. "Are you okay?"

"Sure." I couldn't afford to cry again, so I plastered on a smile. "So, my loyal sidekick, give me the game plan. What are Santa Fe's answers to Nancy and Bess doing nosing around the tiny village of Chamisal? What's our cover story?"

"Glad you asked," she said. "You reporters are not the only ones who make up great stories. My second cousin Ben owns Alex's Safety Lane. He told me to pretend we're looking for spare parts to surprise our *esposos* or our boyfriends, whichever we choose."

"I choose boyfriend and think you do, too; and hey, I like it. Better yet, let's turn fiction into reality. Poor Berg got gypped out of his birthday present, his exclusive Squank portrait of *Elvis*. I'm guessing it was Squank himself, but that's a moot point. So, what do you think? Should I give him a hubcap or a fender?"

"Ah, Mickey, mija, that's what I love about you. No matter where we are or what we're doing, you can find an excuse to turn it into a shopping expedition."

"Well, Berg does have his own jalopy, Dulcinea, his pride and joy. Your brother Rudolpho was explaining to me at one of your mom's dinners that I'm Berg's girl-friend, but that his car is his mistress. My boy, with his French background and aristocratic nose, secretly wants to be a lowrider aficionado."

"Another Anglo succumbs to our native charms."

"Let's have a dress rehearsal for our performance at Señor Martinez's. We're looking for a 1989 Phoenix Red Honda Accord, right? With the right front fender bashed in?"

"*Es verdad*, and I'll go first," she said, "because I can warm Matty up."

"Yes, please go first," I said, "I won't be brave and stop you. And we're pretending to buy spare parts so we can create an auto sculpture for the beloved men in our life."

"Something autoerotic, I hope," she quipped. "Or at least autocratic."

"Indeed, but I'm going for a religious experience. Berg keeps his cars forever. When his cherished car turned thirteen, I bought designer hubcaps as a car mitz-vah present."

Laughing, she said, "Mija, we need you here in Santa Fe to keep us *riendo*."

The rest of the hour passed quickly, and then we were driving past a sign for Truchas and a miniscule ceme-tery colorfully decorated with plastic flowers and figures of saints. I was amazed to see that the tiny village of Truchas now sported a bunch of art galleries. Chamisal—

even smaller—was our next stop, and we were there in minutes.

I glanced outside the window at the Lilliputian hamlet's outskirts, wincing at the ugly "graveyard" filled with junked cars and dead stoves and refrigerators, all now partly covered with bright yellow *chamisa*.

Chamisal wasn't even on most highway maps, but I noted that the streets were better marked than sophisticated Santa Fe, which had very few street signs; when I was a kid we were often told: go three blocks past the *acequia*, cross the arroyo, and turn left at the sleeping dog.

"Read me my tia's directions to Matty's," Lupita ordered.

However remote, Chamisal had the internet, and Tia had emailed a map of her town. I called out the route to Lupita: "To Plaza Road, past the Emmanuel Presbyterian Church, turn right after the rooster to Old School Road. You'll see a worn wooden sign that reads 'M———ez's Shop.'"

We followed her directions with due diligence, but we didn't need the illegible sign or Tia Concha's road map to locate Matty Martinez's place of business. We just followed the yellow brick road of fenders, hubcaps, and worn-out tires.

Matty's shop looked like it had played host to a gigantic demolition derby. The place was strewn with injured cars, auto accessories of all hues, vintages, and sizes. It was a car junkie's dream; car parts for as far as the eye could see.

A man walked out of what looked like an office. He

was short and stocky, with a shaved head bearing ink. As he approached us, I could see his tattoos were of vintage convertibles (Pontiacs, I guessed), one on each side of his skull, front end headed toward his forehead.

"Are you Matty Martinez?" Lupita asked.

He stopped a few feet from us. "Who's asking?"

As agreed, I let Lupita take the lead. She chatted Matty up in Spanish and mentioned all the friends and relatives they had in common.

Matty was clearly not the sentimental type; he eyed my sister with a *why-the-hell-are-you-telling-me-this?* look on his steely face.

I was busily exploring, holding my cell phone's camera at the ready while she tried to distract Mr. Martinez. I poked around. It didn't take long before our host, Matty, began acting really edgy. I was hoping his technology skills were limited mostly to cars and that he would not notice I was snapping pictures of his cars with my phone. To keep him at bay, I played the role of Ms. Self-Important Yuppie Businesswoman. I put on my earphones while barking orders to my imaginary secretary. "Michelle, I want my phone messages, and I want them NOW." I'd seen and heard enough of these bitch-on-wheels, cell-phone queens to know the drill.

I could tell that Lupita and I spotted the car at the same instant. It was under a metal hangar and covered by a year's supply of the *Rio Grande Sun* and torn, old Chimayo blankets. I spotted a petite patch of the Phoenix Red poking through the faded gray, red, and white blankets. I pointed my cell phone camera at the car while barking orders to the made-up Michelle. "Did you order

Berg's cake? When will it be ready? Don't forget to pick up his 1956 Bel Air from the detail shop."

Like a hummingbird zooming toward red sugar water, I darted toward the hidden red car.

"Oh my god, Lupita, look at this. This is exactly the color I've been looking for, for that new red dress I've been wanting to make. This color is to die for." *Snap, snap, snap* went my camera.

When Matty lunged toward me, yelling, "Hey, you girls can't go in there," I thought my words might be prophetic.

"I'd love some nail polish this color," I said, perfecting my Valley girl routine, while swooping under the hangar and helping myself to a paint sample.

"Could I buy one of these spare parts?" I asked, madly clicking pictures of the car and several parts that had become detached and fallen to the ground. "This buggy would brighten Berg's day." I had a hunch I should start recording our conversation and tapped the red record button on my phone.

I had hit a raw nerve, and Matty was clearly agitated. "What would your esposo want with such an old, beat-up car? You girls gotta leave now. I have to take my *madrecita* to the doctor." He glanced anxiously at his watch. "Her appointment is in fifteen minutes."

"But I want those red parts. They're perfect."

"They're not for sale. Besides they wouldn't fit your esposo's 1956 Chevy Bel Air. These here are from a 1989 Honda Accord. You better look elsewhere."

Bingo! The make and year.

"Can I come back with my esposo?" I asked.

"Uh, I'm going on vacation for two weeks starting tomorrow," our host said, looking really uncomfortable. "Bueno bye." He shoved us toward the door.

The minute we were out of sight, I used my multi-purposed cell phone and rang Pygmy and Berg. I had hit the jackpot and wanted to spread the news. Plus, I knew Matty was dialing a few numbers of his own and that the red Honda that hit Mel was about to be buried in a secret car graveyard. When I only reached voice mails, I left messages for both men.

When we were back inside her car, Lupita started to giggle, "Mick, you crack me up. I almost blew it when you pulled out that Harriet Housewife Routine; Mickey Moskowitz sewing a dress. That'll be the day! I could hardly keep from splitting a gut at the absurdity of it."

"Okay, so the domestic sciences of cooking and sewing were never my strong suits; but I was resourceful and learned early how to shop and how to order out." I looked up and down the deserted street and shivered, "Let's get out of here."

Lupita obliged, pulled away from the dirt sidewalk, and accelerated slowly through the next few streets that made up the village of Chamisal.

Soon we were on the two-lane highway headed toward Chimayo, and the surrounding vista of desert hills and blue sky was a stunner, I admit it.

Just as I reached for my bag to retrieve a stash of two bagels, a green pickup truck appeared out of nowhere and tried to push us off the road. We were passing one of the magnificent rock formations just outside of Chimayo. Having good basic training as a reporter, I quickly noted a roadside cross, indicating someone had met their end at this very spot.

As she swerved to keep from rolling off the road, I saw the passenger grinning back at us from the truck. A male Latino, wearing a white shirt, probably a T-shirt. The other thing I couldn't miss was the big insignia in the rear window—a massive coiled rattlesnake staring back at me.

As the truck accelerated and she got us back on black-top, I said, "Did I see that truck parked at Matty's?"

She nodded, watching the truck grow smaller until it was toy-size. "Definitely. And I think that was their little warning not to stick our noses in any deeper."

"I guess we can be thankful the warning wasn't worse," I said, just as I heard a sound that made the hair on the back of my neck stand to attention. An urgent, buzzing sound. Was it the engine? Were my ears needing to pop? Or was it a snake?

"Pull over." I said it calmly but firmly.

"What—?" Lupita looked puzzled as I pulled my knees to my chest and hugged them. "—is that noise?"

"Snake?"

Now the sound grew louder, the vibration so strong I thought I felt it in my body.

She was staring at the floorboards, eyes wide, mouth open. "Look," she whispered hoarsely. By now the car was driving itself, and she yanked the wheel to bring us back from the edge.

"I can't look," I whispered back.

"No, you're right, don't look—"

So, of course, because I've always thought I had a

touch of oppositional defiant disorder, I looked and saw the gray diamond pattern of something that looked like a snake and moved like a snake slithering between me and where Lupita had her feet on the pedals. Keep cool, I told myself, don't panic—the worst thing to do is panic!

I screamed.

And, of course, Lupita screamed, and she yanked the wheel and her beautiful Chevy swerved left and then right and then right off of the road onto the shoulder and into some brush.

"Ahhhhhhhiiiiiiiiiieeeeeee!" I can't tell you which one of us screamed more loudly.

The car bounced and made some cracking noises and jerked to a stop.

"Out!" Lupita ordered, pushing her door open and jumping out. "Mickey!"

I tried to get out. I pushed, and my shoulder screamed with pain, but the door didn't budge.

"Mija, come to me, I'm pulling you out!"

I turned toward her, saw her arms outstretched, and reached to clasp hands. As soon as she had me in her grip, she tugged me toward the open door. Pain shot through my right arm and shoulder, but I kept my mouth shut and scrambled out to safety.

Only when we were out and had run a safe distance did the fear hit fully. Lupita pointed toward the car, and I turned in time to see a huge western diamondback rattle-snake exiting through the open door and disappearing into the brush.

We were lucky: Lupita's treasured Bel Air ran fine. Like me, it had been shaken up. Unlike me, it had no visible damage. Somehow in the unexpected side-shoulder detour, my arm was deeply scraped and bruised, and my shoulder hurt like heck.

I was lucky there had been no return of the Rattlesnake Truck, as we called it now. Unfortunately, we both remembered that it had lacked a visible license plate.

"I think we should take you to Urgent Care," Lupita said. "Or the hospital."

"Oh no, not St. Victim's." I shook my head. The local hospital had a shady reputation, deserved or not. "And I don't think I need Urgent Care, just my own bed and a pack of ice and some antibiotic ointment."

Reluctantly, my sister agreed. And once she got us back on the road, I tried to distract myself from my considerable pain by thinking of something trivial. "Remind me to send Aunt Concha a thank you note."

"Not this time, Emily Post. Forget your perfect Anglo manners. It's a lovely sentiment, but this town is one buzzing big beehive, and the less the worker bees know the better."

"You're right; we don't want the whole village to know that Concha spilled the *frijoles*."

"She's already told the entire Ladies Altar Society at church. But besides being the good guys in the white hats, on the side of truth and virtue, these ladies can actually keep a secret."

My arm hurt like hell, but bantering with Lupita helped pass the time. I was biting my lip in pain, but thanks to her amusing chatter, Lupita talked me into leaving my rental parked in front of the lodge and driving back to Santa Fe with her. Normally, I might have protested; I didn't think my arm was broken, but it smarted like crazy when I moved it. I had learned back at my first driver's ed lessons, when I was sixteen, that it takes every one of one's faculties to drive in New Mexico.

"Mickey, be careful. If these people killed Mel, you may be next," said Lupita as she delivered me to Berg's. "I'll call you to make sure that you're okay."

"You be careful, too. You told Matty all about your family relations, just in case he didn't recognize you as a prominent New Mexican."

"I need to get some pals in law enforcement to get to 'our' Honda before Matty destroys it." She hugged me. "Take care of yourself, mija."

When I walked into our domicile, I could tell right away something was bothering Berg. He had two big bags of Jordan's Almonds and Reese's Peanut Butter Cups in front of him and was chain-eating. Berg takes such good care of himself and his nearly perfect body, I knew something was amiss. When he's working out a problem, he eats junk candy. Fortunately, Berg leads a pretty pure, trouble-free life; otherwise, he might junk food himself into a blimp (a gorgeous blimp, but a blimp nonetheless).

My second clue that something was wrong—after evidence of binge eating—was when Berg didn't immediately notice my wound. Berg is the typical absentminded professor-type, but when it comes to me, he's a mother hen. He was as nurturing as my parents were indifferent. On his desk, he had two blue prints of what looked like little cylinders with a bunch of arrows pointing to openings in the cylinders. Everything else looked like Sanskrit to me. But I knew him well enough to tell that the diagrams weren't what was troubling him.

"I've seen cheerier faces on a bottle of iodine," I said, as I kissed him. "And you have your army of Reese's peanut butter soldiers ready for battle. What's going on?"

"Well, at Merriman's request, I just did a routine check of the laser target inventory for the upcoming experiments next month at the National Ignition Facility at Livermore. One of them is missing, and it's the one we had pinned our most optimistic hopes on for achieving fusion breakeven. It's the latest hohlraum design that researchers from the two labs spent months coming up with. If it can't be found, there will be hell to pay." Berg said this all so quickly I thought he was practicing for a speed-talking contest with my editor. Unlike Brady, Berg only talks fast when he's anxious.

I shook my head, trying to keep up. "Okay, so an extremely valuable laser target has gone missing," I said, as if I were in kindergarten and trying to learn a new language. "Could it have been misplaced? You said the targets are miniscule. Maybe someone just can't see them;

you know how physicists never clean their eyeglasses," I said trying to add a touch of levity to the situation, while slipping my hand into Berg's.

Berg looked dumbfounded and mumbled, "Nobody accidentally misplaces laser targets. They're labeled, placed in special containers, and locked in a vault."

"How big are these things?" I asked. "Are they bigger than a golf ball?"

"No way! Like I told you at the Lodge, they're tiny, not much larger than a grain of rice. Trying to find one outside of its container would be all but impossible."

"Any ideas what could have happened?" I asked.

"Damned right I do," Berg sputtered. "You know that Wainwright had worked in Merriman's lab before taking off on his own. He knew how everything is done here and was familiar with anyone who had access to the vault. My guess is that Wainwright paid one of them to steal it. The simultaneous timing of this theft and his preposterous claim of fusion breakeven is too coincidental to ignore."

"But what would he do with this target?" I asked. "Would it be compatible with his laser?"

"Nah, the stolen target was designed for the NIF laser, a huge machine that cost the U.S. government more than two billion bucks. That's way, way out of Wainwright's league," Berg answered. "My guess is that he's going to claim that the target he stole is a twin of the one he used in his fusion experiment and sell it to the highest bidder. That spoiled brat huckster, Wainwright, has some *cojones* on him; he starts his own lab, but at the same time, he is a big buttinski back here at LANL."

"Right …" I said, waiting for Berg to tell me the rest.

"Wainwright is casting blame on several of my colleagues—he tries to ruin anyone who doesn't agree with him, including my old pal Merriman. So far, I've escaped his accusations, if not his wrath. But he's doing everything he can to place the blame on Dr. Harry Merriman." Berg said quietly. "And he's trying to get him fired. He was on the other team also working on ICF who didn't achieve breakeven. Harry is smarter than Wainwright, so Wainwright has always hated him.

Wainwright tried to hire him to work at his private labs; when Harry turned him down in no uncertain terms, Wainwright was livid. The bastard most likely got one of his henchmen to steal the laser targets and place the blame on Merriman." Berg made a growling sound. "Hell hath no fury like a physicist scorned!"

I frowned. "I've always been partial to Dr. Merriman. You know, you physicists all have predictable behavior issues, but he is sweet. And you shared an office with him—he's the one who played Hawkeye Pierce to your Trapper John?"

"We were the MASH physicists, all right," Berg muttered. "He wouldn't steal a pickle off a sandwich if it had his name on it." Berg helped himself to another Jordan Almond. "We wrote four papers together, and he never even purloined a pencil."

"Maybe Wainwright is just cooking up some more attention to promote his project," I said. "Maybe he hid it just to get his name and his group in the headlines. You know what a publicity hound he is."

"You may be right. But don't get your laptop out just yet, button nose. This is all strictly off the record."

All of a sudden he noticed my injured arm. "Oh my god, Micaela, what happened to you? Does it hurt? Oh, what a stupid question!"

"Lupita and I found the car that ran down Mel."

"What do you mean you found the car?" Berg stared open-mouthed.

He had clearly been too preoccupied to listen to my voice mail. I said, "Lupita's tia heard from her BFF in the sewing circle who heard from her nephew who heard from her … never mind, this will take all winter. The point is Matty Martinez in Chamisal has the car hidden at his salvage yard."

Berg jumped to his feet, reaching for his jacket. "We've got to get on this—"

"Stop, Berg, it's under control," I said, waving my hands in front of his bleary eyes. "Lupita has some of her fed pals on the job. They know about Matty's because it's a cog in the wheel of New Mexico's auto theft ring. They'll make sure the Honda doesn't disappear."

He took a breath, and he grasped my good hand, his eyes on my damaged shoulder.

"What happened to you, Mickey?"

"We were on our way out of Chamisal but … someone is getting really nervous and is trying to remind us to play in another sandbox."

"I'm taking you right to the ER. I can't believe I didn't notice this when you first walked in."

"I don't need the ER. Nothing's broken, and the bleeding's stopped. I took a basic first aid class in New York and know I won't be pitching a no-hitter with my southpaw in the next day or so. But I'm okay."

"I want details," he insisted.

"Okay ... but give me a few minutes before I tell you about the sidewinder in our car—"

"Mickey!"

"Okay, okay." So I told him, and, eventually, he calmed down a bit.

I'm lousy at accepting help; I'm always concerned that if I'm too needy, they'll take away my crown as the reigning Ms. Independence. But for once, I let him wait on me hand and foot. He was good at it. He was the bona fide king of comfort food, the type mother never used to make.

His amazing repertoire today included all my favorites:

— A perfectly toasted cheese sandwich with green chile and tomato slices.

— Macaroni and cheese peppered with green chile.

— Sugar cookies (without green chile).

— A killer hot fudge sundae with the original Bergenceuse chocolate sauce that could serve as a secret weapon in any effort to save the Free World and to remind me and all good Americans what we're fighting for—truth, beauty, and fudge sauce.

After this feast of my favorite nursery foods, Berg said, "Now, I'm putting you to bed, young lady."

"Promises, promises."

"How you do go on. There'll be none of that, not with your injuries. I was thinking more of a soothing bedtime story."

"Like *Lolita* or maybe *Lady Chatterly's Lover?*"

After a few more minutes of this gentle repartee, we bagged the bedtime story in favor of playing Doris Day and Rock Hudson in our own version of *Pillow Talk*.

Berg, my own special blend of Prince Charming and Florence Nightingale, brought me breakfast in bed before he left for The Lab. He was riding up The Hill with Ricky, his carpool buddy, so he could drive my car home. He left me the keys to his beloved Bel Air (from the same litter as Guadalupe's Red Beast) but told me to use it for emergencies only. "I want you to rest that arm."

He gently put an ice pack on said arm. "Eat your breakfast. I made all your favorites. French toast with cinnamon. Broiled grapefruit with honey. Extra crisp bacon. Your own special brew of coffee."

He leaned over and gently kissed me. My boyfriend continued to exhibit the qualities I had yearned for in parents (plus many traits you would never mention to your parents!) He had even found time to make some chocolate mocha piñon fudge for the beleaguered Harry Merriman's birthday. My lad was a jewel. Why was I so reluctant to make a stronger commitment? I thought of Mel's funeral, all the run-over dogs of my youth, and I knew the answer: I'm not so sure that it is better to love and lose. Mel's absence felt like a never-ending knife in the heart. Her death was bringing out the soft, sloppy part of myself at the same time it brought out my instinct for self-preservation of the heart. *My* heart.

It's less painful to go on life's highway as a single passenger. Good God. Now, I sounded like one of Berg's satirical Country Western songs.

Enough of this line of thought. As much as I pretended to be indifferent to the so-called charms of Santa Fe, I had always been secretly fascinated by the dramatic skies. I even started painting them when I lived in New York. Today, there was a hint of early winter in the air; spectacular grey clouds were forming a picture in the sky that resembled a great cathedral.

To change the channels in my mind, I pulled out what I needed and dabbled on my watercolor while nibbling at Berg's delicious *petit dejeuner*. Painting helps me think— and also it helps me not think. I suddenly started noodling and drawing pictures of Squank's *Elvis* painting. I wanted to get it back for Berg. That would cheer him up!

I remembered Squank told me that on Wednesday mornings he went to Albuquerque to the Carrie Tingley Children's Hospital to paint with the children being treated for cancer. On my first visit to his house, he'd reassured me that he took his dogs because they were so gentle with the kids! Hard to believe but lately a lot of things were beyond explanation. If his dogs ever went berserk with anyone but me, I was sure I'd hear about it on the local—and national—news.

I thought back, deciding it wasn't my Chanel perfume; their erratic behavior had something to do with that high-pitched sound I'd heard. Something else to ask Berg about.

As I dabbed cobalt blue onto my watercolor mountains, a non-thought occurred to me: With any luck, I could drop by Squank's house—sans canines—and "collect" Berg's painting. I still couldn't figure out why he would insist upon gifting me a painting for Berg only to steal it back. After all, I had offered and fully intended to purchase it from him. But now we knew he'd done it—the night of Berg's birthday party, while almost all of us were outside on the deck eating cake, Berg's buddy, the reporter from the *Santa Fe New Mexican,* had taken a quick trip to the bathroom. On his way, he'd actually witnessed Squank casually carrying the painting out the front door. At the time, more than a bit tipsy, he'd returned Squank's cheerful wave, convinced that this was part of the evening's legitimate activities. I hadn't given it much thought until now.

With a modicum of dread, I drove Berg's car to the barrio. My trepidation grew as I approached Squank's street. An eerie wind was blowing; it could turn into the dreaded, haunting fall winds, Santa Fe's version of the French mistral. There were all sorts of folk tales connected with these spooky sounds. One I remembered most vividly from my childhood was *La Llorona*, a moaning ghost who supposedly drowned her children in order to spite an unfaithful husband. My mother liked to threaten Mel and me: "La Llorona will drown you if you aren't good." I used to answer her with a defiant, "I don't believe you. There's not enough water in this state to drown a gnat."

Mel and I used to kid that the maddening sounds of

the seasonal winds were the reason so much of the citizenry seemed to be *poco loco*.

As I parked one block away from Squank's house, I thought that I might be joining the ranks of Santa Fe's "wee bit crazies." Respectable reporters weren't supposed to be burglars. That job was better left to Cary Grant in his old, romantic, highly unrealistic 1940s movies. For better or worse, I had become quite adept at picking locks. When I worked the police beat, I did a series on burglaries, and in the process, gained quite a few new skills; one of them was how to pick a lock. When Squank gave me the tour a few days ago, when he turned his dogs into monsters, I carefully observed what type of lock I was dealing with—a good old-fashioned cylinder lock. Pretty simple stuff.

By the time the lock complied, a few cold raindrops were splashing onto me and onto some potted artificial flowers near the door. (It did occur to me then that Squank was the type to leave his key out for everyone and anyone, including burglars, but I'd already gained entrance, so I refused to look under the pots.) I was glad I had thought to bring along a plastic garbage bag to protect Berg's painting from the elements.

I opened the door one inch at a time, holding my breath. Inside, the first thing I didn't do was move—I stood stock-still and listened. No terrifying noises. No deep growling. No scratch of dog toenails on floors. No barking. Just the faint patter of rain.

When I could breathe, I entered his studio, which looked like a kitsch warehouse. He had paid tribute to his favorite icons: James Dean, Marilyn Monroe, Elvis,

Mickey Mouse, and his mentor, Timothy O'Leary.

He'd been busy! There were plenty of examples of his realistic period. (Or should I say copycat period?) There were reproductions of venerable paintings—the *Mona Lisa*, Monet's series of haystack paintings, Whistler's famous mother painting. Was he branching out? The man was versatile. The fakes were decent.

As the wind made a sinister sound outside his painting shack, I decided I had better stop being so cavalier about this whole caper. I, Mickey Moskowitz, award-winning journalist, was breaking and entering. I could be tomorrow's headlines. I had just watched Cary Grant and Grace Kelly in *To Catch A Thief*. The secret was to get in and out in a trice.

I looked through the stack of *Elvis* paintings and realized that my art treasure wasn't exactly an original; it was confusing because the pictures were all so conceptual; they all looked alike.

I had talked him into putting Berg's initials on the guitar; lifting painting after painting, I squinted, almost losing hope. But, finally, at the bottom of the stack, there they were: LB, for Lawrence Bergenceuse!

It seemed like there were a few tiny, new magenta and chartreuse sequins in this masterpiece; it was hard to tell since they were about the size of a grain of rice. The smell of fresh paint indicated that Squank had been tinkering with the painting yet again.

Taking great care with both the painting and my injured arm, I wrapped the *Elvis* in the garbage bag and turned to make my retreat. That's when I heard the patter of dog feet on the floor.

Just as I was about to scream, two dogs appeared around a corner.

Wagging their tails. One was shepherd sized and the other was a teeny-weeny pocket dog. And they couldn't wait to show me how nice they were. And they looked very sleepy, as if they'd just awakened from a lengthy nap.

Adrenalin still pumping, I decided I needn't reach for the bear mace. These dogs were more like adoring puppies, wanting desperately to lick me. Not a trace of the monstrous aggression of the dogs who attacked a few days ago.

I gave them their well-deserved "good doggies" and patted each gently, and then I made my retreat.

I put Berg's garbage-bag wrapped painting in the trunk of the Bel Air. I was taking no more chances with theft. You never know if you'll meet another fanatic Squank collector wanting to make a deal at Hickox and Aqua Fria. In Santa Fe, it could happen!

I went home and fixed some of my outrageously expensive pure Kona coffee I had flown in from Balducci's in New York and that I could barely afford with my new, anemic salary.

Sipping the espresso and nibbling some of Berg's fudge, I pulled out my paints and brushes and painted a quick copy of the Picasso-period *Elvis* painting. Watercolors were a nice escape from writing—all brushstrokes, no words. While all that lovely caffeine floated around in my brain, I pulled out the original sketch I had made of the picture of Elvis strumming his guitar.

I could swear that the two pictures were different. But

they were so abstract, who could tell? It seemed like the one I had just stolen had more sequins on it.

Why would Squank want to steal the picture of *Elvis* anyway? He had scores of duplicates. What was so special about Berg's own private *Elvis*?

Lupita called to see if I was safe and to update me on the stolen red car. "My pal in the cross-border multi-jurisdictional task force to combat our state's auto theft rings has two officers and a tow truck collecting the vehicle so Matty can't annihilate it and leave it in an arroyo."

I smiled, greatly cheered, and said, "I love it when you talk interjurisdictional!"

Berg called twice to check up on me to see if I was behaving myself. I told him I was painting and eating fudge. I figured he had enough to worry about with stolen laser targets, so I conveniently left out my new career as a cat burglar among dogs.

"I'm stopping at The Guadalupe Cafe for some guacamole enchiladas for dinner."

Then, he asked me that question every New Mexico woman yearns to hear, "Red or green?" Without blinking an eye, I answered, "Christmas."

I had fixed a Chimayo cocktail for Berg—tequila and fresh apple juice, a concoction from one of his favorite New Mexican restaurants, Rancho de Chimayo. I handed it to him as he walked in the door, but it was obvious that his mind was a million miles away.

"No thanks, button nose. I've got to go back to The Lab. Just wanted to come home and see how you were feeling and to feed you supper. I knew if you were left on your own, you might forget to eat. And everyone knows the restorative powers of chile—pure Vitamin C and plenty of the Bs. It'll cure anything, even a sore arm."

Berg zapped the enchiladas in the microwave, and the heavenly smell of chile filled the air. His announcement of returning to The Lab suited me just fine. I had been hatching a plan to accompany Berg to Los Alamos to do a little detective work.

With great ceremony, I gave Berg his newly reclaimed *Elvis* painting. I even put on a CD of "Love Me Tender" for just the appropriate touch.

"Did Squank bring it back, or did you have to ask him for it?" he inquired.

I hated to destroy his belief in my innocence. He had been distracted lately—he'd even hinted that the Feds had been nosing around at The Lab because of security lapses. Although the focus seemed to be on Dr. Merriman, even my boy felt the pressure, I knew that. Plus, he was worried for his friend. So, for his own good, I stayed quiet.

But he's too darn smart, and my face is too darn pliable!

"You mean you stole the painting from his studio? Jeez, Mickey, I thought you were in bed reading trashy novels. Instead, you're out committing petty larceny."

"Well, I was just getting back what was rightfully mine. I'm not even sure this gem is really ours. That's where you come in," I said, drinking his Chimayo cocktail, for courage. "I'll explain some things on our drive."

"What drive?" Now Berg was fully on guard.

"The drive to LANL. There are some odd discrepancies ... your original painting, this painting, they're not exactly the same, and yet, they are so … see why I should just explain along the way?" I tried batting my eyelashes, although this isn't my usual tact, and I think a lash got stuck in my eye.

He shook his head. "I don't like the sound of this. What are you suggesting that entails you coming with me back to my work?"

"Well, they do it all the time in the movies when there's something fishy with a work of art." I took another sip of the cocktail, finishing it this time. "How about taking the painting and X-raying it with your fancy machine? After seeing all the paintings Squank has copied from the master, maybe he's got a Rembrandt hidden under *Elvis*'s guitar."

"Well, that's a leap," Berg said, shaking his head slowly. "Couldn't it just be that he is a little … eccentric and maybe he's also a klepto, to boot?"

"Oh, he is eccentric!" I said. "And maybe a klepto, too—very probable, in fact."

"So, that's that," he said, exhaling with a bit of relief.

"Hey, buster, not so fast," I said. "Just because he's eccentric and has sticky fingers doesn't mean he isn't forging art or up to something else—all in cahoots with Leticia."

"Now you've gone beyond a leap to playing leap-frog!" Berg shrugged. "But it's not out of the question, I admit."

"*Voilà!*" I said, standing excitedly.

"But I promised Merriman I'd nose around tonight and see if I could find the lost targets when nobody's at The Lab. Wainwright is really putting the screws on and trying to convince the muckety-mucks that Merriman is a spy."

"God, Wainwright is turning into the 00s version of Joseph McCarthy. What a tyrant! Didn't he help set up that Chinese spy scandal that kept my fellow journalists happy for six months?"

"Yeah, Spy of the Month Club is a great diversion from doing research."

"And nobody knows how to tap into The Lab's paranoia like Wainwright," said Berg, biting into a guacamole enchilada smothered with green chile.

Green chile can make anyone better—even a worried physicist.

He brewed himself a double espresso and said with his impish grin, "Well, I'd better take you with me, or I'll probably have to come bail you out of jail. There are at least 352-and-a-half galleries in town that you might want to pop into to borrow a few paintings. For your own good and the protection of Santa Fe art, I'd better keep you with me at all times."

I turned the radio on to the Oldies but Goodies station. Tonight was Remember Elvis night. We sang along to "Jailhouse Rock" and "Blue Suede Shoes." I felt so comfortable with Berg, the way I'd felt with Mel. I didn't want to get this close. Look what happened to Mel. Loving people meant losing them.

Besides that, I was getting too entrenched in Santa Fe. I was a New Yorker, for God's sake. And I was settling into domestic bliss. I had built my reputation on being a mean and lean New York City reporter. Now I was in danger of turning into Donna Reed.

And I was spending too much time thinking of myself. I was supposed to be finding out who killed Rothschild, what was the story of Squank and these mysterious paintings, and most of all, who killed my sister? Would I ever know the truth about any of this? Well, at least we were hot on the trail of the *Elvis* variations.

An hour or so later, we pulled up to one of LANL's twenty-four-hour secure checkpoints. Naturally, he was on a first-name basis with the security guard; like almost everyone who had ever encountered him, they were great pals. I showed my press pass to my folksy physicist's buddy, Gary the Guard, and with some of Berg's smooth talking and overall charm, we motored on through the checkpoint. Ben Franklin could have learned a thing or two from my boy!

As we approached Berg's building—the same building where the targets had supposedly gone missing—he took his foot off the accelerator. And then I saw what he saw—flashing blue and white lights on top of a car driven by Los Alamos's Finest.

"Uh, oh," Berg moaned. "I think I see Dr. Merriman talking with those officers. "I better go see what's the hubbub."

I nodded. "Looks like Project X-ray will have to wait," I said, "until you rescue him."

He moved quickly—out of the car and jogging to the flashing lights and Merriman.

In less than five minutes, he was back, an uncharacteristically grim expression visible as he slid behind the wheel. I gave him space, remaining silent while he turned the car around and began to drive toward home. After a long sigh, he said, "Dr. Wouldn't-Hurt-a-Fly Merriman is safe for the moment, Mickey, but I fear the FBI will be knocking on his door very soon."

I patted his knee. "Then we'd better keep Merriman as busy as possible away from The Lab."

"Good idea," he said. "And we'll have to hold off on X-rays for now. But most importantly, I need to find out what Wainwright is up to—the dirty dog."

Food has dominated my life since I was sucking baby bottles as an infant, and I've had mother issues ever since. I know this seems extreme, but I almost recall, as a two-month-old wiggle worm, wondering why other babies of my early acquaintance were snuggling up to a real-life breast filled with mother's milk while I was stuck with commercial, sugar-added baby formula. *UGH!*

My Jewish mother managed to champion many of the tenets brought to the new world by the Puritans. She was also, as I've mentioned before, an awful cook. Some people are tone-deaf—well Muriel was taste-deaf. And she didn't believe anyone else should enjoy the sensual pleasures of good food.

In that way, she may well have inspired the wonderful scene in the film of Charles Dickens's *Oliver Twist* when Oliver holds up his empty bowl so innocently and says, "Please, sir, I want some more."

My relationship with food changed dramatically when my parents died and Mel and I were adopted by Lupita's parents. In La Familia Gutiérrez, the amount of edibles resembled the abundance of a Food Network Challenge—spiced up with New Mexico's glorious (and internationally coveted) Hatch and Chimayo green chiles.

The vittles in Mel's and my new home were sublime: carne adovada, calabacitas, posole, sopaipillas, and biscochitos—and became my daily fare. Mel and I ate like queens, for sustenance and pleasure both.

When I moved to the Big Apple, I found myself surrounded by an explosion of cultures and flavors—Thai, Cuban, Country French, British tea (the "high" kind with all the sweets and savories), and venders like Balducci's, D. Coluccio & Sons, and Zabar's everywhere. I had landed in foodie heaven.

Berg and I share this food worship. He loves his calling as a physicist, but I know he's always harbored the dream of being discovered as a great chef on one of those shows like *Iron Kitchen*.

So, when Shackleton approached Berg to ask if he would, by any chance, like to host a prototype or test run of Desserts in the Desert—in the form of a concept party for adults who love desserts and dessert wines, he had a pretty fair idea that the answer would be a resounding, "Yes!"

This was the morning after our trip to LANL, where we had found Dr. Merriman talking to police. After encouraging him to avoid The Lab for now, Berg drove us downtown to the Santa Fe Railyard development.

Berg and Shackleton were both toting their bags down the aisles of Santa Fe's Tuesday farmer's market when Shackleton posed the Desserts in the Desert question, adding modestly, "If it's successful, it's a shoo-in to qualify as a workshop for next year's Santa Fe Wine and Chile Festival."

"I'm thrilled and flattered, my man," Berg told Shackleton. "But is The Adobe Nightmare worthy of the event?" Hearing his worry expressed out loud, Berg looked as crestfallen as a ten-year-old boy who'd failed to make the basketball team.

Shackleton was quick to reassure him. "Your charming abode … is exactly the right size for an intimate, informal initial gathering."

At which point, a very excited Berg expressed his gratitude by purchasing a vendor's remaining inventory of shitake mushrooms, which added up to five pounds and almost twenty-five dollars.

"As for guests," Shackleton said, over spring rolls at one of their favorite stands, "it will be a short list to accommodate and encourage a sense of intimacy and discussion of the merits of the various desserts, wines, and their pairings."

"What about demerits?" Berg quipped, as a very tender sunflower sprout danced from between his lips.

"Who's getting demerits?" I asked as Lupita and I joined them at the small table.

Both men proceeded to explain the newly-agreed-upon partnership of the desserts venture.

Berg quieted as Shackleton waxed poetic: "Envision for a moment: sopaipillas infused with prickly pear sauce; chocolate tacos; biscochitos with crème brûlée topping; key lime flan—"

At which point Lupita spit out a bit of fresh strawberry that happened to land on Pygmy's sleeve—as, interestingly, he had just joined us, too. He merely smiled as he collected the strawberry remnants with a clean and pressed hanky that he returned to his pocket.

"This is absurd!" Lupita said, rising to her feet with passion. "New Mexico has had its unique food for centuries! Now all these foodies want to put their trendy stamp on the tried-and-true!"

"Who can argue with biscochitos?" she demanded, turning to Pygmy—*A very easy mark*, I thought but wisely refrained from verbalizing.

He frowned, looked shocked, nodded, shook his head, and waved his hands—almost all at once and (I imagined) covering every possible gesture of agreement that Lupita might be searching for.

"And who can forget *empanadas* and *tres leches* cake *y flan de limón!*"

She wasn't hiding her anger. She was clearly pissed off! And the fire of her passion only made her more beautiful—oh, dear, Pygmy was a goner!

Berg noted his best friend's acute case of "bitten by the love bug," but he took it in stride, never missing a beat while he munched his crisp egg roll (having already polished off the spring roll). "Ahem … you are so right," he reassured her, "so very right."

Which gave her time to catch her breath, and Shackleton nodded to allow her to take yet another breath.

"However …" Berg began gently. "Can we not consider the rigor of experimentation? True classics will withstand the force and challenges of the tests of time—and they also withstand the machinations of wannabe famous chefs, do they not?"

Lupita, eyeing Berg with all the sharp suspicion she

used to use to break hostile witnesses on the stand, nodded very, very slowly. "Yes …"

Pygmy slid a plate of crisp kim chee pancakes onto the table. Lupita reached out and broke off a piece to nibble, but she wasn't done with her lecture. She shook her head. "We are always apologizing for New Mexico— bad schools, worst child welfare, teen pregnancies, high drug addiction rates, and Albuquerque's status as the best place to have your car stolen—"

Pygmy looked as if a small dark cloud had settled just above his black Russian eyebrows, while Berg nodded sympathetically. I kept my eye on Lupita.

"But!" she said abruptly, voice deepening, hands raised.

Both men startled in their seats.

"When it comes to *comida*, that is our pride and joy, *que no?*"

"Our food and our skies," Berg added quietly.

"Only sissies complain their plates are too spicy," she snapped. "And they should all hop on a plane this instant and fly back to their bland, white-bread homelands!"

Which inspired Pygmy to shout, *"Da!"* while Berg stood and saluted.

Shackleton handled the half-dozen-plus invitations to Desserts in the Desert: A Concept Party for Adults Who Love Desserts and Dessert Wines (a.k.a. "an impromptu prototype party that may become an annual tradition"). The response was unanimously affirmative. Everyone agreed to attend the upcoming Friday afternoon at Berg's. He admitted his sneaking suspicion that Shackleton had anticipated his enthusiastic response and already set preparations in motion. I agreed.

In addition to invites, and the repast and vino (created and donated by local chefs and sommeliers), Shackleton also provided a staff of three to set up, serve, and clean up. He'd even sent a crew of Merry Maids to clean the day before the event.

In my mind, there is no finer culinary event than one where my only obligation is to eat, drink, and be merry!

Friday dawned with a crisp bite of fall in the air, turquoise skies, and a soft breeze to rustle aspen leaves. I spent my morning finishing and filing two light gallery opening pieces for Brady and, for *Art News*, a thousand words on the creative legacy of Leticia Rothchild.

By the time I'd changed out of my authorial PJs, showered, and donned my party persona, it was 3 p.m. and legally time for a glass of sherry. Berg appeared from his office looking and smelling delicious and sporting a bow tie, jacket, and Levis.

By 4 p.m., I was nicely relaxed and ready to eat— although Shackleton's efficient staff had taken over the kitchen, and Shackleton, impeccable in his formal wear, shooed Berg and me out repeatedly.

Pygmy, bearing gifts of flowers and several mysterious containers, arrived ten minutes before the 5 p.m. hour. Trespassing into what was now Shackleton's kitchen— his way eased by the fact he was twice as big as anyone else—he unveiled his offerings with flare. We, who had followed in his wake, watched with bated breath.

Whisking open boxes and bags and letting his Russian accent thicken with each pronouncement, he introduced us to:

"*Syrniki!*" Which we would learn were sweet cheese

pancakes topped with raspberries and mint from his garden and dusted with sugar.

"Chocolate salami!" Which truly looked like chocolate loaves of salami, although I was pleased to learn were made of dark chocolate, crushed milk biscuits, and toasted walnuts—a resourceful invention of Russians during various food shortages.

"And, last but not least, *ptichye moloko* or bird's milk cake!" a gorgeous-looking frosted cake that he explained was a combination of cake layers and custard and crème Chantilly frosting. I gained half a pound just staring at it!

I gained a second half-pound when Lupita placed a tres leches cake on the island next to Pygmy's offerings. "Traditional," she said proudly. "To prove that *mi bisabuela's* recipe can beat the shorts off any Le Cordon Bleu snobs!"

Pygmy grinned at Lupita. "Mine are also traditional— my great-grandmother's recipes! Russians love sweets, and we've been through our share of hard times and food rationings—so we learned to create with what we had at hand."

It was Shackleton who insisted we all toast to universal ingenuity with a small glass of Füleky Pallas Tokaji, a late-harvest Hungarian appellation.

I was surprised that Shackleton poured a fifth glass, knowing his professionalism kept him from imbibing until his duties were a *fait au complet*.

Mystery solved when a deep voice behind me boomed, "I'll have what the man on the floor's having!"

"Brady!" I turned, smiling, and to his surprise and my

own, I gave him a hug. Gosh, was Santa Fe infecting me with the touchy-feely bug?

"No worries," Berg whispered into my ear. "It's just the sherry and the wine." My lad knew me too well.

But now, the party, officially launched, began heating up as invited guests arrived. On the list: Ellen Paddington who came with a sweet, shy-looking young man wearing paint-stained clothes. Moments after Ellen, Shackleton announced the arrival of Sally Pommery, looking California sun-kissed (if a bit tired), accompanied by Joaquin C. de Baca who appeared to be openly grieving for Leticia Rothchild or else suffering badly from the desert's fall allergies, judging by his constant dabbing at his eyes and nose with a bright red bandana. The seemingly ever-cheerful and always-scathingly-critical food writer from the *New Mexican* arrived next, along with Lynn Cline, well-known author of several wonderful books on New Mexico's food, history, and traditions. Dr. Merriman arrived with the first wave and soon disappeared into the kitchen, which I thought wise. The other guests weren't exactly his people.

Shackleton made certain that everyone held a beverage of choice in hand within seconds of their arrival.

"Good man," Berg noted, adding, "Clearly, Shack is oiling the social cogs."

I couldn't help noticing that Berg was staying uncharacteristically close by my side. I wondered why he was hovering but understood as soon as Sally and her knife-obsessed escort Joaquin approached. "How nice of you to host a festive event in your home," Sally said, including me along with Berg. Before I could correct her that it was Berg's only, she added, "It's a welcome change after so many difficult events ..."

Just as I assumed she was referring to Leticia's death, Sally took my hand, and I saw what I took as sincere sorrow on her face. "I'm so sorry about your sister's death," she said quietly.

Joaquin added, "And now Leticia ..." And I noticed the shift in Sally's expression as Joaquin dabbed his eyes, apparently moved by memories of his deceased patron and lover. But before I could really take my full investigative journalist's read on Sally, Joaquin blew his nose—a startling honk that actually made me jump.

And Sally turned away abruptly.

From across the living room, Lupita caught my eye, but I barely had time to wonder what message she was conveying when a shriek terrified us all.

The occupants of the room turned in tandem to see Rosa, the crazy lady fortune-teller who was also Leticia's certifiable cousin, walk into the house with temperamental artist Jamie Inman on her heels. "I knew it!" Rosa yelled at the same pitch. "There is death in this house!"

"Oy," I murmured to Berg. "Please tell me she didn't bring her murderous fortune-telling cards!"

Shackleton swept past us, leaving profuse apologetic phrases in his wake. I made out: "… were not invited … assure you … would never—"

One of Shackleton's servers whisked a tray of small glasses of wine and assorted canapés across the room to present the offerings to Rosa and Jamie. They both accepted a glass and immediately imbibed, and Rosa popped a small chile dipped in chocolate into her mouth.

And just when it seemed things could not get worse, Richard Wainwright strutted in and announced, "I hear this is the place for 'fusion' food!"

Sally, still standing close to us, actually gasped—I assumed at the sight of her husband. Hmmm? And Joaquin muttered, "*Bastardo!*" which needed no translation. Berg groaned but pulled himself to full height, as if readying to fight.

"You do know Joaquin's family name, C. de Baca, comes from the explorer Cabeza de Vaca's lineage," Lupita said breezily, appearing at my side. "Which, as you well know, Mickey, means 'head of the cow'—although he might qualify as another body part at the opposite end of an unfortunate cow."

By the time the final topper of non-invitees arrived minutes later, I was numb. Almost. Although hearing Senator Rendón's voice sent a chill through me.

"I cannot begin to make up for this disaster," Shackleton said clearly as he passed us again to greet the senator.

Although, hark, dear reader, I spoke too soon—the last to arrive, dancing through the doorway and moving to some very privately and internally amplified boogie-woogie was none other than Squank. And I must admit, given the fact he tailed this group, I was actually happy to see him!

"Ooh, party time!" he crowed.

"I need another drink, and make it a triple," Inman groaned loudly.

"—having a good time without me, Sal?" Wainwright

asked his wife as she pivoted toward the bathroom, clearly trying to escape him.

"So, here is the new plan," Berg announced to me, Lupita, and Pygmy, who had joined us. I also noticed Brady leaning in to hear.

"We do not crucify Shackleton, the old bean," Berg said. "Instead, we take advantage of this unfortunate series of events and invitees and turn our little grey cells toward murder!"

The wines poured so freely I feared Shackleton would have to send scouts out for supplies, but ever the impeccable majordomo, he seemed to possess the Jesus touch and make wine from water. He'd understood his orders to keep our guests (invited and uninvited) lubricated and fed and—most vital of all—blabbing! With backup from Shackleton and Brady, our quartet of amateur detectives spread out to gather intel.

We divided the room, agreeing to reconvene after we'd kicked the last of the partyers out. But alas, that time was hours away.

I eased myself toward the fireplace and a group that included Jamie Inman, Richard Wainwright, and Lynn Cline.

Berg, wisely, steered clear of Wainwright, and I hoped he'd keep to that plan. It would be best to end the evening without fisticuffs! Perhaps he would be distracted by Merriman, who sat stiffly on the couch with a plate of food in hand; he was not alone because Magic had curled up in his lap, and I envied the good doctor for keeping some of the best company at this party.

As I weaved between folks, I noticed Ellen and her

young companion gravitating to a corner, off to themselves, although I saw Squank eyeing them repeatedly. It did occur to me that he'd recently lost his art patron. Ellen might be a much better match for his temperament. In turn, he might bolster Paddington Gallery's international visibility, which would be good because right now it seemed to be nearly invisible. I passed Pygmy, who was eyeing the trio of Ellen, her date, and Squank, his ear tuned to catch anything of interest. Being so tall, he couldn't exactly sneak around, but he could charm Ellen, of that I had no doubt.

On the other side of the living room, near the entryway to the small library, Berg and Lupita had Rendón cornered. Oh, better them than me! Sally and Joaquin hovered close by.

I shifted attention back to my group when I heard Wainwright say, "Letty was an expert climber, but lately, I'd noticed she'd been a bit ... well, off her game."

"Off her rocker is more like it!" Jamie offered his pronouncement loudly enough to inform Berg's neighbors on either side of the house and half of Canyon Road. "The witch broke all her promises to me—and don't think she was interested in Joaquin-bloody-head-of-a-cow, not on your life! She was playing some other game!" at which point, he seemed to think he had a knife in his hand instead of his wine glass, and he sent a stream of flowery, nutty Manzanilla arching through the air toward Lynn.

"Oops!" She pivoted just in time to avoid most of the Spanish sherry. I sent her a sympathetic wave as Shackleton arrived with one of his staff to handle the spill. I loved her books because she was such an excellent writer, researcher, and storyteller. (She might get some stories tonight!) A great cook too, I knew, but I skipped her recipes because my only interest in cuisine was eating it.

As she wisely excused herself from that group and headed toward the kitchen, it occurred to me that Rosa had vanished. I slipped into the hallway and tiptoed toward the bathroom. The door was open, no one inside. I continued along the hall to the master bedroom and slowed when I saw the door ajar. I thought for sure I heard the sound of a drawer sliding open or closed. I pushed the door and stepped inside the bedroom I shared with Berg—

—to see Rosa bending over the night table on my side of the bed. I couldn't see what had her attention, but her tarot cards were scattered all over the white bedspread and the floor.

She turned toward me just as I asked sharply, "What are you doing in here?"

She stood very still, went slightly bug-eyed, and stared at me—and let me tell you, if you're going for a creepy effect, try it sometime.

I repeated my question in a quieter tone, adding, "Are you looking for something?"

She smirked. "I could tell you I was looking for the loo, but that would be a lie, and I do not lie."

"Then what are you doing in our bedroom?"

"I have a message," she said, her voice dropping and wavering. "Her death was no accident."

I couldn't help myself, I shivered. "Whose death?"

"Look at the cards," she said, waving her arms to

point out what seemed to be a full, if scattered, deck. (*Even though she was playing with barely a quarter of a deck*, I couldn't help but think to myself.)

She reached out and pointed to a card with a ladder set against a blank wall.

"I don't understand," I said.

"The ascent from dark to light, from ignorance to wisdom ..."

Then she reached for a card depicting a jester dressed in ragged clothes—and said, "The Fool means the end of one journey and new beginnings and trust in the Universe, although this one is reversed, and that signals naïveté, lack of judgment, perhaps trusting too much in the Universe."

I repeated my question: "Whose death was no accident?" Was she referring to Leticia or my sister?

"Take your pick," she said, her eyes narrowed, and her whole being seemingly tense.

"Leticia?"

Rosa pointed to a card, and I shook my head, having no idea what the image meant.

"Temperance ... sounds good, doesn't it? But it's reversed, so it reflects an extreme lack of balance." At that, she laughed a short, deep, "Hah!" She shook her head "They're usually not so literal."

She pointed to another card, and the image was clearly a spire. "And here is The Tower, which when upright, indicates disaster and abrupt upheaval." Her eyes widened so the whites surrounded her entire pupil. "And it all came tumbling down ..." she said, her voice singsong.

The woman could make a fortune taking Bela Lugosi's place in remakes of horror films.

My instincts howled that Rosa was crazy and that I was almost as crazy if I took her seriously, but I couldn't help asking, "So, you're saying Leticia was murdered?"

"I say nothing; it's the cards doing the talking."

Like Charlie Brown who sucker-kicks the ball one more time for Lucy, I took a deep breath and pushed onward. "What about my sister?"

Rosa tipped her head, her eyes, onto me and then onto the cards. When she spoke, she sounded almost reasonable. "The Moon reversed indicates fear. And here …" She pointed to one card whose image needed no explanation: a human figure hanging from a bleak, bare tree. "The Hanged Man … I think in your sister's case, it means sacrifice and martyrdom."

A sob rose up from deep within me, and I clutched my hands to my belly.

Rosa shook her head, and her eyes softened. "See that the card for Justice is touching the others, and I believe that indicates your sister's courage and her search for clarity, for the truth. And you have taken up her cause. You can find true justice—if you can find all the clues."

She paused for a moment before adding, "And if you can stay alive."

My mind jumped right over her last sentence. (*Thank you, denial.*) "What clues?" I demanded, not caring if my voice screeched.

She shrugged.

I stood, confused, not knowing if I were listening to a seriously ill woman off her meds or if Rosa, for all her faults, somehow spoke truths—whether she "saw" them, intuited them, or knew things others didn't.

"I'm going," she said, abruptly beginning to scoop up her cards. "Thanks for inviting us to the party."

My jaw dropped, and I huffed in frustration, again certain I was under the influence of a fruitcake.

Within seconds, there were only two cards left. She turned to me and jutted her chin toward me. "Listen carefully. This card is The Devil, and it tells us about someone caught in addiction, greed, materialism … he is dangerous in his ineptitude—"

Before I could ask her who she was talking about, she continued.

"—and this card, The Emperor reversed, means tyranny, a mad lust for power at any cost."

"Who is he, this devil, this upside down emperor?" I asked, my voice trembling.

Rosa scooped up the last cards and flashed them at me. "You mean who are 'they'?" Again, she simply shrugged. "Only the cards can answer." She turned toward the door. "What do you take me for, a looney-tunes huckster?"

I followed her into the hallway, and just before we reached the living room, she swirled around so quickly I stumbled back a few steps.

"Be very, very careful. One thing I do know—you are dealing with very dangerous people, and they are all here tonight in this very house!"

I couldn't take my eyes from her, staring as she clutched Jamie by his jacket sleeve and tugged him along to the door and out into the darkness.

I studied the people in the room: Did the cards refer to Joaquin C. de Baca, to Rendón, to Wainwright?

Squank? Sally or Ellen? After all, women could be killers too, even though less often than men.

Abruptly Lupita was by my side, clutching my arm. "Mickey, mija, are you okay? You're white as my tia's whiskers."

I nodded, even as I still shivered. "I'll tell you all about it when we have privacy—but right now—" I broke off as Shackleton gently pressed a small toddy glass into my hand. As I raised the drink to my mouth without hesitating for an instant, the scent of honey and whiskey soothed my senses, and the warmth eased its way to steady my stomach and my nerves. Bless the man.

Lupita read my mind and spoke quietly. "*Él es un mago.*"

Indeed, she was absolutely right; Shackleton was a magician.

By the time the "guests" had left or been shooed out the door, I felt one hundred years old. Surveying my friends as we gathered around the kitchen island, I knew I wasn't alone in feeling like a centenarian. Lupita, Pygmy, Berg— and our backup men, Shackleton and Brady—were joined now by Lynn and the inimitable Dr. Merriman.

"I can offer aid and comfort in the form of edibles, even if I cannot impart miraculous recovery from the events of this evening," Shackleton told us, still looking impeccable and fresh. How did he do it?

"I have very strong, very dark espresso, decaf or real, Kona, courtesy of Ms. Mickey. I also have chamomile tea and honey. And, of course, various *digestivos*: Talisker Single Malt Scotch Whiskey, St. Agnes XO brandy, Courvoisier, Armagnac, and several liqueurs."

Within minutes, we were settled around the kitchen table, savoring our various lubricants.

Berg cleared his throat. "Who wants to start?"

Shackleton appeared quietly from nowhere. "If you will forgive me, I'll share my information and impressions first, so I can then concentrate on cleaning up and sending my crew home."

We all stared at him or nodded, and Berg said, "Yes, my man, please go on."

"Well ..." He looked pensively at Berg. "I begin with Richard Wainwright—"

Seeing Berg's instant scowl, Shackleton lowered his head. "I know, I'm sorry."

But Berg waved him on. "Then we get him quickly out of the way."

Shackleton frowned. "I witnessed him telling Joaquin C. de Baca to sober up. Wainwright said, 'How many disgusting drunks do we need at this shabby attempt of a party?' He was referring to Arturo Rendón, if I read his look and his expression correctly."

There seemed to be general agreement in our group that Shackleton was capable of reading minds, never mind expressions.

"And now I must apologize to our venerable doctor ..." Here Shackleton looked quietly to Dr. Merriman, who promptly blushed. (*How could everyone not love this man?* I wondered.)

"Wainwright made a point of singling you out ... perhaps for the sake of the several journalists present—not one of whom took the bait."

Brady nodded to himself, no doubt in silent praise of journalists around the globe.

Now Shackleton focused on me, and I sat up straight. He said, "You were spared, Ms. Mickey, because you were otherwise occupied, being confronted by Leticia's very distinctive cousin."

I nodded, shivering. "It's doubtful I was spared anything. Rosa might be off her meds, but she's not crazy when she implied that both my sister Mel and Leticia were murdered. She frightened me."

Everyone took a breath, aware the air seemed instantly cooler; they also took the moment to sip more of their liquid courage.

"It's medicinal, so drink liberally," Pygmy said. Lupita looked up at him and smiled.

Brady tapped a cocktail fork against a plate now empty of Lupita's enchiladas. "Mickey, when you went looking for Rosa, and Ms. Cline wisely sought refuge in the kitchen with Shackleton's assistance, I took over with Wainwright and Jamie Inman."

My heart seemed to squeak excitedly. "And?"

"Not surprisingly, they were speaking past each other—might as well have been on different planets."

Berg snorted. "I'd be happy to strap Wainwright to a rocket and send him to his own planet."

"Preferably a black hole."

Everyone looked at the speaker, slightly surprised by the sound of his voice. Dr. Merriman smiled impishly before tipping his head to look much like a preverbal child expressing half-hearted remorse.

Mirroring Merriman, Brady tipped his own head.

"What did surprise me was the way Inman kept deferring to Wainwright as the expert on Leticia's state of mind."

"Hmmm," I said. "We know Letty collected lovers like some people collect stamps—Inman, Joaquin ..."

Lupita jotted a note on a napkin and said, "I'll get ahold of a list of her paramours."

Berg reached out and took my hand in his, but he addressed his words to the group. "I can fill you in, if Lupita doesn't object, on our time with Rendón."

"No objection, Your Honor," Lupita said, smiling just a little.

Berg nodded. "I guess we can say that he knows how to hold his liquor—but it might be more accurate if we say, it holds him, because he's basically pickled—the results of decades of alcohol dependency. He needs AA desperately. He did say he used to let Leticia house her VIP guests at his family ranch. When I mentioned that our medical investigator views Mel's death as suspicious, he became even more squirrelly than normal. And he teared up."

Lupita's gorgeous eyebrows arched expressively. "The exchange heated up when Sally and Joaquin joined in and she got in Rendón's face—"

"Almost literally in his face," Pygmy added.

Nodding lightly, Lupita continued, "And Sally accused the senator of pressuring Rothschild for kickbacks on any action—"

"As in money earned from sales with those very impossible prospects," Pygmy said quickly.

Lupita slapped the table with her palm. "Rendón yelled back that Pommery acted like a spy, even while turning a blind eye in her own house! C. de Baca and Rendón almost went at it *mano a mano* at that point."

I shook my head. I'd managed to miss a lot during my brief encounter with Rosa. "Someone tell me they were watching Squank," I said, speaking quietly.

A young female server busy removing her apron said, "He's at least one enchilada shy of a full combo plate—and I'd say he's missing the *refritos*, too."

Now, Lynn spoke up, smiling warily. "He puts on a good act. Looks shy and elfin-like, but I watched him watching all of you, and his focus and attention was quite—amazing. Although he views the world through an artist's eyes, so I guess it's not surprising."

"Maybe it's more surprising he plays dumb so well," I said.

"And looney. He's made it work for him. He could pass for Dopey of the Seven Dwarfs, but he even has international collectors."

Pygmy took over, adding, "Who apparently pay small fortunes for his *Elvis* art."

I made a face. "Well, his dogs were anything but dwarfs. When they were attacking me, they certainly seemed larger-than-life and anything but cute." Berg squeezed my arm.

Lupita waved a knife (butter knife) in the air and said, "I know everyone thinks Ellen P. should be nominated for sainthood up there with Mother Teresa. But she has a dark side."

"No doubt," I added, "brought out by all that dreadful herbal tea."

"Doesn't everyone?" Pygmy asked softly. "Have a dark

side, I mean? Even the kindest soul, when pushed to the brink ..."

Lupita cocked her head, eyeing him speculatively.

His cheeks flushed a bit. "Or is it my Russian soul?"

"I think you're right," Lupita said, surprising all of us (only in the sense she'd admit Pygmy was more accurate than she). "In my business, *Madre de Dios* knows I've seen everything." She bit down thoughtfully on a piece of Pygmy's cake. "Still, what motive would be strong enough to get Ellen Paddington out on a cliff, literally?"

"I agree; it doesn't make obvious sense," I said, shaking my head.

The conversation drifted comfortably for a while to food and murder mystery books, focusing fondly on Agatha Christie and poisoning scenes while plates were polished, and drinks quaffed.

Then the amateur sleuths of the Desserts in the Deserts' soirée returned their "little grey cells" to the local murders. The things Rosa had said were beginning to show up on everyone's radar.

Questions flew: "What did Rosa mean by her inscrutable comments? Were Mel and Leticia murdered by the same person? If yes, who done it? Or was Rosa right when she referred to the greedy and addictive devil and the tyrannical emperor as two people, both capable of murder? And what the heck did she mean by 'find all the clues!'"

"I need answers," I said, standing abruptly. "I can't keep on wondering who hurt Mel, who killed my sister."

Lupita put her arms around me, and Brady patted my head. I felt claustrophobic and loved—and those emotions together confused me miserably.

"Much still needs to be revealed," Berg said, using his best Poirot voice.

"Holy cow," Brady said, sounding very much like the sports announcer Harry Carey.

As Shackleton dismissed his staff, slipping money into their pockets, our group began to quietly break up. The day had been long.

"I'd personally like to blame everything on that Trump clone, Wainwright," said Berg, as he carried glasses to the sink. "He's a mediocre scientist who thinks he's the next Oppenheimer."

"Or speaking of the Narcissist's Parade," said Pygmy, our art expert, "That clown Rendón is pretty full of himself; he's a pedestrian artist who thinks he is channeling Picasso."

I stirred a generous helping of sugar into my espresso, searching for answers in the swirling darkness. Was Squank sly or dangerous or both? He was definitely extremely eccentric—but was it in the harmless way of many Santa Feans, or was he deranged? Was Ellen as pure as she seemed? What about the parade of narcissists— the overinflated Wainwright and Rendón, who controlled much of the money flowing into the state? I couldn't help but hear Rosa's words in my ear: The Emperor and The Devil. Or what about bipolar and unmedicated Rosa, the fortune teller with a penchant for crashing parties, this time with blacklisted, unsellable artist Jamie Inman as her date? Diane Mott Davidson beware: your cooking/catering books are being invaded by the Mickey Mousse Club!

Inheritance is a funny thing; some people inherit money, a few inherit the wind. I inherited a gene for disquietude and dread, which I was trying desperately to overcome. My parents had two words that dominated their life: "work" and "fear." Fear filled our home like a giant balloon—fear there would not be enough money, fear someone would get sick (and therefore couldn't work), and fear that Henny Penny was right and the sky was falling.

My mother could have served in Washington, DC, in the president's cabinet as the secretary of Fear and Foreboding. Most Jewish mothers dispense chicken soup; mine served up soupçons of Anxiety.

Fortunately, Mel and I were blessed with a fairy godmother, our Aunt Millie, a wild and zany pistol-packing mama who erased many of the trepidations we were taught daily. She was my father's sister, but she somehow got the extra chromosome for Fun and Adventure.

Aunt Millicent was the black sheep of our family, and therefore, naturally my role model. She looked Fear in the face and told it to take a hike. She rode horses, she climbed mountains, she told outrageous tall tales, and in the Yiddish parlance that Senator Rendón was so fond of malapropping, she was a mensch!

She introduced me to *Charlotte's Web*, *Eloise*, *Anne of Green Gables*, *Little Women*, bought me my first bra and my first drink. She took me on my first real trip and showed me there was a big, interesting world out there waiting to be explored. My mother abhorred traveling, feeling there were too many peculiar foreigners inhabiting the planet.

Aunt Millie collected husbands the way I used to collect charms for my bracelet, but she retained genuine affection for all of her assorted spouses. She once told me, "I learned something precious from each of them." My free-spirited aunt is no doubt the reason I'm a journalist today; if I had listened to dear old mom, I'd probably be a clerk at the Five & Dime.

It was for my Aunt Millie—and Mel—that I was going up to the mountains today. I have to admit, I'd rather be home sipping java and dabbling on my watercolors, but sometimes you've got to face your fears and wrestle them to the ground.

"*Estás loca, mujer!*" Lupita muttered to me now, calling me "crazy."

If there is such a thing as reincarnation (and most of Santa Fe believes there is), Aunt Millie would be by my side today. And, I admit, Lupita was totally akin in spirit and style to my own Auntie Mame—afraid of nothing.

Let me share some context: With Lupita by my side, I was making my way up to the Y to see if I could reconstruct what happened to Leticia. After the events of Desert Desserts, my conversation with Dr. Merriman, Pygmy's report of the autopsy, the red car, and Mel's unsent letter to me, I was convinced that the answer to Mel's death, the missing target at The Lab, Rendón's weird behavior, and Berg's stolen painting might all be intertwined; if I solved one of them, maybe everything else would fall into place.

I was panting while Lupita seemed to be barely breathing. Looking for a suitable rejoinder to her statement about me being crazy, I said (between labored breaths), "you may think I'm five cans short of a six-pack or not firing on all cylinders, but I know EXACTLY what I'm doing."

And suddenly, I started to snicker, then laugh, and Lupita couldn't stop herself, and she joined in my laughter, and soon we both collapsed to the ground, almost rolling in hysterics.

By the time we calmed down, I was wiping tears from my eyes. And I thought I noticed a sheen to my sister's eyes, too.

"I miss Mel," I said softly.

"Me too, mija." Lupita wrapped her arm around me and pulled me in for a brief hug. Then she hopped to her feet—truly hopped from sitting to standing—and offered her hand to pull me up more slowly.

Once, when we were in high school on a Girl Scout jamboree in Hyde Park in the foothills of the Sangre de Cristo Mountains, we met up with some *pachucos* who thought our Girl Scout troop would add some nice notches to their belt. They clearly didn't know with whom they were messing; even back then, Lupita had her black belt in karate.

After Lupita cleaned the clock of two of the trouble-makers, the rest of the gang of not-so-merry men went dashing back to the woods and left us alone. Our Girl Scout troop leader was so impressed she asked the Juliette Gordon Low House in Savannah, Georgia, (the birth-place of the

Girl Scouts) to create a special merit badge for Lupita that reads "I Own You."

Besides being a good chum (in the best girl detective sense), Lupita had a practical reason for trudging up to the mountains with me. I had commissioned her to do a photo layout on the dramatic, ever-changing New Mexico skies for *The Maverick*. Twice a year at the paper, we do special supplements featuring photo essays of New Mexico; these are our most popular issues, making me think, again, that Eliza Doolittle knew whereof she spoke when she said, "Words, words, words, there isn't one I haven't heard … show me!"

Lupita was typical of the Renaissance women New Mexico is famous for; these multitalented, resource-ful, strong women grow in plentiful crops along with the state's beloved green chile—women like Georgia O'Keeffe, Laura Gilpin, Willa Cather, Mabel Dodge Lujan, Agnes Martin, and of course, Lupita Gutiérrez.

Lupita was as handy with a camera as she was with a karate punch. She told me that the Lost World Plateau near the Y was the perfect spot to begin shooting her series of timed sequence photographs of the magnificent New Mexico skies. I was happy for the company, and for her overflowing cup of bravado—even though I knew a part of her plan was to keep an eye on me.

We synchronized our watches and agreed to meet back at The Red Beast at 5 p.m. She gave me my own key to the car so I could get in and out of the elements if my journey proved fruitless. She also gave me one of her famous lectures.

For better or worse, Lupita never forgot that she was two days and thirty-two seconds older than me, and once we became sisters, she took this older sister role very seriously.

"Mija, you know I adore you, white as you are, and since we were *niñas*, I've always tried to take care of you."

She stood up, towering over me with her extra half an inch, making my diminutive five feet seem like Toulouse Lautrec.

"Girlfriend, here's a little advice."

I sighed because she loved giving advice (whether you wanted it or not). It was mother's milk to her. Sometimes, I don't think she was aware she was acting as council; it was an occupational hazard—it's just what she did.

Her words were always wise ones, but we were both as strong-minded as they come; stubborn me didn't always like to hear anyone else tell me what to do, even a person I loved and admired.

She set her hands on her hips. "Okay, chum, I know this may be falling on deaf ears. I know you've been trying to be the perfect niece for Auntie Millicent, which always makes you preternaturally brave. Then, understandably, you want justice for Mel."

I started smiling; it was hard to turn away from the

commanding and loving ways of my soul sister and best chum. And she was correct that I had become obsessed with finding answers, not only to the mystery of my sister's death but also to questions about Leticia's death—how an experienced climber could suffer such a disastrous fall and what Squank meant when he said: "... yellow day."

"But remember, don't do anything foolish. For one thing, you could easily get altitude sickness up here in the mountains at 8,500 feet. It takes a while to adjust from going to sea level to the mountains. Just going from sea level to Santa Fe with its 7,000-foot altitude can make you very sick."

I mugged a sour face. "But I grew up here."

"Like that gives you natural immunity. No way. Don't you remember when my cousin David Gonzales spent the summer in Quebec, came back, and entered the Santa Fe Labor Day Marathon?"

"Didn't he end up in the hospital?"

"Yep, altitude sickness coupled with dehydration did him in." Lupita shook her head. "Mick, I know your parents (may they rest in peace) were a little neurotic—okay, nutcases—but there is some truth to those bone-chilling stories they fed you daily."

I began to protest, but she cut me off.

With a sweep of her arms, she said, "This land is treacherous and unforgiving. And, honey, you are a damn Easterner used to that land of Oz they call New York City. And hey, city slicker, it's a whole lot more dangerous out here in the Wild West."

She sucked in a breath but barely slowed her speech.

"And I know you are being facetious when you're always telling our whole clan that your mantra is: 'I'm a mental and moral giant but a physical coward,' but, girlfriend, there's a lot of wisdom in that expression!"

"My sister, my heart," I said, catching a quick breath. "Say it over and over 'til you believe it's true."

"Then, as our great late governor Bruce King used to put it so colorfully," she continued, combing my hair with her fingers then placing my wool ski hat, which had been dangling from a coat pocket, on my noggin, "Ladies, it looks like we're in for some weather."

The ugly gray skies were spitting snow.

"I really think I should go with you," she said as she gave me one of her signature bear hugs. "Whenever you get that faraway look, I know you think you are Super Woman, and that makes you a dangerous wild card."

I admit, for a second I hesitated and almost came to my sensible senses—but then I pictured Mel and heard her whispering my name and knew I'd do anything to find the truth about her death. I took a quick breath and mustered my chutzpah.

"Hey, missy," I shot back with my big mouth, "the only thing I've seen you climb was a stair-stepper, and you've only got one day to do the favorite feature in *The Maverick*; the angry skies are just begging to be photographed. And I'm your editor, so get to work!"

"Remember our meet-up plan—but if the snow gets serious, scrap 5 p.m. and head to the car ASAP."

"Okay, *'mana*," I said.

She hugged me again as we parted ways, admonishing: "Enjoy the climb and let whatever happens happen. Who knows on what branch the *paloma* will stop?"

"Happy shooting, photo queen," I said with a flippant tone I didn't feel.

Gazing up at the formidable Jemez Mountains in the distance, I was already getting that queasy feeling in the pit of my stomach that I often get at the beginning of a climb. Once again, I remembered my parents telling Mel and me, "Stay away from the mountains; they eat little girls like you."

My mother had a friend who was killed in a climbing accident. Mel and I were fed gruesome tales of Marva's crushed bones and her bloody skull, often at the dinner table while we were eating our overcooked vegetables and rubber-tough meat.

Even though Aunt Millie had told us that Marva was an overconfident, reckless climber whose equipment included a canteen filled with Bénédictine brandy, my mother's dire warnings now returned to dance around in my head and turn me once again into an insecure nine-year-old. Add to that the warnings from Lupita, turned Mother Superior, and I was more than a little anxious.

All my life, I'd heard that the only thing I had to fear was fear itself. Easy for FDR to say. I found fear itself to be a formidable foe, one I've been battling most of my life.

Before most climbs, I invariably fast forward to a scenario of me lying on the ground, face down, looking like my imagined version of crushed and bloodied Marva.

If I ever invested in psychotherapy (which I'll probably never do), in one session, I would no doubt learn that my tough-broad, hard-boiled persona was a defense mechanism, my way of holding an often-terrifying world at bay.

Enough digression; focus on why you are here, I snapped at myself: to see what Squank meant by a "yellow day," to figure out how an experienced climber like Leticia could fall to her death on a challenging face—but not one that should have proved fatal.

I found myself smiling, reverting back to the brave nine-year-old who loved girl detectives, realizing I also had come on this one-woman expedition to discover "clues."

I signed in at the Tsankawi trailhead to the Y, writing the time of arrival of 2 p.m. and estimating that I would be through with my sleuthing climb at approximately 5 p.m. I noted the entry of three other climbers who hadn't yet signed out (and whose handwriting, if possible, was worse than mine) scrawled in the notebook. I wondered why this popular climbing area was so deserted. Did everyone else know something I didn't know?

My anxiety level escalated as I looked around. The weather did NOT resemble a poster from the New Mexico Department of Tourism promoting the charm of climbing in New Mexico. The sky was a coal grey, and a light snow continued to spit in my face. Maybe I should have taken Lupita up on her offer to accompany me.

I told myself I was behaving like a big baby; where was my valor when I needed it? I remembered Aunt Millie giving me flying lessons (which was not on my top ten list of things to do) and telling me the only way to conquer your fears was to do the things you feared the most and pretend you love them.

I reminded myself that while I wasn't a "hardwoman" (climbing parlance for world-class climber), I really wasn't a "bonehead" (rank beginner) either. I had taken six months' worth of lessons at the in-house climbing gym at *News View*.

I even took several climbing workshops in the Shawangunks on the Hudson River, taught by expedition mountaineers, Don and Alice Liska. I was a diligent student, but let's put it this way—Ms. Liska's title of "world championship record holder for women's altitude" was in no danger of being usurped by me. I had done my homework, but I was not a natural. I hated heights, hated depths even more, and liked my feet planted resolutely on *terra firma*. And I was fearful of taking on a climb solo.

I reached into the pocket of my parka and located, among the gum wrappers, unidentified buttons, and the key to The Red Beast, a St. Christopher medal given to me by Lupita's mother.

Tia Maria had taken me to the Albuquerque Sunport when I moved to New York City. At the gate, as I was ready to board the plane, she pressed this same St. Christopher's medal into my hand. "Christopher is the patron saint of travelers; he will protect you." I wish she had given a similar medal to Mel.

"Okay, stop stalling," I said inwardly. "The sooner you start, the sooner you will finish—now there's a catchy bumper sticker for you."

I put on my red Petzl helmet that matched my red and black GoLite Reach parka. God forbid, my climbing outfit wasn't perfectly color coordinated and accessorized! I adhered to my Girl Scout motto "be prepared" and put my LED flashlight, my newly acquired Los Alamos Mountaineering Club Climbing Guide, and a whistle into my parka pocket.

I broke out my collapsible ski pole and used the easy-descent gully to access the gorge where I would begin my climb. I pretended I was here on assignment and talked out loud describing my climb to myself as if I were writing a story. This technique relaxed me a little, putting me back into professional, reporter mode.

"I am using my ski pole to balance on the difficult basaltic borders. Now I am descending into the gorge and traversing about a quarter mile up-canyon to the base of the cliff section known as Portillo."

I started chuckling to myself, which either meant I was relaxing and getting the hang of this climbing gig or was about to come unglued. I decided to give myself the benefit of the doubt and go for the former. I was feeling so exhilarated that I stopped my one-woman reporter routine and began whistling a few tunes from *Annie Get Your Gun*. Crooning show tunes always cheers me and sometimes activates my braver self. I stopped my Bernadette Peters imitation and took out my climbing guide to verify that I had arrived at the face where

Rothschild's accident took place. Yep, here it was, the cliff with the intriguing name of Cat Burglar. I glanced over at the 5.10d face route, which called for fixed bolts and showed chalk tick marks. Difficult—make that impossible for me—but not for Ms. Rothschild. And yet, this was where she had breathed her last.

I shuddered, then I gingerly started up the easy class 4 route where I was going to look for any clues I could show my chums. You have to be *poco loco* to do technical climbs—and as Rothschild proved, you could end up dead.

What I was doing was precarious enough. I started shivering, an activity not highly encouraged in climbing circles. Instinctively, I pulled my loose parka around me and put my LED flashlight and whistle into the front pocket. The sky was darkening, and I might need the flashlight on the way back down.

I switched my musical repertoire from "Anything You Can Do, I Can Do Better" to my own rendition of "Breaking the Code" sung to the tune of "Staying Alive" from the 1977 disco film classic *Saturday Night Fever*. ("Breaking the code" in climbing lingo means figuring out the moves on a rock route.) Sometimes I show off how much I know, even if only to impress myself, to keep my courage intact.

Suddenly, I saw something glittering in one of the handholds. At first, I thought I was channeling Ms. Drew in my desperate attempt to find clues; then, I worried hypothermia was setting in and my reasoning was unsound.

But no, there it was, no hallucination—on the black

basalt cliff the next step up. Feeling like I was on a Girl Scout treasure hunt, I scrambled up to the ledge, where a pair of tortoise-shell sunglasses lay wedged halfway beneath a cleft in the rock. Taking care and wearing my climbing gloves, I nudged them out to take a better look—distinctive, trendy, expensive, and … familiar? Did I remember Rothschild wearing glasses like these? I wasn't sure. Vuarnet, very retro. And suitable for a style-conscious woman or man. The more I examined them, the more I was certain I'd seen them on someone. But, moment by moment, I was less certain that someone was Ms. Rothschild.

How could the investigators have missed them?

I was like a woman possessed. I was going to solve all of these cases; move over Columbo and Monk! The sun suddenly came out for a moment, and something above me caught my eye. Acting like the Mad Woman of the Mountain, I climbed up to an area that was new to me and where the climbing became more difficult and exposed. In a vertical crack to the left of the challenging face route where Leticia had climbed, I saw something green fluttering from a small branch. A small voice inside me whispered that I was treading on dangerous ground, that I was way out of my league here. I also heard Lupita's warnings to take it easy. I ignored this and listened to another stronger voice telling me to keep going; I had almost reached the holy grail.

The stronger voice won. Who did I think I was? Wonder Woman? I didn't care; I was on a quest. I eyed the narrow ledge leading out to the branch where the green item flew like a flag. The ledge petered out about halfway across the steep face, very exposed, but with small crimpers and decent foot purchase. As I got closer, I thought I recognized the flapping object as a piece of canvas from some kind of protective case.

I knew what to do. I'd just sidle out along this ledge and reach the evidence with my ski pole. My inner cheerleader shouted, *I can do this!*

I put one foot in front of the other. I realized, that as a reflex action, I was holding my breath. Carefully, I took the ski pole out and tentatively jabbed at the tuft of canvas, which I could now see had insulation.

Damn, I missed it. I took another baby step and poked at the branch with my ski pole. It came loose and, in slow motion, like in an anxiety dream, fluttered down. I reached out to catch it and a rock crumbled under my left foot. This noise acted like a wake-up call, and a bell went off inside of me.

What the hell was I doing? I certainly was not heeding Lupita's advice. Like I was having an out-of-body experience, I assessed my situation: I was spread-eagle on the face of this precarious balance! Had I totally taken leave of my senses?

I looked down and realized with one false move I—like Leticia—could plummet down the wall to the jagged rocks below and skewer myself like a cube of raw sirloin.

I had been so fixated on emulating my girl hero that I must have blocked out everything else; Lupita was going to read me the riot act. Climbing is all about keeping your mind in the present moment—very Zen. The mantra for this slightly insane sport is: "Focus, focus, focus." Getting distracted could get you killed.

But something else was distracting me. Below me, yellow fragments of broken glass shimmered, and I thought maybe I was looking at pieces of black plastic or metal. There was no way I could physically reach that lower ledge now—but my mind connected the canvas case with the glassy rubble.

I hadn't been merely distracted; I had been mesmerized. Suddenly, I was aware that I was freezing. Worse than that, I was shivering again and developing the death wobble in my legs.

The symptoms of hypothermia flashed through my bewildered mind.

I stared at the ledge I was on, like I was watching it in a movie. It was quickly filling up with an opaque layer of snow. Why hadn't I noticed this?

How did I get myself on high-angle rock with fresh snow? Could this be real? It had to be the granddaddy of all nightmares—didn't it? Soon I'd wake up in our never-finished Canyon Road adobe with a cup of hot, steamy espresso in my hand.

I tried to focus, get centered, assess the situation, and make it right. This getting things wrong and spacing out was so out of character for me. I was the poster child for planning ahead; non-spontaneous/anal-retentive was my middle name. But I had not been paying attention because I was so fixated on my fictional childhood detective role model, and now I was on the narrow ledge of a face with no rope or belayer.

My hands felt frozen; my fingers numb. Could I have fallen into the same "hypothermia trap" that caught so many tourist-hikers and climbers in New Mexico? I was having trouble holding on to the face. I was snow blind.

I thought I glimpsed something or someone in the distance walking toward me. Was it another climber coming to my rescue—or a snow mirage?

It didn't matter; it was like Pascal's wager about whether God really exists; it's better to believe until proven wrong. If my so-called climber was merely an apparition, I would find out soon enough.

I think I called out—at least I tried to yell, "Hello! Help!"

From out of the nowhere a figure appeared wearing a helmet and carrying what looked like a rock climber's rope. Rescue was on the horizon; I was the endangered heroine of an Alfred Hitchcock movie with Cary Grant to the rescue. I smelled a strong and expensive scent; familiar, and yet something was off …

Wham! My head seemed to crack open and light exploded! I was falling—cold air rushing past—and the world went black!

Where was I, Dante's Purgatory? The sky gleamed the color of a steel blade, and a mixture of snow and hail pelted me helter-skelter.

I felt like I was in a bad silent movie playing in slow motion. I was here, and yet I wasn't here. Could my body-double have been drugged and dumped in a cave filled with cement?

My mind groggy, the only thing keeping me awake was the most searing pain I've ever experienced. My upper back felt like the main entrée at a Japanese steak house, and razor-sharp knives plunged into my shoulders, preparing Mickey Teriyaki.

Everything seemed surreal; what was that pink stream of liquid running down my knee? Was it my blood mixed with snow or merely an illusion? Could I have stepped into a Salvador Dalí painting?

How long had I been here? And where was here?

The reporter in me took over. She was the survivor; the terrified little girl (somewhere deep inside me) who had screamed for help.

Okay, ace reporter, I said to myself: "Who? What? Where? When? How?"

Who? Me, unfortunately.

What? I'd taken a bad fall.

Where? I appeared to have hit the rock apron at the base of the wall only to be deflected into this stand of juniper trees.

How? Color me baffled.

I decided to put the journalistic Five Ws on the back burner and focus on the here and now: saving myself.

A sharp, strange taste filled my mouth; as I ran my tongue over one of my front teeth, I felt a ragged edge. I wiped my chin with my parka sleeve, and a trickle of blood dribbled down my fingers. Amid juniper branches, I took off my glove, and like a blind woman reading Braille, I studied my face. My chin and cheek had gashes in them and something slick—blood, I assumed—was everywhere. To paraphrase Macbeth, "Who would have thought the woman to have so much blood in her?"

My pain was so intense I couldn't identify where it was coming from. I glanced at my left hand, which resembled steak tartare. The skin was loose and hanging, flapping in the sharp, cold wind; doing the Charleston all on its own.

Could this be a dream? If so, I'd like to change dream channels—this one was too creepy. And painful! But I couldn't remember a dream where I'd ever felt pain; usually the "dream" emotion I experienced was embarrassment for running down an arroyo stark naked.

I tried to think, but there was nobody home; a layer of gauze seemed to be wrapped around my brain. I forced myself to concentrate and realized that I must have taken a "screamer" or "grounder" and had free fallen to the ground.

It was my nightmare—falling, falling into a void of midnight blue, of black ice, of total emptiness. I remember hearing a terror-filled scream. Was it mine? I heard the words repeated over and over, "Make it stop. Please make it stop."

Then a crash, a thud. Nothingness. Where was I? Was I dead?

A cold chill of reality hit me as something inside screamed, *If you don't act quickly, you could die.* Shivering, I was palpably in the grips of shock and hypothermia. My prime directive: *Survive!*

Moving like an arthritic old woman, I positioned my arm to reach inside my ski vest. Every gesture was agonizing. Even breathing hurt; had I broken a rib?

With the speed of a tortoise on an unusually slow day, I arduously pulled out my flashlight and whistle from my parka pocket. I blew the whistle for all I was worth, but I had almost no stamina left, so I hoped Lupita—or someone—would hear me. I was taking no chances on being rescued; I maneuvered the flashlight to fit into my hand. Using the code Lupita, Mel, and I had invented back in our Girl Scout days, I blinked the light on and off. The beam bounced around like a spotlight at a circus as the overcast sky was turning black.

I thought of Mel on that bleak, friendless road and wondered if there was a plot afoot to rid the world of the Moskowitz girls. Then my mind went blank; I was back in the abyss.

So far, being dead was the best thing that has ever happened to me—and so very different from anything that I previously imagined about the experience. No bright lights zooming toward me and no zipping through celestial wormholes. Just love, comfort, and food, glorious food.

It was more like an episode of *Downton Abbey* with me being waited on hand and foot by a gaggle of caring, loving servants. Being an English aristocrat with servants galore was one of my most enduring fantasies when I was among the living.

Was it possible we human beings had gotten this death thing completely wrong? Mr. Mark Twain would be relieved that in the afterlife, we weren't all hanging around in stiff white robes singing pious music and playing harps.

Maybe with death, we are allowed to fulfill all the dreams we meant to get around to but never quite did. Could it be that death equaled the ultimate do-over?

Glorious things kept happening: my mediocre little secret sketches that helped me think morphed into the most sophisticated art show ever. And these diminutive pictures, only viewed by Mel and me, were suddenly the talk, the buzz, of this happy hunting ground.

And the visitors to my show were from my afterlife A-list: Michelangelo, Claude Monet, Mary Cassatt, one by one, they filed by my white eternal light and all generously offered me suggestions to improve my sketches and, thus, my thinking about the mystery of Mel's (and my own) death.

Michelangelo, who looked like a thug, said he was looking to get rid of some of his large apprentice staff—since I was the new kid on the block and a one-woman band, he could loan me some free labor to help with the investigation—an offer I couldn't refuse.

Monet wanted to know if I needed any workers to tie my haystacks. He was paying union wages to the Haystack Honorarium and had plenty of hayseeds to go around.

Cassatt pulled me aside with this startling advice: "Listen up, my dear child, to my wisdom—I don't impart it to just anyone. I've learned a few things on this art journey, the first one being that art and diapers don't mix. Stay blissfully single and enjoy your delicious solitude. Kids do make fetching subjects and, of course, it's what the masses expect of us women artists. Take my word for it, for every kid you produce, ten years of painting go down the drain. Be smart. Rent a kid instead." (I could have sworn Mary delivered this speech in a Brooklyn accent, but what did I know.) I wondered: If I were dead, why was she telling me this?

I reflected back on all the existential discussions about death I'd had with both Mel and Lupita over the years. What did it all mean?

—Was it meaningless and nothingness?

—Was it pure white space? Was it Dante, after all?

—Did we truly understand Sartre or just pretend to?

My only regret is that I wanted to spread my good news. Can you imagine the type of work Woody Allen might produce if he didn't have the ultimate threat of death hanging over him? (Or if he and everyone else knew how much fun this was?)

"MICKEY, MICKEY, I NEED TO TALK TO YOU. IT'S GOD."

OMG, there really was a God, and he was trying to talk to me. I had seen little in my brief life to prove that there was a benevolent, loving God holding court somewhere in the neighborhood. I never believed he/she existed.

I would like some face time with the Big Guy or Big Gal. He/she/it seems to be conveniently out of town at a convention when something is going on in my household. Hmmmph. Where was he when my cat died of cancer? Where the hell was she when Mel was killed? And why was delightful and wise and daring Aunt Millie dead of a stroke while my cranky, nasty ninety-nine-year-old Aunt Mac was holding court in the cushiest retirement home I'd ever seen in Savannah, Georgia?

"Mickey, it's Lupita." Oh, THAT Guad.

It was Guadalupe Gutiérrez, which cheered me enormously. Now I didn't have to explain all this heavenly rapture to her; she could experience it for herself. And could this afterlife be any better than having one of my closest chums with me for all eternity?

But wait a minute. As much as I loved her, I didn't

want her to be dead. And if this were The Promised Land, where was Mel? Why hadn't she come floating by?

"Mickey, you've got to wake up."

For someone now engulfed in the spirit world, I was surprised to realize I could still experience physical pain. It felt like someone was slapping me on my cheeks. While I'd believed that my eyes were wide open, they blinked open now, and daylight through windows splashed me in the face.

"Okay, Ms. Moskowitz, if I keep this up, I'll lose my job in the DA's office when it's reported in the local press that the DA was seen beating up an injured victim. It would be very bad for my sterling reputation. So, how about a cup of coffee, made from your own Jack and the Beanstalk coffee bean selection? I smuggled it into the hospital, specifically hoping that a café au lait might rouse you, Sleeping Beauty."

"But I'm dead."

"The reports of your death have been greatly exaggerated. After the accident, we decided that it would help keep you alive if the outside world thought you were dead."

I must have looked as surprised and confused as I felt. "What? Everyone else thinks I'm dead, too? Where am I?"

"Secretly tucked in a corner private room at the hospital enjoying some very powerful pain-relieving drugs. Someone pushed you off the cliff—we found footprints in the snow that weren't yours, but we couldn't ID the brand of boot. Brady; the police chiefs in Santa Fe, Los Alamos, and the San Ildefonso Pueblo; a couple of FBI agents; the Pope; and I decided that whoever it was ought to think he did you in—mission accomplished."

"But," I said in a weak, sluggish voice, "I thought I was an angel."

"You may have flown up from Brownies to Girl Scouts, but honey, you're no angel."

As euphoria does, mine wore off a few hours later along with the most pleasurable effects of the pain drugs. In reality, my surroundings resembled nothing close to Heaven—at least the Heaven I had been experiencing in my delirium. My room, although adequate, lacked the amenities of a spa—or even a AAA-rated motel. I'd run low on the goodies delivered by my friends, and even though I'd been here for less than three days, I feared bedsores might be imminent. I love pampering—as much as I hate bed rest.

I was working to maneuver my injured body out of bed when the door opened, and Lupita walked in, pushing a wheelchair.

"For me?" I chirped, aiming for manic cheer. "How thoughtful—but it doesn't match my outfit."

"Your outfit happens to be hospital PJs," she said, smiling.

I was admiring the bandages on my wrist and ankle along with plentiful bruises—moaning in pain, of course—when Pygmy stepped into the room, looking unexpectedly handsome in his work scrubs. He winked at me and said, "We've been busy making a plan because we don't want you to get so bored you go AWOL from your safe house—errr, safe hospital. You know you're susceptible to The Hurry Sickness."

'I've been playing with my Jell-O and talking to ghosts, so I'm going crazy, but I'm still here," I said. "But from your cat-ate-the-canary expressions and the sight of that picnic basket, I see big changes on the horizon."

"Don't start sounding like Crazy Rosa reading the future, but changes are coming if our gamble works," Lupita said.

At that very moment, Berg breezed into the room, triumphantly displaying a large valise stuffed with what looked like official documents. His loving smile and jaunty stride, I have to admit, gave my heart more than a little jump-start.

"Okay," I said, eyeing the valise. "I assume this material has something to do with Wainwright and his audacious announcement that he achieved fusion breakeven. Please, oh please, tell us that he was wrong."

"Oh, he failed big time!" Berg exclaimed. "The FBI raided his lab and gathered all the information they could find about his experiment. They passed this stuff on to the research team at Livermore and to Dr. Merriman and me at Los Alamos for them to interpret the data."

"The FBI," I exclaimed, "Why were they involved?"

"Well, you know how Richard loved to claim that he built his project using only his own money? Turns out that while he was still employed by LANL he managed to skim off a few thousand bucks here, a few thousand there from the DOE annual budget. This discrepancy was passed along to the FBI and when they started digging into his shenanigans they discovered that Wainwright had been trying to cut a deal with either Iran or North Korea to sell his sensitive fusion research results to the highest bidder. Both these countries are anxious to get into the game and are more than glad to have a scientist from the U.S. help them get their program started."

Pygmy and I both gasped as we let this information sink in. "You're telling us that he was consorting with a hostile nation?" I cried.

"Yeah, that's the really bad news," Berg answered in a calm voice. "Our saving grace, no thanks to him, is that his results were a sham, as these reports show. His neutron counters were not properly calibrated so that most of what he claims were fusion neutrons were spurious counts – he had accomplished exactly nothing! *Nada! Rien!*"

I breathed a sigh of relief, as Berg continued. "Here's an intriguing side story. It seems that one of the two countries had offered to pay him $2.5 megabucks in exchange for a sample of the laser target that he had developed. According to one of these reports, he had arranged to conceal this sample target in a piece of artwork that they had already contracted to buy from Rothchild's gallery, but that this artwork has not yet been received by the buyer."

"So now it's up to us to find this needle in the haystack?" Pygmy asked. "Where do we start?"

Suddenly, it all came together for me. "Do you remember the screaming match between Squank and Letitia about the sequins on your Elvis painting? Well, suppose somebody with access to the targets concealed one of them in a sequin and included it among all the other sequins on Elvis's vest. Talk about hiding the secret in plain sight."

"Oh, Micaela, you're a genius," Berg shouted with delight. "If you're right, and I bet you are, the folks at the lab will be able to find it. Once they do, we'll be able to verify the FBI's contention that Wainwright has been conspiring with a hostile nation, even if that effort was a resounding flop."

"Speaking of Wainwright," I inquired, "what's going to happen to him?"

"Don't worry about Dickie," Berg answered. "He's under house arrest pending the investigation. This isn't some minor traffic violation, this is espionage, possibly treason. He could land in the slammer for life. So for now, he can't go anywhere without his own personal GPS ankle bracelet."

"This calls for a celebration," Lupita exclaimed. "My Mom and mi hermana Jacquelyn just fixed us a batch of enchiladas, so let's dig in." Pygmy expressed his appreciation with an enthusiastic nod.

While we were noshing, I said, "There are still a bunch of questions that need to be answered, like 'Was Letitia in on this subterfuge?' or 'Did she organize it so that she could take a cut?' or 'Did she even know about it?' And what about Squank? It was his painting that got this whole mess started in the first place."

A chilly internal breeze blew a few more clouds away from my frontal lobe, and with new thoughts, my shoulders drooped. "I can add theories to theories to connect all this to Leticia's death fall ..." My body would have drooped even lower except my bruised back hurt too much. I sighed for all a sigh was worth. "But, most vital of all, what does this have to do with Mel's murder?"

Lupita hugged me very, very gently. "We've got surprises in store for you, mija, I promise." She spoke with an ominous pleasure that triggered more chills. "Some interesting security footage, some anecdotal evidence, and … well, let's not spoil all the surprises."

"When will you tell all?" I asked, my heart beating as quickly as a child's.

"Soon," Berg said quietly. "But right now, we need to get you dressed—and what does a style queen wear to her own memorial service?"

I stared at them, wondering if my medications hadn't fully cleared my system after all.

"Don't worry," Pygmy said, "you are not hallucinating, Mickey."

Lupita nodded, producing an expensive shopping bag. "And I've got your queenly wardrobe in my hot little DA hands."

I stared at my friends, my gaze moving from one to the other. Their excitement hit me fast and hard, like a *good* kind of virus. "Let the games begin!" I cried.

Dear reader, if we found ourselves in the middle of one of my favorite English mysteries, we would have gathered everyone into the stately library or a British conservatory dripping with greenery. High tea or sherry would be served as Hercule Poirot or Jane Marple interrogated all the suspects in the most civilized of fashions. When the last biscuit or tea sandwich had been consumed, the dignified English sleuths would, with great ceremony and style, blurt out the name of the killer to the astonished assembly.

Here in northern New Mexico, however, we were fresh out of English conservatories and fussy libraries. What we did have was an understated, simple retreat called Evergreen, a lovely spot for ceremonies smack in the middle of Santa Fe's National Forest.

At the beginning of Hyde Park Road, Evergreen stood as plain as a simple country church. The modest stone building, equipped with comfortable chairs and vast views of turquoise blue skies and mountain ridges, was ideal for memorials, even fake ones.

The best part, from my standpoint as a girl detective wannabe, was that the Evergreen actually *did* have a secret room.

Nobody knew why. Nobody cared except me, and I have to admit that it was a pretty cool place to hang out while watching my memorial.

This "surprise" had come about hurriedly after the spirited debate in my hospital safe room. My DA sister had directed officers to retrieve the evidence I'd found on the cliff face where Leticia and I had both been attacked—in Leticia's case, fatally—her murder being an accepted fact in my crowd by now. It made sense that the murderer had tried to kill me, too, if I was getting too close to the truth. But that was only an "if": We needed rock-hard evidence—and, yes, pun intended—and we were here to find it.

Pygmy and Lupita both had called in favors owed by forensic scientists and techs in New Mexico's State Crime Lab—but the results from analyzing the sunglasses and the broken pieces of glass and, what the Lab called, a Carbon Fiber Reinforced Thermoplastic material (determined to be bits of a digital camera flash) were not back yet. Being the narcissist that he was, Wainwright often carried a camera to capture those Hallmark moments—with himself as the centerpiece.

"Any minute now," Lupita assured me.

In the meantime, how were we going to prove anything at all?

In my fiction writer's mind, our theory was as good as gold—but my journalist's mind said something else altogether. We needed real facts and incontrovertible proof. Lupita had promised surprises—and they would need to be of Penn & Teller or David Copperfield caliber. No small order.

In addition to my damaged hand and sprained right ankle, bruised back muscles made walking difficult, so I watched the memorial unfold from a wheelchair I occupied in the secret room. Lupita squeezed my hand, promising me we would get justice. We had a serious agenda: to catch my would-be killer, my sister's killer, and Leticia Rothschild's murderer—and to discover if the murders were connected. (My gut growled that they were.) As if all that weren't enough: to discover who was the real Squank, a madman killer or a harmless Santa Fe eccentric? And to unravel the mystery of his infamous Elvis painting?

Oh, yes; then where was the matter of the theft of our nation's secrets to be sold who knows where...

Lupita, the star of many a high-profile trial (and also a real ham) was enjoying her chance to play a combination of Harriet Vane, Cordelia Gray, and Jane Marple. "I need to strike the right tone of grief and determination," she murmured, straightening her collar. I was a little jealous, but I reminded myself that not many people get the eerie thrill of attending their own memorial service.

I had a surprisingly good view of the audience of three dozen or so "mourners," and I saw friends like Lynn Cline and Dr. Merriman and Shackleton. I also saw maybe-friends, like Sally Pommery and Ellen Paddington—and maybe-not friends, like Rosa, the psycho fortune-teller, artists Jamie Inman, Joaquin C. de Baca, and the inimitable Squank, who stood hovering restlessly at the edge of the group. There were those present whom I could only think of as enemies: Senator Rendón and Richard Wainwright, who sported a suspicious bulge around his ankle. A faint, red LED could be detected blinking through the fabric of his slacks. True to what Berg had told me, the Law was on to him and his suspicious activities at the Lab, placing him under "intensive supervision," otherwise known as house arrest; placing this GPS leash on his person. He was accessorized with the most captivating of bracelets.

I was hoping I'd recover fast enough to give (whom I believed to be) my sister's murderer a swift kick in the derrière before he was carted off to jail in a bright orange jumpsuit and chains.

Because Lupita was in charge of the memorial, she had kept it simple. Two large and brightly cheerful arrangements of sunflowers graced each side of a lectern—and, on a side table, more traditionally gloomy floral arrangements brought by attendees. Behind the lectern a four by six-foot screen displayed a montage of photos of Mel and of me projected digitally: a recent photo of Mel on her bicycle, Mel holding a rescued owl at the Española Wildlife Center, Mel on horseback with Senator Rendón at his ranch, a younger me with Brady hunched over his desk putting final touches on my first story, my professional headshot from my various bylines, and a playful picture of Mel and me as kids on a teeter-totter. By the time the photos ran through their loop, I was wiping away tears—as were many members of the audience, the very clear exceptions being Richard Wainwright (who simply looked imperious), Joaquin C. de Baca (who seemed to be floating on downers), and Rosa the fortune teller (who looked as if she'd gone off her meds).

Thinking of this whole intertwining and overwhelming drama, I shivered in the chilly October morning and missed Mel more than ever.

It was comforting to see that my dear, no-nonsense boss Brady would be the keynote speaker. With Brady's let's-get-to-the-point approach, we knew we weren't going to be subjected to lots of cutesy, flowery phrases. Brady was a straight shooter, the king of the left-handed compliment; his highest praise was something like, "Kid, your story was not half bad."

Brady solemnly approached the lectern. To most of the audience, he was a true journalistic machine, showing no emotion or sentiment. But this complicated, wonderful man had been my mentor, and I knew him better than anyone. I caught the tiniest glimpse of a trembling lip and collapsed shoulder—and I recognized his grief. Horrified, I turned to Lupita. "Does he really believe I'm dead?"

But Lupita eyed me in her cool DA fashion and said, "Brady knows the truth, mija, but his outrage at the thought of Mel's death and your near death will keep his performance authentic."

And, as if on cue, the show began.

"Life is strange and often tragic, and the good die young," said Brady in his deep radio announcer voice. "Mel and Mickey Moskowitz, two of the finer and most accomplished young women I've been privileged to know died within a month and twenty-five miles of each other.

They say life is an accident waiting to happen, and Mickey's whole family was cruelly taken from us by one misfortune after another. Mickey and Mel's parents were tragically drowned in a boating accident in Lake Superior when their allegedly untippable catamaran flipped over during a fierce windstorm. Unlike Mel's situation, no foul play was involved, just bad timing.

But Mel's demise is not so black or white. Mickey is convinced that her beloved sister was deliberately hit and forced off the road to her death, and the older sibling returned to Santa Fe to prove that her sister's death was no accident."

In reaction to Brady's assertion, murmurs arose from the unsettled audience.

After the briefest pause, Brady continued: "Unfortunately, in the slack boys-will-be-boys way of doing business in this understaffed, underpaid, and laid-back state, Mel's death was filed under police shorthand: 'happens all the time/probable hit-and-run.'

Because Mickey was not part of the good-old-boys network, her phone number and e-mail address were put in the dead letter office; Mick was left completely out of the loop. Business as usual 'round here, especially if your family hasn't been running the town for the past 400 years. As they say in this nepotistic neck of the woods, 'If you want to know about crime, you have to do your time.'"

As if on cue, Lupita gave me a thumbs up and crossed to the "unsecret" door to the chapel and outside to make her entrance as Brady moved toward the conclusion of his pretend eulogy.

"The powers that be apparently didn't know that Mickey and Lupita were sisters; the whole adoption had been rather clandestine. And Mickey rarely asked for help from anyone; she was the reigning Ms. I'm in Control." Brady looked to Lupita, who now stood by his side.

"But Lupita, with all her power and connections, is involved now. So, police, stop hiding behind your badges; Lupita's got your number, and this case will be solved!

It was totally out of character for Mickey to venture out for a climb on a day when the weather was so foreboding. I cannot begin to fathom what it was that prompted her to tackle such a difficult project during such unpredictable weather. My journalistic instincts lead me to surmise that Mickey's sudden, out-of-nowhere cup of bravado was related to Leticia Rothschild's death at the same site just a few days earlier. Now, tragically, the ..." Brady's voice broke, and you could tell he felt he needed to turn the microphone over to others—and I wondered if he'd missed his calling as an Oscar-worthy thespian.

He gave a small cough and pulled himself together. "The best reporter I've ever trained will never be able to explain exactly what her motivation was. I'm very much beginning to believe someone was after her and did her in." He gave one of his finest Brady scowls to the audience; and, as far as I could tell, every member of that audience squirmed under his laser beam gaze. Behind Brady, a photo of me that was taken by Lupita the day of my climb flashed onto the screen. Staring fiercely at the audience, Brady said, "We'll get to the bottom of this, and I'll see that this story runs in every daily in the country. Mickey deserves the best."

Looking dejected, he handed the microphone to Lupita.

"Thanks, Brady. Mickey would have been pleased with your talk—short, heartfelt, and to the point."

Lupita, with tears in her eyes (I told you she was a good actress), looked resolutely at her co-star.

"Brady, you may be right. The DA's office has found evidence that may prove that Mickey's death was no accident."

The audience reacted just like we wanted them to: with the appropriate amount of shock, awe, and discomfort.

"Let me provide some background to my sister's demise." She continued in her cool, steady voice, "I was with Mickey at the Lost Plateau on a photo shoot for *The Maverick* to capture the dramatic autumn skies. As far as I knew, Mickey was going to hike around a bit to see if she could answer questions she had about Leticia's fall to her death. My job was more fun.

As I was arranging the photos, my nephew Jeremy happened to be visiting. Jeremy, who is autistic, has some amazing gifts and discovers things in pictures that I would never see. He can look at two almost identical scenes and home in on what makes one different from the other."

With a few swift keystrokes on a computer, three pictures flashed up on the screen behind Lupita. "The three pictures projected behind me look pretty much the same, but they are actually remarkably different in one crucial respect."

Lupita pointed to the photo on the far left. "Look at the small red area at the bottom of the picture—when we enlarge it and zoom in, it turns out to be The Red Beast, my 1956 Chevy Bel Air."

I'd been doing my best to sit quietly in my wheelchair, but I was chomping at the bit to make my dramatic appearance. Still, I held myself back.

Lupita said, "If I zoom in even more, we can make out my license plate: 2487WL "Share with Wildlife.""

Picking up a laser pointer, Lupita explained, "Look more closely and you'll see Mickey and her backpack."

I was beginning to feel claustrophobic, and I couldn't stay still. I craned my neck and shoulders forward to see as much as I could. Hurry Sickness struck me full force. Even as she kept speaking, I knew I should be discreet and stay hidden, but a combination of hubris and adrenaline tipped my body forward until I was almost levitating out of the wheelchair.

Aiming her pointer, Lupita said, "Turning our attention now to the middle photo, the one taken only thirty minutes later, you'll be able to see what caught Jeremy's attention.

I am referring to this small, grey object—next to my laser pointer—thirty yards or so away from my red Bel Air, which is still in the same location as it was in the first slide. Jeremy, in his exacting way, noticed that it does not appear in the previous photo. Zooming in, we discover that this object is another vehicle—a classic Jaguar X-KE with the Vanity license plate, 'FUSION.'

And in the third photo, the mysterious steel grey Jaguar is gone. What we concluded is that the vehicle is owned …"

Richard Wainwright bolted up from his seat, yelling, "Hey, that's my Jag-you-ar!" (as Brits like to pronounce the word). All hell broke loose—and my wheelchair came to life—like a scene from *The Nutcracker*—and I was holy rolling through the low doorway into the gathering for my memorial, zooming down the incline (who knew it was so steep?)

Several of my mourners pointed and stared at me with

open-mouthed, horrified expressions a la Boris Karloff; others gasped or shrieked—offering winning auditions for a horror movie! Several called out, "Mickey!" while Rosa the fortune-teller and Squank both let loose falsetto, ear-splitting screams. But I was so hell-bent on nailing this entitled bastard that I temporarily forgot that I was dead.

My wheelchair picked up speed, and in my peripheral vision, I caught sight of Berg and Pygmy both darting toward me—but almost every molecule of my attention was focused on Wainwright, all color drained from his face, who stood in the center aisle.

That center aisle was my lane—and even as people quickly jumped out of my path while others scrambled—I'm happy to report I ran over at least one set of tootsies belonging to my nemesis, Senator Rendón. He yelped, and I would have backed up to roll over him again if I could. To my surprise and joy, I kept rolling toward Mr. Jag-you-ar!

Just before we collided, I caught a look of true bafflement on his face—and then, I was enveloped in the cloud of his L'Homme cologne.

Wainwright stumbled backward as Berg reached my side. "Are you okay? Mickey! I almost had a heart attack!"

"I-I-I-I'm okay," I stuttered, aiming one shaky index finger at Wainwright. "His cologne! I smelled it when I was attacked on the rock face! He's the one who tried to kill me!"

A collective gasp went through the audience, and all eyes focused on Wainwright. The crowd fell silent as good old tough-speaking, never-misses-a-beat Lupita concluded her speech. "Ladies and gentlemen, as I was saying, in the third photo, the mysterious steel grey Jaguar is gone. Our opinion is that the vehicle owned by Richard Wainwright was present at the Y's climbing rocks parking area at approximately the same time as Mickey's fall. How do we know this? We discovered that her watch stopped at 4:37 p.m. when the impact broke the crystal."

Her eyes bored into Richard's. "Dr. Wainwright, do you have an explanation for what we've just seen?"

Our production number was staged perfectly.

Lupita tossed me my cue: "I can't help but wonder what else Mickey thinks about this surprising turn of events?"

I knew this was serious business and this man had wanted me dead, but I have to confess that being the ghost of honor at my own memorial was a total hoot. I felt a teeny pang of guilt for having such a good time, but THIS WAS FUN!

I pointed to the monster, Wainwright, and in my loudest voice yelled, "*J'accuse!*"

I had to admit that my actions were a little on the melodramatic side, but hey, the bastard had tried to kill me. Let's face it; pushing me off a mountain was definitely not an act of love.

Events moved quickly after my collision with Wainwright. Once the mayhem died down to mere hubbub, many attendees were eager to take their leave after expressing their relief and congratulations at my resurrection. However, Wainwright appeared content to remain at the Evergreen, answering Lupita's questions as long as he stood in the spotlight (in this case he caught a sunbeam casting through ponderosa pines). His level of hubris was astonishing, but (I was realizing) also quite useful. As Spinoza once noted, "None are more taken in by flattery than the proud, who wish to be first and are not." He's still right.

We were now clustered around Wainwright as attendants cleared surrounding chairs and flower arrangements. Rendón sat with shoes off, flexing his toes and shooting me dirty looks—*Go ahead and sue me,* I thought. And Squank and Crazy Rosa seemed to be loitering around the edges of everything, as if deciding whether to go or stay.

Wainwright personified the vision of nonchalance and amused indifference—you'd never know from his calm demeanor that a GPS tracker, removable only with bolt cutters, was wrapped around his ankle. He focused on me and asked, "What exactly are you accusing me of doing?"

"Murder to start with and then add conspiracy to—"

Lupita cut me off, with a near-shout—"Premeditated murder!"

She shot me a look that ordered me not to chime in at this moment, and I drew my lips into a flatline: *these lips are zipped*. But why? What did my brilliant sister have up her sleeve? *Watch and learn*, I told myself.

Lupita stood tall, arms crossed, face stern. "When you're convicted of murder in the first degree, you will go to prison for life, Dr. Wainwright."

"I have never in my life committed murder, premeditated or otherwise," he said—sounding unnervingly convincing to my ears.

Lupita appeared unruffled. "I've yet to meet a murderer who wears his confession on his sleeve."

Wainwright shifted posture, as if readying to make his exit. "This is absurd, and I'm getting bored. Show me an ounce of proof to back up your accusations."

"Your Jaguar? Same day, same time? What's your alibi, Wainwright?!" Berg snapped.

Wainwright scoffed (a verb I could never quite picture until I saw him do it). "You might have proof my Jag-you-ar was there, although with Photoshop, I doubt that you can even prove that much incontrovertibly. And either way, you have nothing to prove I was driving my car."

My stomach lurched a bit, I admit. Was it possible he wasn't my attacker? *Not possible*, I told myself. Images flashed through my mind—images I'd worked to block:

the shattered glass, the camera bits, the intense and recognizable stench of his cologne.

Time for flattery; I composed my expression to convey admiration, and I even fluttered my eyelashes. "You are quite an amazing man," I said, lowering my voice in the hopes I signaled intimacy and not a croaking frog.

Apparently, I came close enough because he shifted in his chair and nodded in agreement. "I am nothing if not amazing."

"Amazing enough to follow Leticia on her climb and lie in wait to catch her by surprise."

Wainwright's smile only looked all the more smug. "I could certainly outclimb Letty, and I could also outsmart her—when it served my purposes. But I had no reason to want her dead; her connections were with international art collectors, and art collectors have money. She introduced me to several top investors in my lab." He shrugged, brushing a pine needle off of his jacket. "I found her irritating and irrational at times, but I was fond of her, and I also found her useful."

"It's bad enough that you are a complete charlatan, Wainwright," said Berg as he ate a scone from the memorial spread. "But the fact you've convinced young, naïve scientists from LANL, NM Tech, and Sandia Labs— as well as clean energy advocates—that you're the new Prometheus… you're a born fabulist."

Then, in his most sarcastic voice, leaning into Wainwright's face, Berg announced, "But I have wronged you, Richard, and I want to apologize. I always knew you were a lousy scientist, but I was unaware of your crack talents as a first-rate killer."

Pygmy, who had also hit the scones, nodded with utmost seriousness. "By my definition, a killer of anything that doesn't serve his purposes."

It was all I could do to hold myself back from screaming—*You killed Melissa; you killed my sister!* Berg wrapped his arm around my shoulder; he knows me too well.

Wainwright eyed us all with disdain. "Oh, if it isn't the Hardy Boys. How cute. But sadly, clueless." Then he stood. "Excuse me, boys—" He looked to Lupita and to me: "—and ladies. If you have any more questions, I will refer you to my solicitors." And with that he turned and walked past the cleaning crew to the path that led to the parking lot.

"Wait! You can't just—"

I didn't get the rest out because Berg clamped a hand over my mouth.

Lupita leaned forward to whisper, "Don't say another word until I say so, okay?"

I nodded, and Berg removed his hand. "I'm sorry, my love; I hope you can forgive me."

"Your hand smells of peanuts," I said with a huff. "But okay, obviously all of you know something I do not."

Lupita nodded. "Well, for starters, Wainwright is right—we don't have enough evidence to take him in for questioning, much less make an arrest."

"But the sunglasses and his cologne and his car and the broken pieces of camera I found before he attacked me?" I was trembling with outrage.

Pygmy coughed quietly. "We're still waiting for results on the items you found, Mickey, although we're hoping for viable fingerprints. And we have to analyze the photograph of his vehicle more closely. As for his cologne, we haven't developed the forensic analysis that can capture 'ghost fragrances.'"

"But …" Darkness threatened to shroud me like a cloud.

"Mija, cheer up," Lupita said.

And Berg and Pygmy added almost simultaneously, "We have a plan!"

Don't ask me how we ended up this way: seven of us divided into two vehicles staked out a half block from each other in the cold and dark on the street outside Squank's home. We couldn't use Berg's Beauty or Lupita's Beast or any other car the slightest bit distinctive—or, apparently, comfortable either. Stakeouts demand invisibility or the closest thing to it. And that is how Pygmy, Berg, Brady, and I ended up in Pygmy's (Lotta Burger-eating fanatic) mechanic's MINI Cooper, while Lupita and her colleagues Captain Ruiz and Sergeant Martini from the Santa Fe Police Department were cozily huddled in the back of a Ford van.

Brady insisted on getting in on the show by citing boss's privilege. And to keep us amused or at least awake during the stakeout, I'd had some white chocolate infused with lavender from The ChocolateSmith delivered. (Santa Fe is a foodies' mecca, and I know where to go to get the goodies!)

But even the best food can't solve everything—we were sated, but we were also cramped, bored, and shivering because rain was turning into snow and the wind was rocking the MINI. And coming from inside the

100-year-old adobe, we were forced to listen to Squank sing muffled Puccini arias to his sometimes-killer dogs. He was no Placido Domingo. The dogs sang along, and they stayed more on key than their eccentric master.

I know I said, "Don't ask," but I was wondering myself: *How did we get in this uncomfortable predicament?*

Flash back two nights ago to the evening of my fake memorial, after we packed all our props from the Evergreen Chapel and drove down the mountain to convene at Berg's. Magic greeted us (Berg first, me second, Brady third) with arched back, ankle-brushing demands for dinner, and that reminded us of the signature green-chile posole stew leftovers. As we set the pot to a very low simmer, Pygmy announced, "Eggs, milk, yeast, salt—we'll have my blinis in minutes!" As the upper third of his long frame disappeared into the refrigerator, we heard, "*Nyet … da … nyet … da!*" He reemerged holding several glass containers out to us. "May I have your permission to include some of your lox and cream cheese and capers and sour cream as possible toppings for the blinis?" With our approval, he went happily to work whipping up the simple batter.

Not to be outdone, Lupita moved to the *armario*-slash-liquor cabinet, where she selected various bottles of the strong stuff. A quick grind of my dark coffee beans and she had a pot brewing as she gathered ice, olives, cream, whipped cream—not all meant to go into the same mug or highball glass.

With food and beverages of choice, we settled around the rustic wooden table. For a few minutes, we were all too busy masticating and imbibing to speak. But soon, we began to review the actions and revelations of my faux memorial, and theories began to emerge.

Not shy, I piped up: "Why isn't Wainwright wasting away in solitary confinement? Why isn't he being tarred and feathered? The man tried to kill me, and I'm convinced he's hiding something about Mel's death, and he's strutting around like the cock o' the walk! A tagged rooster, but still ..."

Berg sighed so deeply that we all turned to look at him. Magic, on his lap, looked up and mewed at his human. "I hate to be the bearer of bad news, but I just got an alert on my not-so-smartphone: Wainwright's PR folks have managed to turn his 'story' into a persecution narrative, and he's becoming a cause célèbre. Clean-energy advocates from around the globe are applauding him as the persecuted hero who, against all odds, is advancing the important cause of thermonuclear fusion: the unlimited clean-energy source."

Brady moaned. "Which means, of course, that there will soon be Wainwright groupies all over town, protesting on his behalf, most of them, in the best Santa Fe fashion, having no earthly idea what thermonuclear fusion is."

Pygmy chimed in, "What do you want to bet you can already buy R.W.THERMONUCLEAR.FUSION souvenirs online?"

Lupita held up her tablet and sure enough, www. DefendWainwright.com was already up and running— complete with T-shirts selling at 3/$49.95!

I shook my head, comforted only by a last bite of

blini, cream cheese, and lox. Swallowing, I said, "I'm pretty sure some of his fans will believe Thermonuclear Fusion is the name of a rock band." Tears welled in my eyes, but I blinked them back. "It's looking more and more like he's the celebrity of the hour!"

"And making the most of the publicity," Berg said darkly. "All the while holding court in his pricey, over-sized playpen on the golf course at Las Campanas."

"A community known for its healthy helping of hu-bris," Brady said, nipping a posole nib from his spoon.

"Sorry to show you this live video from outside Wainwright's home," Lupita said. "But it's better to know what we're dealing with here."

I looked even though I didn't want to—and saw a dozen protestors in front of a huge, and obviously hugely expensive, home backed by a golf course with moun-tains in the distance. A glance at the protesters' signs showed they were comparing Wainwright to Robert Oppenheimer. *We often pay a heavy price for free speech in this country!*

"That's heresy," Berg said darkly. "Oppenheimer was tortured by his unleashing of the atomic bomb, tortured by his vital participation in opening Pandora's Box, even as he believed the knowledge would be let loose upon the world one way or another. Better it come from America than Germany."

"While Wainwright …" Brady paused to swallow his stew. " … is an imposter and egomaniac with no scruples whatsoever."

"Exactly," Berg murmured in disgust.

"And the imposter is worshipped by these scientist

types and the just plain dense, as is so often the case," Brady said, setting down his spoon. "You make a half-way decent posole stew, Berg," he added, with his usual Brady-effusiveness.

"Thank you, sir," Berg said quietly.

Lupita lifted a scoop of whipped cream from her glass mug of Irish coffee and flourished it into the air. "It comes down to hard evidence. We all know this. Wainwright is his own Teflon Don—so we need to undertake extreme measures to bring him to justice using all of our resources—lawful resources."

And, it was at that moment, everyone froze at the *tap-tap-tap* at the kitchen door.

I admit I almost screamed when I saw the wild-eyed, wild-haired apparition through the window.

"Squank!" Pygmy shouted as he lunged for the door.

"Wait!" Lupita yelled—followed quickly by, "No, don't wait! Hurry, let him in!"

Pygmy complied, and Squank almost fell into the kitchen. Teeth chattering, dripping puddles onto the floor, shivering, he stuttered, "S-s-s-stormy—w-w-w-want—m-my—El-el-vis—p-p-p-painting—p-p-please—" And then he collapsed into a heap.

Minutes later, after a quick examination by Pygmy, Squank, wrapped in a blanket and sipping hot chamomile tea, managed to communicate that he had come looking for his *Elvis* painting—that may or may not have been Berg's birthday *Elvis*.

There was no way Squank could have his painting back; it was evidence in an espionage case.

"I'm sorry, Squank," Pygmy said, softly but firmly.

"Your painting is being examined by investigators because evidence points to it—and to you—participating in an international smuggling ring headed by Leticia Rothschild."

Yes, Pygmy was overstating things a bit, but Squank's reaction supported the use of overstatement. He almost fainted again! Bolstered by Berg and Brady, he spluttered his story: "I never—I only—I did what I was told or Leticia would have the city take away my dogs and kill them and they would never let me adopt again and I would end up in prison unless I did whatever she told me to do!"

Silence reigned for several seconds while we all absorbed Squank's confession. Lupita, never one to miss an opportunity, leaned forward to confront him with some indefinable mix of authority and empathy. "And Richard Wainwright did not come to your defense, did he?"

His eyes bulged, and a shudder ran through him, and he shook his head. "You-you-know-everything?"

We all nodded.

He took our word for it. "Wainwright didn't help me at all! He called them 'mangy horrors' and promised he would see to it that they starved to death unless I did everything they told me to do."

After a small and quiet conference held out of his range of hearing, Lupita presented this proposition to him: "I think there's a very good chance you will be able to clear everything up—and demonstrate your innocence—if you cooperate with us and our plan. All you have to do is agree to wear a teeny-tiny wire and invite Richard Wainwright to a meeting." Here, she clasped her hands like a choirgirl. "And I promise you that each and every one of your beloved doggies will live out their lives in comfort, if not luxury!"

And so she closed the deal.

That brings us back to the four hours spent squished into the MINI Cooper and the freezing-rain and quickly metastasizing ill-humor—and the drastically mood-reversing effect of the sighting of a steely gray Jaguar, license plate FUSION, pulling up to the curb far from any streetlight and less than a block from Squank's home.

We all hunched down in our seats as a stealthily acting Wainwright wrapped his long overcoat tightly around himself and covered ground quickly between his car and the house. We'd told Squank to keep his porch lights off, so as not to frighten Wainwright away from their appointed meeting.

Squank opened the door and Wainwright slipped inside. Pygmy noiselessly opened the car door and scuttled over to the police van. Only one day out of my wheelchair, Berg and Brady each took one of my arms and helped me in after him. After some initial ear-piercing squawks and squeaks and ear wax-clearing noises (and yes, Lupita and her law enforcement officers had run a pre-check for audio), we picked up the first seconds of Wainwright barking at Squank and dogs growling in response.

"Why the hell did you drag me out in this hellish weather, you idiot?" Wainwright began.

"I-I-I know what you and Leticia were up to!" Squank sputtered.

I closed my eyes and imagined him huddling in a

corner of his living room while the dogs focused every doggy molecule on bullyish Richard Wainwright.

But Wainwright sounded half-panicked, raising his voice to shout, "What were we up to? You're a moron, so tell me what we were doing? And call your stupid dogs off! Now!"

I have to say, if I was in that kitchen facing those dogs, I wouldn't be using words like "moron" and "stupid," but hey, that's just me.

Now Squank came through—I wasn't the only one afraid we'd lost him to Wainwright's bullying. But the wire crackled, and he yelled, "You can call me names all you want, but I'm no moron, I'm a genius! And you owe me moola! Lots of moola! You thought you were using me, and I'd never figure out about the paintings, what you did—but you're wrong, and it's going to cost you! And just so you know—you made my dogs crazy with your gadgets!" Ah, that accounts for the high-pitched sound I was hearing during my first visit to Squank's.

Wainwright's silence was, as the cliché goes, deafening. Well, it would have been except the dog's nonstop vocalizing took away from the full effect. And when Wainwright did speak—very slowly—his tone gave me the chills. "What do you know about the paintings?"

Lupita had coached Squank to hold back as much as he could so Wainwright couldn't claim he'd been coerced or "led" in this recorded exchange.

One of Lupita's detectives had also taken charge of getting visuals, videotaping Wainwright's arrival, and also getting some additional footage from artfully placed GoPros inside.

"I'm asking you one more time—what do you know about the paintings?"

The threat in Wainwright's voice chilled us in our already chilly vehicle.

"I-I-I—"

We held our collective breath. Squank had been warned to stick to the script, but no one really had any hope that he would or that he was even capable of holding to any script.

"You sold secrets!" he hissed.

Wainwright hissed back—"What did you say?"—and we could all hear the consternation in his voice.

"Those paintings were for my patrons," he said, audibly outraged. "My collectors love my work, don't you know. And you hid your secrets behind my genius and sold them to enemies. You are a spy!"

"Who have you told about this?" Wainwright asked, his voice steely now.

"W-w-what?" he chattered.

"I'm asking … Who. Else. Knows."

A shiver ran through me and doubled back through my body. The dogs' growling rose in pitch.

I jumped in my seat when he broke out in singsong: "I won't tell you, and you can't make me!" He kept up the chant, and his dogs' snarls drowned out much of the conversation—or, more accurately, the threats—from Wainwright and shrieks from Squank, who screamed, "Don't shoot me! Help—help!"

Everything exploded.

Lupita and her detectives leaped out of their van and raced toward the house. Pygmy followed. Brady and

Berg were in close pursuit. I didn't move. I knew I'd help most by not trying to help—especially when I heard the snarling dogs go berserk. I didn't need to pile on any more injuries.

A gunshot!

Squank yelled, "You tried to kill me!"

Wainwright screamed, "I was aiming for your killer dogs. Get them off me!"

"Admit it!" he yelled back. "You sold my work to enemies, you sold secrets!"

"Okay, yes, yes, yes! I confess, now call off your hounds before—"

Leticia and her officers burst into the room.

"Police! Drop your weapon! Squank, call off the dogs!"

I tried to keep track of what followed, which was basically cacophony.

"Leticia was the boss," Squank squeaked. "But you were her partner!"

"She wasn't the boss of me!" Wainwright yelped— whether or not he knew he sounded like a toddler, or whether or not he cared, was a mystery. "She did what I told *her* to do!"

"You told her to use me!"

"And I was using her. That's why I had to...." Wainwright's other confession dropped off mid-sentence.

Predictably, within minutes of the police intervening, Wainwright claimed entrapment and took back every word. That didn't matter because investigators would be working nonstop to shift through the evidence.

But luckily, the evidence I had collected before he tried to kill me provided fingerprints, as did the broken flash he used to trigger Leticia Rothschild's epilepsy attack which, in turn, caused her to fall to her death. One way or another I believed we had Leticia's killer.

But what about bringing justice for Mel?

I accepted a perfectly prepared cappuccino from Shackleton with a smile of deep gratitude. For the moment, I was content to sit back in the Eames armchair and inhale the dark, sharp aroma of Paulig Juhla Mokka coffee while Sally moved boxes and went through shelves and closets with admirable focus. We were in the guesthouse she occupied at Leticia's gallery and compound. While federal agents and local law enforcement were busily taking apart Letty's hacienda and the business office—they didn't seem to be stopping Sally from reorganizing. I wasn't sure why.

As for me, I was there by invitation, thanks to Shackleton, having a private moment with Sally. Of course, I had my notebook in hand—with Leticia gone her ghost still seemed to fill every inch of the property. No one could argue the fact that Leticia Rothschild had been a true character. My profile of the gallery owner, international art maven, and embezzler of government secrets and technology had become investigative journalism with a tad of obituary thrown in, too. And my editors—in New York and in Santa Fe—were excited about Wainwright's role in the saga—if I could make the connections. "There's a book in this for you, Mickey," Brady gushed (for Brady, that's gushing).

"Are you worried about your husband?" I asked, when Sally paused for a moment with a small ornamental box in hand—she seemed to be looking into another world.

She blinked, and her eyes widened as if I'd just appeared via *Star Trek's* transporter. "The police let him go ... they couldn't hold him for long without more concrete evidence ... he was defending himself against wild dogs—"

I knew those dogs, and I could sympathize, but only to a very tiny point. I said, "Sally, he had a gun, and he threatened Squank." I kept my voice gentle. Sally brought out a protective streak in me that surprised—no, more accurately—shocked me. I'm not the protective type.

Both Lupita and Sally herself said that she was co-operating with investigators and that the FBI's forensic accountants were poring over files in Wainwright's lab and Leticia's gallery—and they were looking for enough evidence to gain a search warrant for Rendón's offices.

Suddenly, Sally sank down into a comfortable chair. And she managed to do it gracefully. "I told the agents, yes, I helped Leticia ... I helped her adjust the books, her records, to account for very large sums of money coming from accounts in Cypress. At first, I had no idea the money wasn't coming from legitimate channels, but when I found out ... I was already involved." She covered her face with her hands.

Meanwhile, I was pondering her verb choice, "adjust the books," thinking "cook the books" was more accurate. And Sally was nothing if not intelligent, even if her choices (take marrying Richard Wainwright, for example) were less than smart. (I've lived in my own glass houses when it comes to bad dating choices.)

A tear leaked from beneath her hand, and she raised her head to look at me, those beautiful blue eyes reddened. "I never believed Richard was involved, at least not at first." Saying his name must have turned on the spigot because the tears streamed down her cheeks now, dripping off her chin. She wiped her face with the palms of both hands. "We've been married for twenty years. I fell madly in love—I gave up my budding acting career in New York and L.A., and that was no small sacrifice. I still love Richard."

As she gathered herself, it crossed my mind that Sally wasn't a positive role model for marriage and she was overinflating the potential of her acting career. As far as I knew, she'd done a few commercials—one for a Japanese version of Charmin toilet paper and one for hemorrhoid cream—where she'd looked convincingly pained—and she'd had a bit part in the flying dog movie … sorry, I can't recall the title.

She clapped her hands, startling me. "If I learned or even suspected that Richard was selling America's secrets to hostile foreign governments, I would have come forward in an instant." She shook her head hard. "I don't believe he's a traitor. I can't believe that. But …"

"But what, Sally?" I'm a journalist, and it is my job to press, so I did—even if I couldn't vouch for the rest of my declaration. "You'll feel better if you get it off your chest, whatever it is."

She started crying again. "I just can't believe he'd hurt …"

I reached out to touch her arm gently. "I've seen enough in this life to know that each of us could be capable of acts we never thought we'd commit." I took a deep breath. "Is it possible he's capable of murder?"

"I never thought—I couldn't believe—I can't believe—but I've never seen him as angry as he was with Leticia! Whatever she did to him—it festered—"

"Go on," I urged as softly as I could.

Sally was hiccupping now, weeping, gasping air. "The day before the climbing—her death—they had a horrible fight! I overheard them yelling but I—I only walked in on the end. When they saw me, they fell instantly silent." Sally went silent, too, looking around us; I reached for the tissue box and handed it to her, and she continued. "They didn't think I heard anything, but I did …"

I leaned so far forward in my chair I almost fell off the edge. *What did you hear?*—I screamed in my head.

She looked at me, clasping for my hand, those blue eyes blinking back still more tears. "He said he would kill her."

I gulped the last quarter cup of my coffee. "Why didn't you go to the police?"

"I didn't think he'd go through with it—I didn't even believe I'd heard him correctly. But then she died! And then, just a few days ago, I saw his credit card statement …"

"What was on it, Sally?" This wasn't my usual role, eliciting confessions connected to murder—usually my job meant writing about jealous rivals in the art world and enraged artists who received bad reviews from those in power who guard the gates of celebrity … hold on, maybe I did write about this kind of confession.

I squeezed Sally's hand, and she squeezed mine back.

I said, "You are cooperating with the police, and you cannot hold back secrets. That could ruin the deal you have with prosecutors. A judge won't look kindly on withholding crucial information."

Sally nodded and swallowed with difficulty. "He'd ordered a very expensive camera with a rapid-fire flash; miniaturized, high-tech. You know how he loves to take selfies, but I wasn't sure why he needed such a fancy camera."

My scalp prickled as I pictured those broken bits of metal and glass on the rocks where I'd fallen—evidence already linked to Wainwright by at least one perfect fingerprint.

"Then I put it together," Sally whispered. "I'd never been able to believe Leticia would fall off that cliff. She was ruthless at everything, including rock climbing! She would demand that the rock hold her up! Unless …"

"Unless what?" I couldn't help it; my voice came out a croak. The air around seemed to crackle with tension, and Sally shivering wasn't helping to calm me down.

"Unless it was her epilepsy." Sally pulled back a bit, wrapping her arms around herself. "She took medicine religiously. She never climbed unless she'd taken all her precautions. She had a checklist—"

Something brushed against my arm and I jumped, barely muffling a scream.

"I'm so sorry I startled you!" Shackleton bowed, his face filled with true remorse. "I only brought some Evian for you both."

Sally gulped her water, and I sipped mine as my heartbeat slowed from racehorse to race mule.

Shackleton excused himself, and Sally finished the

last of her Evian. "Richard knew about her epilepsy. It was the reason she often appeared drunk. And she shook sometimes when the meds were wearing off. He asked me about it last year because he was concerned."

I nodded. "I saw the symptoms at C. de Baca's opening. And the autopsy showed WHAT?" I focused my laser look on Sally. "So are you saying the camera flash ..."

"Rapid, very bright light can trigger seizures," Sally said quietly. "That's why we kept the light dimmed in the rooms she used most. Remember those videos in Japan that were so bright and flashed so quickly they caused seizures in children?"

I nodded. I remembered vaguely. I wanted to poke her to spell it out, but I kept my mouth shut, my lips zipped. Silence is one of a journalist's most powerful interviewing tools.

And finally ...

"Richard is a world-class climber. He is a genius. He threatened to kill her, and he was involved in a scheme to sell our nation's secrets ..." Sally embodied misery. "And, yes, I believe he was on that ledge with Leticia and he managed to disorient her with his camera flash. And if she didn't fall, then maybe he pushed her when she was seizing. Maybe that's how the camera got away from him, too." Sally dropped forward in her chair, her forehead barely missing a coffee table. "I feel sick to my stomach now that I've said it out loud—"

I would have comforted Sally at that point, but I didn't have time.

Something disturbing had developed in the courtyard between the gallery and the guesthouse. Refined and gentle Shackleton was shouting; he and another man exchanged obscenities. Sally stood so quickly I thought she'd fall over. I jumped to my feet just as Wainwright strode into the room.

"You witch!" he screamed, lunging toward his wife.

"Help!" Sally dodged—looking like a woman who has learned to escape an abusive man.

"You lying bitch, don't you try to get away from me!"

Sally and I were both attempting to keep a loveseat between us and Wainwright. I grabbed a tall, slender lamp. And Shackleton—who had rushed into the room behind Wainwright—wielded the first makeshift weapon he could find, a sculpture of reclaimed Lab parts that had been sitting on a pedestal in the courtyard.

"Is she telling you lies about me and Letty?" As Wainwright moved toward us, looking as if he would scale the loveseat with ease, he snarled another word that rhymes with "bucking" and one that rhymes with "stunt."

I started to swing the lamp when Wainwright had one leg up on the loveseat's brocade upholstery, yelling, "You think you can set me up for your sins and get away with it, you evil, treacherous—"

Suddenly, Pygmy, Berg, and Brady joined the party. *Whack!*

Shackleton's sculpture hit its mark, and Wainwright crumpled to the floor.

"Get the police!" I yelled to Squank as I wrapped my arms around Sally just before she fainted, pulling me with her to land on the faux bear rug.

"I told you he wouldn't know a neutron counter if it hit him on the head," said Berg.

And what about Mel? She was the reason this crazy investigation started in the first place. We'd ruled out Wainwright and Leticia and C. de Baca—and even Squank and Crazy Rosa had solid alibis. But Rendón who was the wild card in this equation surprised me by calling with an invitation to his ranch in nearby Galisteo.

It was an easy drive, even with lingering maladies that confined me to a wheelchair.

I found Rendón seated in his leather armchair, which was burnished with his ranch brand, AR-BAR. A very large oil painting, mounted over a massive fireplace, depicted Rendón and his wife posing in front of a vast panorama of New Mexico. But the grand presentation was noticeably spoiled by stuffing protruding from cushions and the chair's tattered underskirt.

Around him, the rustic and very expensive furnishings and decorations of the old hacienda were in disarray where federal agents had scoured every possible hiding space—searching for more evidence of Rendón's collusion with Wainwright and Leticia Rothschild. At worst, they'd sold our country's secrets; at best, they were guilty of tax fraud. Rendón would certainly do time—but how much had yet to be determined.

Even as he awaited the agents who would take him away, he treated me graciously, inviting me to sit (to mitigate my pain, I accessorized a space on a loveseat by adding a mismatched pillow). I noted the grayish pallor of his skin and the bags beneath his eyes, seemingly large enough to hold some spare change. I could understand why Mel had been so charmed by her boss yet, in this moment, I could see right through him.

One FBI agent stood outside the door to Rendón's study, while Consuelo, a lovely older Hispanic woman, served us chamomile tea. It took effort for her to mask her distress, but I sensed how worried she was for Arturo Rendón.

I couldn't help but find my eyes drawn to the hunting trophies mounted on the study walls—heads and horns and hides of magnificent animals I assumed Rendón had killed.

"How could my sister have ever worked for you?" I asked, gesturing to the macabre spectacle of death.

"She forgave me because I gave up hunting for her," Rendón said, slowly. "She wouldn't let up on her lectures until I finally quit. She was fiery, a pistol, once she set her mind to something. Or as your family would put it, she kvetched until I conceded."

There he goes again, I thought, that meshuggeneh Rendón, speaking Yiddish to me. What a schmuck!

Oblivious of me or my thoughts, he smiled faintly, looking past me, but his eyes seemed focused on some other time and place. He said, "I cared for Melissa as if she were my own daughter."

My spine felt stiff as steel, and I needed that strength to ask my next question. "Then why did you kill her?"

I didn't truly expect an answer. We had no proof that Rendón was responsible for Mel's death. But Lupita had heard whisperings about a connection between Rendón and his nephew who dated a woman who was friends with the postmistress of Chamisal and whose husband played at the weekly poker game that often included Manny-of-the-red-Honda.

But, still, no confession.

I'd made a vow to Mel—a vow from my heart to my sister that I would bring her killer to justice. And no matter what evidence we lacked, my journalist's instincts kept pulling me back to Rendón. So, here I was, sitting not six feet from him when he put his hand to his heart.

"I swear, on my mother's grave and on the Holy Mother and Our Lady of Guadalupe, I never meant to hurt Melissa."

Arturo Rendón went on to confess that he'd "borrowed" the red car from the parking area at his fundraiser after drinking heavily at the event.

A quote from *The Great Gatsby* flashed through my mind. "They were careless people, Tom and Daisy—they smashed up things and … then retreated back into their money… and let other people clean up the mess they had made."

Mel had confronted him after overhearing an indiscreet conversation with Leticia about some special bookkeeping they were doing. "Mel had her suspicions," Rendón told me sadly. "She was nothing if not smart.

And considering the ways I'm positioned politically, I could have intervened."

I was right: Rendón was a political hack with no moral compass. He said he tried to calm her, but she went racing off on her bicycle. So he followed. Drunk. Upset. In no shape to be driving.

"The sun was in my eyes, and she was just ahead of me, and then she wasn't—you know our New Mexico sun! Then as we got close to Nun's Corner, the sun shot through my windshield again like a blade, and I blinked—only for an instant—I swear! I felt a thump—just a little thump—the car barely shuddered—so I thought, 'Oh no, maybe I hit a fox or a small deer!'"

But she was right in front of him; why would he think I'd believe this? He was trying to trivialize Mel's death, and I was getting angrier by the second.

"I felt so bad, and as I continued down the hill, I glanced into the rearview mirror but I didn't see anything—and anyway, what could it help to stop?" Tears streamed down his crumpled face.

That's called "hit and run." Maybe you could have saved her, you bastard!

My heart felt hard, but I leaned forward to hear the rest of his words.

"It was only … when I got home I fell into bed … but soon after Consuelo rushed in with the news. That Mel had died in a bike accident up by Nun's Corner. Then I knew for sure it was me."

He buried his face in his hands, but still, I heard him say, "I couldn't face that I'd hurt her. I'm a coward."

"Hurt her? Try, killed her!" I didn't disagree. I pressed

the bright red record button on my phone to turn it off.

Two days later, Berg drove me to the site of Mel's death. I was trying to learn something from this devastating experience; otherwise what was the point of living through it. I was trying to be more in the present and put The Hurry Sickness in my New York City suitcase.

There is something sobering, after all, about being the very last survivor in your clan. The clarion call of mortality was shouting my name and I knew, this time, I had better listen.

The very day that Lupita pronounced those crushing words: "Your sister is dead," a bone-chilling river started forming inside me. Since that life-changing moment, I've been trying to thaw this glacial freeze.

I realized that my topsy-turvy love-hate relationship with Santa Fe would continue. My town is charmingly eccentric—goofy, some might say—but the people I love are here. And though I would never admit it to anyone I could feel Mel's spirit all around, giving me some comfort and closure.

I knew that I would be intermittently coming back to this crazy quilt of a city because I had established the Melissa Moskowitz Urban League; I had asked Ellen Paddington to be in charge of this foundation.

I was secretly trying to be more contemplative. Lupita—whose personality was halfway between Mel's and mine—bought me a copy of Thornton Wilder's *Our Town* with Emily's graveyard monologue highlighted: "Oh Earth, you are too wonderful for anyone to realize you."

This quote just kept rolling around in my mind as Berg and I made our way to Mel's shrine.

I carried flowers, and Berg lugged a rather large stone engraved with the name of the new foundation, and a dedication to my sister.

We'd just stepped over the roadside railing when Berg and I both stopped in our tracks.

Someone had already erected a roadside cross and Star of David for my sister. The wood had been polished and smoothed, and the artisan had carefully etched "Melissa Moskowitz" into the wood. Flowers and stone carvings—prairie dogs, a wolf, a robber jay, and a deer—surrounded the base of the cross. Other offerings were tucked into every possible space: food, and a bottle of beer, and an energy bar; and then there were personal items, like a bracelet, a tiny gold cross on a chain, and a baseball cap embossed with "Save the Prairie Dogs" protecting a tiny bird's nest. And Mel's Environmentalist of the Year medal sparkling in the sunshine.

There were flowers everywhere—a dazzling profusion of vivid wildflowers—interspersed with more buttoned-up arrangements from local florists.

As we added our stone and flowers, tears streamed down my face. But I knew I was smiling, too. Berg's arm wrapped around me felt warm and comforting and right.

"I miss you, Mel," I whispered. A jay called out, and wind stirred the trees.

"I miss you, but I know you're with me always—in my heart. You make me better—you make me stronger. Now I know to be more present, to notice the wonders of life, and to show more gratitude. You have shattered me, and you have changed me. I love you, dear sister."

Berg and I walked back to the car, arm in arm. It was late afternoon, and the sky was flooded with an intense, blinding, bright yellow light. As Lupita might say, "With patience you gain the impossible."

EPILOGUE

Dear Reader,

I love books where at the end everything is tied into a neat little bow. Sorry! This isn't one of those tomes. Life is messy and so is my indecisive ending. Should I marry Berg and ride off into the sunset? Will we live happily ever after? What about my crown as Ms. Independent? Berg is the boyfriend of the century and I adore him, but my past history with bad boyfriends didn't exactly turn me into Annette Funicello. Biological clock? I don't think I even have one. Maybe all will be revealed in my next book.

As we left Mel's shrine, I held tight to Berg as we were enveloped in our own sunbeam. I was about as content as I get which would make this scene about as close to a happy ending as I am capable of writing. This seems like a good stopping place, so I'll say *adios*.

Or as we say around here in romantic, historic, diverse *La Villa Real de la Santa Fé de San Francisco de Asís*,

BUENO BYE!

Acknowledgements

Hillary Clinton may get by with just a village but my thank you list resembles the Chicago phone book!

For starters, I live with my favorite character, literary or otherwise. We have danced a waltz of words for lo these fifty years, as certified wordsmiths we toss words across the room with abandon. Anxious adverbs collide with comely commas and no-account nouns bump into seductive semi-colons. My physicist husband with the soul of a poet has been by my side every step of the way. Thank you, David.

And gracias to Laurie McDonald, who is good at so many things including the production of the smashing book cover. We are quite a team, two anglo women living in the land of mañana and suffering from The Hurry Sickness. She is, in the best girl scout fashion, reliable, creative, helpful, resourceful and is as impatient as I am – I couldn't have done it without her.

Sarah Lovett, writing coach extraordinaire: talented, kind, amusing, filled with ideas and fun. As Melissa was to Mickey, my brother Bob has been to me: supportive, sensitive, simpatico. Kathy Harms, a lovely worker and friend; Jeanie Fleming a fine photographer and a great friend; Jacqueline Rudolph my favorite illustrator; and world renowned mountaineers Don and Alice Liska for giving me a crash course on rock climbing and providing poetic names for geologic features.

Carol and George Price for manuscript reading and friendship, and John Sherman for going through the manuscript with a fine-toothed comb. General good guys who kept me afloat: Carol Jewett Baer, Valerie Brooker, Susie Sonflieth, and Michelle Ouellette.

Cameo appearances of real people Lynn Cline, Eileen Pink, and John Sherman. Fellow writers Mary Gay Rogers, Elaine Pinkerton, and Jan Wolcott. Best friend to writers Dorothy Massey, owner of Collected Works Bookstore in Santa Fe.

Thanks also to Monica Harman and Colleen Goulet from Outskirts Press for their guidance and patience.

About the Author

Peggy van Hulsteyn has written for *Cosmopolitan, Mademoiselle, Modern Bride, Country Living, New Mexico Magazine, American Way,* and newspapers such as the *Washington Post, the Los Angeles Times, the Miami Herald, the Kansas City Star, the Chicago Tribune, the San Francisco Examiner, and USA Today.* Her work has appeared in Australian periodicals and been translated into Japanese, Spanish, Dutch, and Portuguese.

During her career, van Hulsteyn was assistant travel editor of *Mademoiselle* magazine in New York City, south-eastern director of publicity for American International Pictures in Atlanta, owner of an award-winning advertising agency in Austin, and advertising lecturer at the University of Texas. Van Hulsteyn won the Southwest Writers Workshop Storyteller Award for Best Novel for her murder mystery in progress. She was awarded first place for nonfiction by the New Mexico Press Women for her book *Mind Your Own Business.*

Van Hulsteyn has practiced yoga for over forty years and was diagnosed with Parkinson's disease over twenty years ago. Her feature article describing the benefits of Yoga for people with Parkinson's was presented in both the American and Chinese versions of *Yoga Journal* and received a rousing response from around the world. She then wrote the book, *Yoga and Parkinson's Disease* which appeared on the Michael J. Fox Foundation's recommended reading list and which the CEO of the National Parkinson's Foundation called "a must read."

Van Hulsteyn, who attended the University of Missouri Journalism School, holds a degree in English and journalism from Indiana University. She lives in Santa Fe, New Mexico, with her physicist husband.

CPSIA information can be obtained
at www.ICGtesting.com
Printed in the USA
LVHW051340280121
677618LV00010B/427